Between
Two
Worlds

LUWAM A. TESFAYE

THE WEIZERIT TALES~BOOK ONE

Cover and interior design by Mary Ann Smith

Illustrations by Nejla Shojaie

Edited by Holley Bishop

Hardback ISBN-978-1-7375142-0-6

Paperback ISBN-978-1-7375142-1-3

eBook ISBN-978-1-7375142-2-0

Library of Congress Control Number: 2021913496

Tesfaye, Luwam

Between Two Worlds / Luwam Tesfaye

To Grams-
I wouldn't be the woman I am today without your guidance, love, and
dedication. I wish you were here to see this book come to life, but I know you
are smiling down on me from heaven. I pray we all make you proud.

CONTENTS

Index of Characters

ANNABELLA LORENZO FAMILY

Annabella Lorenzo (also known as Weizerit)- main character
Lorenzo Kidane- government official and Annabella's father
Yeshimebet- wife of Lorenzo and Annabella's stepmother
Emama- Yeshimebet's mother
Ababa- Yeshimebet's father and first cousin to Emperor Haile Selassie
Mikael Kidana- Annabella's uncle
Yonatan Mikael- Annabella's first cousin. Son of Mikael
Marta Mikael- Annabella's first cousin. Daughter of Mikael
Moges- Lorenzo and Mikael family member and caregiver
of their family home in Eritrea

ANNABELLA'S GRANDDAUGHTERS

Gabriella   Hiyab   Bilen   Awet   Natsenet

Key Characters in Addis

THE IMPERIAL FAMILY

Princess Saba- Annabella's best friend and daughter of Emperor Haile Selassie
Princess Maryam- Daughter of Emperor Haile Selassie
Ras Dawit- Princess Maryam's husband
Princess Makada- Daughter of Princess Maryam and Ras Dawit
Princess Zewditu- Daughter of Princess Maryam and Ras Dawit
Prince Addisu- Son of Emperor Haile Selassie

HOUSE STAFF

Lekay- Saba's childhood nanny
Berhana- Annabella's childhood nanny and head housekeeper
Mekonnen- Annabella's family home gardener
Tadesse- Annabella's family driver
Marcos- Berhana's husband and Mikael's driver

OTHER CHARACTERS FROM ADDIS ABABA

General Kebede- Proposed to Annabella
Ato Hagos- Local goldsmith
Behailu- Ato Hagos's son
Kasahun- Driver hired to take Annabella to Asmara from Addis Ababa
Lemlem- Kasahun's on and off girlfriend
Ato Zerihun- Marcos's friend
Weizero Beletish- Ato Zerihun's wife
Ato Fisseha- Café Owner in Addis Ababa near Parliament

Key Characters in Asmara

BANCO DI ROMA STAFF

Signora Lucia Barattolo- Bank Director
Signore Roberto- Signora Lucia's husband
Signore Antonio- Bank Hiring Manager
Daniel Kahassay- Finance Spokesperson
Nigesti- Press employee
Saba- Press employee
Gebremeskel- Press employee
Tekleab- Finance employee
Asmara- Finance employee
Teclino- Finance employee
Alem- Finance employee
Meheret- Signora Lucia's secretary

OTHER CHARACTERS FROM ASMARA

Signore Membrahtu- Local carpenter
Signora Tsega- Signore Membrahtu's wife
Ahmed- Palace driver
Mario- Owner of Alba Restaurant

Prologue

September 1987
Addis Ababa, Ethiopia

The morning Miriam called, I was outside drinking coffee on my front porch and doing my daily prayers. I was sure it was one of the ladies from my women's business association calling to complain about the new bylaws I passed the night before.

"Almaz, tell whoever it is that I am not home. Those women from last night have been calling all morning!" I yelled to the maid, annoyed that I had to interrupt my prayers.

The telephone rang again. "Hello." I could hear Almaz, and seconds later I heard her footsteps coming outside instead of the words I had told her to say.

"Emama," she said. I hated it when she called me that. It reminded me of my own grandmother, and I was not that old.

"For the last time, call me Signora Bella. I am not your Emama. I told you to tell those women that I am not home. I do not want to be interrupted during my prayers."

"Signora Bella, it is your daughter. She says she is calling from a different country."

"My daughter?" I asked, wondering why one of my girls would be calling me on a random Friday morning. "Which one?"

"I do not know. I did not ask. Should I go ask now?"

"No, no, I'll come talk to her," I said, getting up from my chair.

"Hello?"

"Mama, it's me, Miriam. She is here. You're a grandmother now!"

September 2019

That phone call occurred over 30 years ago. And now, here I am in my eighties, an immigrant living in the United States in Alexandria, Virginia, just mere miles away from most of my family, or at the very least what is left of them here. A part of me wants to believe I'm living up to the grand promise I made to myself so many years ago: that I would stay connected and close to my grandchildren at any cost possible. Yet my circumstances, like those of so many others from Ethiopia and Eritrea, have changed drastically over the years and have forced us to live in faraway places. I know deep down in my heart that had our situation been different and had our countries been safe, I would not be an immigrant today. I would go home to my people and live the rest of my days sitting on my porch, smelling and sipping coffee, ground and roasted that same morning; listening to the wild laughter and swift footsteps of my cherished grandchildren and enjoying the perfume of incense wafting on that crisp, dry East African air.

Now that my five granddaughters are all in their twenties, I believe it is finally time to share my story with them. It is time to revisit old wounds and heal from them as well.

I gathered all of my granddaughters together one day in my younger daughter's family room where they snuggled together on the big sofa. There would be no television or internet today as I made them surrender their phones and the television remote. The room was bright yet chilly from the air-conditioning set in the high 60s, where the girls seemed to love it. We all wore sweaters, and I added my favorite gabi (blanket) and sat near the windows to bathe in the warmth of the late day sun.

Then I began my story.

"I was never the shy one, never the one to hold back and let others define me in any way. No kings, nor queens, nor communist leaders could stop me from living the life I wanted for myself. But life sometimes has other ideas for us. It's funny. We think we are always in control, but listen to me, and listen well, I'm going to share a story that will not only show you that life has its own way of making you change your path, but that it will also always bring you back to the center when you think you are lost. All stories start with a beginning. For mine, we will begin in 1957. I was twenty years old and had my whole life ahead of me. I remember this year especially because this was the year it all started."

"All what started, Grams?" My youngest granddaughter Natsenet was the one to blurt out questions first. "Do not interrupt me and you will see." I looked at her sharply and then continued on. "Later I will give you the details, but first let me explain why I am telling you this." I looked at each of them one by one to make sure they were paying attention.

"Never allow yourself to feel like a victim. No! We are strong, independent women who will always rise from any situation thrown our way. Girls, I want you to promise me that you will always stand up strong and proud. What I am about to share with you is my story. It is an Ethiopian story, an Eritrean story, an African story, and an international story. It will display a rich and well lived life. I do not want you to dislike or think ill of anyone who hurt me or intended to hurt me, because that was and is my job and my job alone. I dealt with my pain, and you girls will have to deal with yours. I am telling you my story today because, against my better judgment, I did not take the time to tell it to your mothers and I will always regret that. Had your mothers understood the importance of their strength, had they not been sent away and sheltered from the struggles we had to endure in Ethiopia and Eritrea when they were a little younger than you, well, then maybe things might have been different between us all today."

I had thought hard about how I would tell my story to these innocent young women. They had not seen famine, death, and the other atrocities that came with war. They did not know the callous realities or the pain of war. No, these young women were sheltered just as their mothers were before them. Sheltered because their father and I saved them from the pain, yet that caused more heartache in the long run. Therefore, I refused to make the same mistake twice. I wanted to protect their innocence, but also prepare them for the real world that was so much less forgiving than the one they were so very fortunate to be raised in. They needed to know how easily people could hurt their loved ones or betray them without realizing the damage that was done. I thought about how I had raised my own girls and wondered if their lives would have been different if I had shared these stories with them. Could I have been a better mother and maybe a better friend to them? Should I have kept them near to me after we fled Asmara, Eritrea, and arrived in Addis Ababa, Ethiopia? Would things have been different today? Well, at the very least, God was giving me another chance with my granddaughters, and I would do better this time around. I wanted to be a part of their lives no matter what was happening in the world around them. No war, no famine, no betrayal, not even the saints and angels could hold me back from my family. I was going to be sure that I made a big impression in their lives. By telling my story and having them understand why I am the way I am today, maybe, just maybe, they will not only understand the world better but also understand me better, too, and strengthen our bond.

CHAPTER 1

Life in London 1957

Every Sunday started out the same ever since I could remember. Wherever I was, whatever was going on, I always made sure to find a Catholic church nearby where I could attend Mass. My faith was always what kept me going, especially through all the hardships I endured. Plus, attending Mass somehow made me feel connected to my biological mother, a woman I had never met except for the seconds after my birth.

"What was she like?" I would constantly ask my papa, Lorenzo. The answer was always the same: "Just like you," he would say. He told me stories of her bravery and beauty whenever he could, but somehow it was never enough. The church always felt like home because that's where I lived until my father finally came to get me when I was two years old. The nuns at Saint Thomas in the south of Ethiopia named me Weizerit, a name meaning "Miss," that my father later changed. The sisters of St. Thomas were my caregivers after my mother died in childbirth and my father, being a high-ranking officer and always on secret missions for the emperor, could not take care of me immediately after my birth. My mother died and was buried at St. Thomas, and for that alone, a piece of me has and will always be connected to the Catholic Church and especially to that chapel.

So, on this Sunday I was excited, yet wary of the unknown as I entered a different Saint Thomas Cathedral far, far, far away from my home country. I was in London, England, and I had grown fond of the city. The year was 1957. In a few days I would graduate from King's College; I could barely contain my excitement to receive my first degree. Up until the night before, I had been ecstatic to return home to Addis Ababa and start my career in foreign affairs, following my father's footsteps. My dreams of the future came shuddering down in the form of a telegram with horrible news from His Imperial Majesty, the Emperor of Ethiopia. I was to be wed to a powerful senior general, General Kebede, after graduation. My heart felt so heavy as I read the words on the telegram.

> *ANNABELLA,*
> *THIS IS TO INFORM YOU THAT GENERAL KEBEDE HAS FORMALLY REQUESTED FOR YOUR HAND IN MARRIAGE. THE CEREMONY WILL TAKE PLACE UPON YOUR ARRIVAL IN ADDIS ABABA.*
> *- OFFICE OF H.E. HAILE SELASSIE*
> *EMPEROR OF ETHIOPIA,*
> *ADDIS ABABA,*
> *ETHIOPIA*

I felt knots growing in my stomach as I read the words. I read each word so slowly and repeatedly that it made me dizzy. I prayed there was some mistake in the translation. I hoped that this was meant for a different woman. However, in my heart I knew neither were possible. This was not the first telegram to change my life. It spun me back to the first telegram I received with horrible news. That telegram announced my father's sudden death. My father was the only immediate family I had in the world, and I found out he was dead through a sheet of paper. Nothing about this telegram brought me happiness. Maybe I should have been happy to gain a husband, a new family. Marriage to the general felt only like another death. This death was of my own ambitions, dreams, and the version of myself that I so adored. Both news crushed me with sadness. Both announced an untimely death.

I never imagined a life where I was wed to a man I did not know. A man I did not love. A man I did not choose for myself. I had heard of and witnessed multiple arranged marriage ceremonies for years, however, that was always from a distance. Then again, what did I imagine my life would be like? Was I truly to believe that I would graduate from King's College and go back to Ethiopia to work as a diplomat? And not just any diplomat but the Minister of Foreign Affairs! Ever since I was a small child who watched her father stay up late to write speeches for the emperor or discuss Pan-Africanism with other political leaders, I was drawn to his work. I loved listening to him talk at conferences and hearing stories of his work at the dinner table whenever I was home from boarding school. Continuing his work and legacy was as important as breathing air to me. Without it, I could not live, and now all that was being taken away from me. "Bella, get some sense into that thick head of yours," said Saba, my best friend and roommate, who also happened to be a princess. "Father will never go for it. You have brilliant ideas, but do not forget you are a woman."

In response, I gently threw a pebble at her leg and a sudden look of hurt appeared on her face.

"Well, that serves you right, telling me my dreams cannot come true. You do not know if it could happen or not, so why should I stop dreaming?" I scolded Saba for saying what I was thinking myself but was too afraid to say out loud.

It was the day before graduation, and the weather was as beautiful as London could get in May. The sky was blue, and I looked forward to the day ahead. I could not wait to see my family lined up to witness me being handed my degree in Political Science the next day. Even though my biological mother and father would not be in the crowd, my stepmother Yeshimebet and her family, whom I grew up with and loved very much, would all be there. These days I cherished them more than ever. They stood up for me when I needed it most after Papa passed away, and they took full responsibility for my upbringing alongside the imperial family. I could not wait to see the mother who raised me, and tell her about the telegram I had received. I hoped that my grandfather, who was the emperor's first cousin, could and would talk to the emperor on my behalf.

The church service was beautiful and as always, I sat in the front pew praying and looking up at the statue of the Virgin Mary. Today was a different kind of prayer. Today, I begged for my deliverance, my freedom. I prayed for hope, for a new life, and as always, I prayed that my mother and father were safe in heaven with God. After Mass, I stayed behind for my favorite ritual. Closing my eyes, I tried to picture my parents at Saint Thomas 20 years earlier. My father left my mother there, where he knew she would be safe until he could return from his secret mission. They were meant to start their life together upon his return. Young, scared, and pregnant, he left her on the steps of that church in the middle of the night with instructions to stay quiet and hidden until things were safe again. How brave they must have been. How scared they must have felt. I closed my eyes extra-tight, trying to picture my mother during those days-rubbing her pregnant belly, praying, and helping the nuns at the church. How difficult her labor must have been for it to take her life. Why would God take her away? I battled these thoughts all the time. The only thing I had remaining of my parents were stories and a huge legacy my father left me when he died. I would have given up all my wealth and the titles I inherited for just one day with my parents. Just one day!

"Amlakay Getaya, my God, I know you have a reason for everything you do in my life. Whether good or bad, you have full control and will always guide me in the right direction. Please Lord, help me understand not only why Papa and Mama had to die, but also why this marriage proposal has happened. Is this for your glory? I cannot believe that this is what you have in store for me, Lord. I have never been one to argue with you, but I know deep in my heart that it is wrong and I need your help. Please keep me strong and vigilant in my faith as I fight for my freedom. I pray that you will always keep my family and friends safe and that you will stand by me in everything I do. I ask for all this in your name. Amen."

Upon finishing my prayer, I got off my knees, genuflected at the end of the altar, and walked towards the door. I made sure to do the sign of the cross with holy water from the church and then slowly walked out of St. Thomas and headed straight to Harrods for my weekly coffee date with Saba. I smiled, thinking about how we had officially made Sunday afternoons at Harrods our "ladies' time," even though we lived in the same apartment and did pretty much everything together. I looked at my watch and realized it was far past two, which was our normal time to meet. As I rushed to get on the train that would take me to Knightsbridge, I thought of how sacred these Sunday coffee dates at Harrods had become, and how I had grown to love Saba as a sister. Her Royal Highness Princess Sabawork and I had been classmates and best friends since the first grade.

Saba waved at me from the café, and I was excited to see she had secured our favorite seats and already had my cappuccino waiting for me.

"Oh Saba, how I love you! Thank you for this — it's been a long night and I have been thinking about this cappuccino since six this morning," I said.

"What took you so long? I was worried your drink would get cold," Saba said. She went on to tell me excitedly that Sebastián, our usual waiter, had saved our seats for us. It amazed me how our time in London had changed us. Even simple things like reserved seating were seen as a pleasure now, when back home in Ethiopia it would be considered perfectly normal.

"I got caught up praying for our future, speaking of which, are you excited to graduate and go home?" I asked.

"I'm honestly not ready to leave all this. If this was home, we would not have been able to sleep in and simply walk into any café for cappuccino, let alone enjoy it in peace. I would have guards and protocols to follow. I have grown to love this freedom and I'm not like you, Bella. I do not have big dreams of saving the world, or my country for that matter. I just want to be happy and enjoy the simple things in life," Saba said, sipping her cappuccino.

"I understand, Saba, I really do, but your country needs you. We are blessed and fortunate to have come here and received an education. Do not forget we came with every intent to go home and make change, remember?"

"No, you came to do all that. I just came to be with you, and come on, this is London after all! Even after the war this is still my favorite city. I could not let you have all the fun alone. Enough of the sad talk! Are you excited about graduation, and your life afterwards? Have you given it any more thought?" Her face showed concern, but there was a hint of laughter as well.

"Yes, and honestly, I'm scared! I just do not understand why your father would think marrying me off to General Kebede is a good idea. For one, he is at least twice my age. And Saba, I do not want to get married now. I want to become the Foreign Minister. I want to rebuild our country and do so much more. I want to finish what my father started — working towards creating a united Africa where we all stand with each other, so colonization never happens again. Why allow me to come to England for an education and then not allow me to use it? Why marry me off right after graduation? I just do not understand!"

"You know Father will never say no to an education. He believes too much in the power behind a book and in learning. He wants to modernize and mobilize Ethiopia, and the best way to doing that is to educate our people. Still, it's one thing for you to be educated and another for you to actually practice in that field, especially given your status and prestige. A good education will serve you well as the wife of such a great man. Who knows, you might still be able to become the Minister of Foreign Affairs, only just as General Kebede's wife."

"Even thinking about that gives me chills. I cannot, I will not, marry him. I refuse!"

"Okay, how about we keep enjoying our drinks that are not so warm anymore, and order our food for now? We can worry about this problem later. I'm starving."

I agreed to stop talking about the general and my arranged marriage, but I could not stop thinking about it. I had to find some way to stop the marriage.

The day of graduation, I woke up bright and early to attend a short daily Mass at St. Thomas Cathedral before heading down to King's Hall on campus. I was excited about my big day, but also dreaded the fact that this meant my time in London was coming to an end. I was ready to go home, just not ready to become a wife. I walked into the church and right away I saw a familiar and loving face that instantly made me smile.

Of course Yeshimebet was there. My stepmother always loved coming to this church whenever she came to visit. We embraced with hugs, and as I smelled that familiar Coco Chanel #5 scent, small tears started trickling down my face.

"What's wrong, my daughter? I know you missed me, but I believe you are supposed to cry when I leave, not when I arrive! Come, come now, where is that beautiful smile of yours? I have missed you so much and I am so proud of you. We all are. I know your father is smiling down on you from heaven right this minute."

"Oh Mama, it's so good to see you. I have missed you so much! I have so much to tell you. I got a telegram from the emperor and it's horrible. He wants me to marry General Kebede! All my plans and hopes are slipping through my fingers, Mama. I do not know what to do. Please have Ababa talk to him. I cannot get married, especially not to General Kebede. I have too much life left in me to marry an old man like that."

"Hush, child! Slow down. I cannot understand when you talk fast like that. We got word as well of the marriage proposal, and Ababa approved it already without my consent. Darling, we only want what is best for you. Think of what this will mean for you. You will be the wife of one of the greatest generals in Ethiopian history. All over the world people will have the utmost respect for you and this will be good. It will secure your future. You are part of our family and have prestige already, but a union like this will keep you safe always. The world is changing, darling."

"What do you mean, keep me safe? I will not do it, Mama. I refuse! I want to be a part of that change in the world, not married to an old general who is part of the past. Why do you think I came to England to get educated? So that I can come home and help rebuild our country! I want to bring Africa together and work towards ending colonization. You know, finish Papa's work."

"You can do all those things in due time, Bella. Being a wife will not stop you from your dreams."

"Mama, we both know what will happen once I'm married. I'll be expected to do my wifely duties, have children, stay home, and run the household. I cannot even imagine how I could ever live like that."

"With time you will enjoy those responsibilities, they will become routine, and you will have plenty of time to do the things you love and want to do. You will also learn to love the general. He is a good man, Bella. Just give it some thought."

At that point, hearing Yeshimebet talk like that, I knew my situation was hopeless. Even she thought it was a good idea. I decided to just continue praying and let God take over. I knew this could not be my life. I knew deep down in my soul that my life was meant for something completely different. We prayed together in that church, and as I was praying, I felt tears coming. "Lord, please help me, help me." I could feel Yeshimebet's warm, gentle touch on my shoulders and with that, I started crying even more.

On graduation day, my mind was so troubled that enjoying my time, and even smiling, was hard to do. Never being one to shelter my feelings or hide my emotions, I was open about how I felt, and people usually either took to it or shied away from me because of it. On this particular day, it took a great deal out of me not to speak my mind to my loved ones. I had every intention of giving my grandfather and even the emperor a piece of my mind, and as I marched towards them during our graduation celebration event at the Ethiopian Embassy, it was Yeshimebet and Saba who held me back. "Annabella Lorenzo, do not dare go over there and embarrass yourself and this family. I forbid it!" Yeshimebet scolded. "Yes, Bella, calm down," Saba chimed in. "Think about the words that will come out of your mouth if you go there now. Father has good intentions, and if you think you will prove him wrong, this is not the place. Let us think this through and find another way. Trust me, I will not let the marriage happen if you are against it. We will find a way." I calmed down and smiled at my best friend and stepmother. Hearing Saba's willingness to fight for me brought me some relief, so I tried my best to enjoy the rest of the beautiful party.

The next week in London went by fast, with many graduation parties and friends to see before we all went back home to our respective lives and countries. Saba and I were heading back to Addis Ababa in a few weeks, and we wanted to enjoy our last days in London. Saba had somehow managed to postpone my wedding a few months, and for that I was extremely grateful. She also promised me that she would make sure I got a chance to speak with the emperor once we were home. I knew that if I could personally explain my reasons as to why marrying the general was such a bad idea, he would agree with me, and we could all move on from this ordeal.

The last few days in London were bittersweet, yet we had fun doing our usual things. We shopped and sat at our favorite café in Harrods. We spent countless hours at Buckingham Park, reading and enjoying the sunshine, and we danced the nights away at all our favorite nightclubs. Saying goodbye to London was poignant, but I was ready to go home and bring change to my people. On our last day, we stood in our apartment and felt overwhelmed saying goodbye to it.

"So many memories here, Bella. I do not know if I'm ready to leave it all behind."

"I know, Saba, I know, but it's for the best. We have to go home. It is time."

We closed the door and walked away from our cozy flat in the West End. We had our driver take the scenic route to Heathrow Airport because we wanted to get one last look at the beautiful city we'd come to love. We knew we would be back in London again, but most likely only to visit. We were both in tears for the entire ride. As we made our way to the terminal, we managed to find some relief in the idea that our lives were just beginning. One chapter was now closing, another was about to begin, and there would be many chapters. When I looked up and saw an Ethiopian Airlines plane parked on the runway, a smile appeared on my face. "Saba, look! Home, here we come."

Ethiopian Airlines D3 plane and Airport *Addis Ababa*

September 2019

"I do not understand, Grams. How can your own family want you to marry an old man you do not even know? Do they not love you?" Segan asked.

"No. It was because they loved me very much that they wanted me to wed. Back then, that was how things were done, my darlings. It was a different time, when women did not have the right to decide what their lives would be like. In fact, our only purpose back then, according to the men who were in charge, was to get married and have children. I was young and naïve and assumed I was immune to the same rules because of my education level, but I was wrong. Listen and learn how your grandmother challenged and changed all of that."

CHAPTER 2

Going Home to Addis Ababa

The flight from London to Addis Ababa was a mere seven hours, and while Saba slept the entire way, I stayed up to work on my talking points for the emperor. I had been working on this for weeks and felt fairly sure that I could recite the entire speech with my eyes closed, but the perfectionist in me could not rest. It wasn't enough for me to know my speech, I wanted to also ensure my facial expressions and body language would reflect and be resilient for my cause.

"I know you believe with all your heart that this is right for me, I know you think my family would want this marriage for me, but that's exactly why I cannot do it." I was proud of my speech and knew in my heart that he would listen to me.

I had known the emperor throughout my childhood and had always found him to be kind, generous, and reasonable when need be. Though he was feared by many, and accused of being brutal at times, with me he had always been a second father. I hoped he would see the child in me and push aside this wedding agreement, or even better, see the educated woman and respect my careful arguments and heartfelt wishes.

We arrived at Lideta Airport early in the morning on July 6th, 1957. I remember the date clearly because it was my father's birthday. Apart from a light drizzle, the weather was beautiful. I took deep breaths to inhale the cool, crisp air, and put my hands out to feel the raindrops that were lighty falling. It felt good to be home. From the plane's exit doors, I could see the mountains far away and our family vehicles parked by the terminal. Yeshimebet, Saba's older sister Princess Maryam, my cousin Yonatan, and our drivers were now all within walking distance of us. Saba and I loved spending time with Yonatan who was a little older than we were and studying to become a lawyer in the south of France. I wanted to go study with him as soon as I could and had already sent in my applications. This was part of my plan in following my father's footsteps, and it would be a huge stepping stone for me to get into the Ministry of Foreign Affairs. I knew that with a law degree attached to my name, doors would open even further for me. "Well, well, well, look who finally decided to graduate and come home," Yonatan said as he grabbed us both into his arms and gave us a hug. "YONATAN! Oh, how we've missed you," both Saba and I said at once.

"Excuse me, what about me, your mother? Remember me?" Yeshimebet pretended to be insulted, as did Maryam.

"And me too, madam, your wonderful sister who made time to come pick you up because I know how much you love an entrance! Come here and give me a hug."

"Oh, Maryam, how I have missed you. How are you? How is that husband of yours, and how are the kids?" asked Saba.

"Everyone is doing great and very excited to see their favorite aunty. Now that you are back, you must come stay with us in Asmara. Dawit is now the governor of Eritrea and it's such a beautiful place. Bella, you must come as well."

I felt a surge of despair, hearing Maryam talk about Eritrea. I was Ethiopian by birth and loved my home, but my father's blood still poured through my veins, the blood of Eritrea. And although I had not been to my father's homeland, I still felt very connected to it. It wasn't long ago that the Italians finally left Eritrea, only to have the British come for a certain amount of time. And recently outsiders within the United Nations came to the decision to federate Eritrea with Ethiopia, making what should have been two nations, one. My loyalties stood to both countries, but deep down I wanted liberation for Eritrea. I could never openly speak of these desires with the imperial family or even my own family, for that matter. They were content in the way things were, and anything that took away from that contentment was not tolerated. The only person that understood me was Yeshimebet's mother - my grandmother Emama.

We drove to the Jubilee Palace where everyone was anticipating our arrival. I loved the drive from the airport to the palace because this way I could see the full view of the beautiful city. How alive I felt, how free! Other African countries, including Eritrea, were not given the same privileges. Having seen a bit of the world, I knew how vital these freedoms were for the people and for our own growth as a nation. Although I had never been to Eritrea, Papa had told me stories of how the Italians treated our people when they colonized the country from 1870-1941. How they subjugated the Eritrean people and made them feel like they were incapable of doing anything without Italian oversight. How they took over our cities, slept with our women, and killed men who they thought might rebel against them. The Italians had forced Eritrean men to fight Ethiopians in the battle of Adwa: fight against their neighbors, their brothers. I knew that the Italians made sure not to educate the local people, and instead turned them into servants. I tried to imagine all that they could achieve if given the same freedoms as Ethiopia. Of what Africa could achieve as a whole if given even a glimpse of freedom.

At the palace, we were greeted by our closest friends and family. I longed for my father and remembered the last time I had entered the imperial palace with him. I was home for the holidays from boarding school in Cairo and was looking forward to spending time with him. We were in his office when the call came for an urgent council meeting and, instead of staying in the office alone, I pleaded with him to take me. It was in that meeting that I knew my life was destined for public service. I wanted to be just like my father. His grace, his power, and his kindness were impressive, and even when all seemed hopeless, he was able to motivate his colleagues to keep pushing.

"Bella?" Yonatan's voice startled me from my thoughts.

"You're physically here, little cousin, but your mind is definitely far away. Is everything okay? Talk to me."

"Yes, sorry, I was remembering the last time I was at the palace with Papa.

I attended a meeting with him, and Yonatan, you should have seen him. He rallied everyone together, gave this powerful speech, was perfect with his words, and put a plan in place for a brighter and greater Africa. Not just Ethiopia or East Africa, he was working towards a greater Africa as a whole. He was so ahead of his time. So brilliant. After the meeting, we came here to give a full report to the emperor himself and Papa let me stay and watch it all. Anyway, sorry. I just miss him so much."

"We all do, Bella. I know it must be so hard for you, and I can understand. He was like a father to me, too. He mentored me throughout my high school years and college, and then encouraged me to go to law school. He saw something in me even when my parents and I did not. He knew I was destined for greatness and I promise you, Bella, I will continue his work. We both will."

Just as I was about to respond to Yonatan, I locked eyes with Lekay and saw she was coming towards me. Lekay had been Saba's nanny throughout our boarding school years and had always taken good care of me as well. I had missed her dearly while we were both away in London.

"Hold on Yonatan, I'll be right back".

I walked away from Yonatan and into Lekay's open arms.

"Lekay, oh Lekay, how I have missed you!"

"I have missed you too, *Yene Lij*, now let's get you upstairs and out of these travel clothes. After all, Princess Saba and you are the guests of honor today."

Get-togethers at any of the palaces were never casual. They were more like grand balls, but with with family and friends. I was happy that Lekay took me upstairs to change and had my clothes brought from my grandfather's home. Both Saba and I looked beyond beautiful in our elegant gowns. As usual, Saba made her grand entrance and I followed roughly five minutes afterwards. I knew the drill, I had done this plenty of times before. We walked together until we reached the main staircase and Saba was announced first, followed by her younger nieces and nephews, and then me. I always got knots in my stomach when I heard my name called at these events. All eyes watched my every move as I swept down a long set of stairs and into the grand ballroom. I could not help but think of Papa as I walked down those stairs. He would have been so proud to see me today, as a graduate, all grown up and ready to face the world. Although these parties usually seemed excessive, today I actually yearned for it. I felt closer to Papa and was thrilled to be home and surrounded by my loved ones.

I walked down the stairs and through the long entrance hallway to greet the emperor and queen, and formally thank them for such a beautiful event. I kept reminding myself that now would not be the place nor the time to talk about my upcoming wedding. "Stay calm, Bella, stay calm," ran through my head over and over again. I curtsied as I always did, and seconds later the queen gave me a nod and called me closer to her for a more private welcoming.

"We've missed you and that wild daughter of mine. It's good to have you back home again. Is it possible you have grown even taller? What were those Brits feeding you, dear?"

"Oh, the usual. Biscuits with tea every day, and tons of fish and chips," I said with a smile.

The queen smiled back and then the emperor spoke.

"Annabella Lorenzo, how proud your father would have been to see you today."

As the words came out of his mouth, I could feel tears forming in my eyes.

"Stay calm. Bella, stay CALM!" I kept reminding myself.

"Saba tells me that you would like a meeting with me to discuss your upcoming wedding. That is an excellent idea. We will discuss it later this week in detail. Today is your day to celebrate your accomplishments."

"Yes, Your Highness. Thank you so much!" was my humble response.

I did not know if it was because of my jet lag or the emperor's wedding comment, but my festive mood evaporated seconds after our encounter. I was ready to go home and be with Emama. I knew better than to ask my mother or my grandfather Ababa to leave. This party was partly in my honor, and as part of my duty, I smiled for another three hours until Yeshimebet finally pulled

me away from the Duke of Harare and told me that we could leave if I was
ready. I smiled at her and turned back to the duke, apologizing for cutting our
conversation short and explaining that I had to go home. As we made our way
to leave the palace, I looked for Saba to say goodbye and was happy to see her
with Yonatan, lingering by the exit door.

"I'm going home. Talk to you soon," I told them.

"I'm right behind you cousin. I'm still tired from my trip," Yonatan said.
Saba waved us off with: "You two are old people in those young bodies. The
night is still young! Please stay."

"No thank you. Mama saved me once already and I doubt she will do it
again," I replied. "I'm going." Yonatan, not one to ever say no to Saba's charm,
decided to stay. I always secretly hoped that they would end up together. My
two favorite people together forever; now that was a love story to tell. At that
moment, I wondered if I would ever be able to find someone that would love
me the way I saw Yonatan loved Saba, or even the way Papa loved Yeshimebet.
Genuine, deep love. That's what I wanted for myself and knew I could never
have with the general. If only Saba knew how blessed she was! Saba had not
noticed Yonatan had feelings for her and when I mentioned it, she dismissed
the idea and told me that they were friends, nothing more. That, in fact, she
saw him as a brother. Maybe it was because she knew the script of her life
would always be written for her: who she would marry; what title he would
have; what family he would come from. She wasn't given the opportunity to
pick and choose. And yet, somehow, I was being matched with a powerful general and Saba was not.

As we reached the gates to our family home, my heart started racing with
joy. I was excited to the point that I did not realize our driver had not stopped
the car completely when I opened the door and dashed out to see Emama.

"Darling, darling, she is taking a nap at this time. Let her rest, her health
hasn't been the best these days. You should rest as well, while Berhana unpacks
your suitcases for you," Yeshimebet said from behind me.

"I'm fine, Mama. I'll be in the gardens if you need me. Call for me once
Emama wakes up." With my ball gown still on, I walked to the gardens to see

what Emama had been growing this season, and to take some time to think without people around.

Full of beautiful flowers from daisies to forget-me-nots, this garden was a sacred place, where one could relax, pray, or simply daydream. Emama's garden was unlike any other I had ever seen. Maybe it was the way each flower glowed as the sun shone on it, or the way the fragrance of the roses hit you as you walked into the gated garden. Emama had planned each section of this area on her own. There was a pathway leading up to the beautiful wooden gate, and when that closed behind you, it was like you were in a different world. There were endless rows of flowers, and in the middle of all that was a beautiful greenhouse with the most exotic flowers. A little past the greenhouse was the cutest little bungalow, complete with two benches and a hammock. This is where all our family portraits were captured and where Emama took her daily afternoon tea. I grabbed my speech to the emperor from my brassiere, having stored it there in case he brought up any wedding discussions at the party earlier. I read my speech again and again until my attention drifted away to the beauty of our home, from the architecture, to the landscaping, to the exquisite décor, and to the bountiful gardens. There was space for everyone and everything, and best of all, it was always full of love and lots of people. The most important inhabitant was, of course, Emama. She made everything magically better, especially meals. She was the glue that held us all together.

No matter what was going on in our lives, everyone came together to eat family meals. It was tradition in Ethiopia, and most countries of Africa, that meals were to be eaten as a family. Stores, government offices, and even schools closed every day at noon and re-opened at 2:30 for the afternoon shift. This tradition of eating together, drinking coffee on the front porch, and then taking a short, relaxing nap before returning to the real world was something I cherished. It was like we were in our own little bubble every day for two hours. We could eat good food, laugh, and discuss what was in our hearts. Even though I saw most of these people again at night, dinners weren't as memorable as our lunches together. Maybe that's because Emama cooked alongside the many servants to make each meal more delicious than the one before, or maybe it was because my cousins and aunts typically did not come for dinner but never missed lunch. Whatever the reason, I was glad to be home again and to get back in the kitchen with Emama. She was the daughter of a prominent general during Emperor Menelik's time and had been groomed for royalty from an early age. She knew how to handle any situation, and was tough yet gentle at the same time. I loved that she always spoke her mind no matter the circumstance. "You're just like your old Emama, Bella darling," she would always tell me, and I would smile from ear to ear upon hearing it. She was my female role model. When Papa married Yeshimebet, it was Emama that took me in and raised me as her own granddaughter, never making me feel like a step-child. Instead, she was always fighting for me, especially after Papa died.

I knew Emama would never agree to this marriage with General Kebede, and I could not wait to discuss the telegram with her in the kitchen, since that was our favorite place to spend time together. Now that she was getting older, she did not travel as much or attend the grand balls anymore, but she always somehow managed to know everything that was going on.

"Bella, Bella, where are you, child?"

My day dream was interpreted by Berhana's voice calling for me from a distance.

"Annabella Lorenzo, your Emama is awake and asking for you, so come now," yelled Berhana. I started running for the gates, past the greenhouse, and past all the beautiful flowers. Giving Berhana, my old nanny and our house-keeper, a hug along the way, I dashed towards the main house. There I saw Emama for the first time in what felt like forever.

"Emama! Oh Emama!" I said as I ran to be in her arms. After a long embrace, Emama started talking.

"Bella, my Bella, you are home at last! This house has been horrible without you. No one to cook with me, and I think your mother is trying to kill me with all this healthy food. I'm an old Ethiopian woman. I need meat and butter, or at the very least pasta - rich, full of butter and tomato sauce pasta." I laughed and whispered in my grandmother's ears.

"It's okay, Emama, I'm here now and I'll make sure you get to eat whatever you want. I even brought your favorite chocolates."

"Oh, bless your heart. This is why you are my favorite grandchild. Come in front of me, let me see you properly. *Ende*, Bella, you have gotten so thin, did they not feed you in London? You're so beautiful and tall, very elegant. Those Brits know how to make a young lady out of girls. What happened to those skinny legs and that chubby tummy? You see all my yelling finally paid off."

It was just like Emama to take credit for something while also making you feel bad about yourself. "Yes, Emama, I feel great. I guess all the walking we did in London impacted my calves and stomach. Well, that, and the food wasn't all that good, nothing like our meals anyway. I'm so happy to be home, but I have a problem."

I leaned in closer to Emama, hoping that what I had to say would only be heard by her.

"It is about a marriage proposal for me. We can discuss it later, though."

"Darling, I know what that stupid husband of mine agreed to and I will not have it, not one bit of it. I have my own plans for you, but as you say, we shall discuss it later."

Emama and I embraced again, and I could not keep the happy tears from tickling down my face. I was beyond happy to be home and with the people I loved so dearly.

"No, no, no! I just told you your face looks so beautiful, why mess it up with tears? Come, come, tell me all about London. Did you meet any handsome men? Any soldiers?"

I blushed at the thought of discussing my love life with Emama, but I knew better than to lie or keep a secret.

"Well, I did go on a couple of dates, but nothing serious. I was too busy studying."

"Rubbish! You go all the way to England and come back with no good stories? Pure rubbish! In my day, we came home with lots of stories to tell our friends. I want the stories you told Yonatan and Saba all about," Emama scolded.

"Honest, Emama, there is nothing to tell. Saba was with me all the time and we spent a lot of time in our West End apartment. We socialized a great deal and met wonderful and interesting people from all over the world, but other than that all I did was study. My grades are impeccable, Emama. You should be proud of me."

"I always knew you were the smartest woman in the world. No need to be proud of something I already know." I laughed and took her comment as a compliment.

"Now let us go have some tea in the garden. Lead your Emama to our favorite place, please. These legs are having trouble walking these days and I want to save my energy."

We went out the door and headed for Emama's garden, with Berhana following behind to serve the tea and homemade cookies. Once we reached the bungalow, Emama dismissed Berhana and looked straight at me.

"Bella, I'm working with Princess Maryam to get you out of Addis and away from General Kebede. I hear he personally asked for your hand in marriage, and I do not trust him. I'm scared he has a hidden agenda and is using you as bait. I need you safe and away from here, away from him."

I could not believe my ears.

"Emama, you cannot go against the emperor's orders! That will be considered treason and I will not have you punished on my account!"

"Oh, hush, child. Leave the emperor to the queen, the princess, and me. What is he going to do, throw an old lady and his daughter in jail? Anyway, he should know better than to wed a child to a grown man. Times are changing and you are different. You have dreams for your life and they do not involve getting married right now. Had someone fought for me when I was your age, who knows what I could have become."

With those words, I felt that my future was now secure at least. I did not know how Emama was going to get the job done, but I knew that at the end of the day, I would be a free woman.

I remembered my conversation with the emperor from earlier that day. He knew I wanted to talk to him about some things regarding the wedding.

Saba had not given him all the details, just that I wanted time with him. He had agreed to it, so it only felt right that I still meet with him. Now, given this new information, whether I expressed my reluctance to wed General Kebede at that meeting would be something I needed to discuss with Emama first.

"Emama, I set a meeting with the emperor to talk about why his idea to wed me off to the general is bad. Should I go through with it? I saw the imperial family earlier today and the emperor even brought up the wedding. He thinks it's a great idea and I believe he thinks I am going to agree with him." Emama shook her head in dismay, "Oh Bella, you are just like your father. Always trying to do the right thing and fighting for what you believe in. I am so proud of you, my darling. So very proud! Take this old woman's advice though, do not go to the palace and share your thoughts with the emperor. It will not go as you plan. Since you already arranged a meeting, go there and discuss the wedding, as he believes that is what you intend to do. Tell him you need time and that you would like General Kebede to agree to you working within the Ministry of Foreign Affairs and that you will keep your father's assets under your name. Help him understand that if the general is asking for your hand in marriage, it should be because he wants you, not your money. Let's see what he says about that. Since he has already agreed to postpone the wedding, which I hear General Kebede was not too pleased about, we now have more time to plan your escape from the city."

"Emama, where will I go? How will this work? Will I ever be able to come home?"

"Bella, I pray it will only be temporary, but I intend to send you to the place you should have gone years ago with your father. You are going to your father's homeland, Bella. You are going to Eritrea. There you will make a life for yourself and do what makes you happy."

I smiled. I knew exactly what Emama meant.

We sipped on our English tea, quiet for some time, both of us lost in our own thoughts. I was thinking about how much I would love to have homemade Ethiopian coffee instead of English tea, but I knew Emama would never drink coffee in the late afternoon, as it affected her sleep pattern. She was lost in her prayers and thanking God for returning her beautiful child home.

"Saints Michael, Gabriel, and George, I knew you would not disappoint me. You always provide for my family and show us your greatness in the end. Now hear me and make sure you tell your boss up there this child will leave Addis Ababa and start a life of her own. She will not get married to that general. I do not wish anyone harm, but Michael, you can tell me honestly, what does he want with my grandchild? Shame on him!"

Emama was famous for having these real conversations with saints, angels, and sometimes, even the Virgin Mary, Jesus, and God himself.

The next morning, I woke to the sound of Mekonnen, our gardener, fighting with Joy, the poodle that Princess Maryam had given me on my eleventh birthday. Joy was ten years old and lately liked to sleep in the garden, making a huge mess out of Emama's rose bushes. *"Itchi belegay hegi hegi kezi!"* He was yelling and pushing Joy with his broom to get off the roses and out of the garden. I opened my bedroom window and called for Joy to come to me, hoping to not only calm Mekonnen but also to hug my dog and save her from his wrath. I walked towards the garden and Joy came running, ready to lick me and have me rub her belly.

"I have missed you too, Joy, but you know better than to sleep on Emama's plants. You're going to get us both in trouble. Come on inside, I brought you a special treat."

By the time I got back to my room, Berhana had already had the house-maids make my bed, and they were now cleaning my room.

"Oh, it's good to be home," I thought, walking away from my room and into the dining room, where I found Emama doing her daily Rosary with Yeshimebet.

The two of them had been doing Novenas for as long as I could remember, and I loved joining in on their prayer sessions whenever I was home. Today was no different. I ran back to my room, picked up my new favorite rosary that had been blessed by Pope Pius XII himself, and went back into the dining room. I sat alongside my mother and grandmother and started to pray. With each Rosary decade, I could feel my heart getting more and more at ease. I knew good things were coming and I continued to thank the Virgin Mary with each Hail Mary I completed. As we closed out the prayers, I whispered one more Hail Mary for my intentions to get married to a man I loved. Whoever he was, wherever he was, I wanted him to be safe, healthy, and full of joy and love. Yeshimebet and Emama smiled as they heard my last intention.

"Bella dear, you already know who you are marrying. I'm glad you are praying for him, though. A great marriage is one built on prayer life," Yeshimebet said.

With that Emama rolled her eyes and said, "Let this poor child get some food in her so she can come help me in the kitchen." "Emama, you know the maids can cook lunch. I do not know why you insist on overseeing it every single day," Yeshimebet said.

"Ende, are you crazy? I will not let a maid feed my family anything that I have not seen or touched or placed on that menu myself. It's the principle of the matter, Yeshimebet darling. I fed your father and all of you for all these years and will not give someone else the honor now that I am a little sick. I already talked to the angels and told them that when it is my time to go, I'll let them know and I will go peacefully. They do not want to deal with me up there for now, so I'm fine down here, feeding my family."

I burst out laughing, loving how blunt and honest Emama always was. While I laughed, Yeshimebet simply shook her head.

"All right you two, get yourselves into the kitchen. The family will be here at noon as always." And with that, Yeshimebet walked away.

I walked into the kitchen with Emama and got to work just like old days. On the menu that day was tomato soup, homemade pasta stuffed with ricotta cheese and mozzarella, chicken cutlets, and lastly, Emama's famous crème brulée. Lunch was always a three-course meal at our home, followed by traditional coffee on the front porch. It was a big production that happened every day at noon regardless of what was going on in the world or within the family. Emama would order everyone around in the kitchen and check each dish to make sure it was up to par. If there was anything she did not like, she would make the maids do it again. I loved being in the kitchen with her. I loved learning new recipes and seeing her techniques. We made magic in this kitchen, and I always felt so honored to not only learn from her, but to also share these moments. I also enjoyed the fact that my family would be eating food I made for them, made with love and care!

As we finished cooking, I placed my apron down and told Emama I was going to go take a shower and get dressed for lunch. I could already hear my family gathering together in the living room.

Lunch was served in the formal dining room, and it was here that I saw all my family for the first time in months. We all hugged and embraced, and I was the toast of the table. I talked about my time in London and how rapidly the city was changing after the war. Ababa raised his glass and spoke up just as I finished, "Bella, our Bella, it's good to have you home again. Cheers to ending one adventure and starting a new one." Emama spoke up and changed the subject, suspecting that Ababa was about to bring up the upcoming nuptials.

After lunch came our coffee time, a celebration I had desperately been waiting on. I had not had good coffee in so very long, it felt almost foreign to me. All it took was one sniff of that good Ethiopian Bunna to bring me back. In all my travels, I have had coffee from all over the world, but nothing could ever replace the smell, taste, or ritual of pure Ethiopian coffee, especially with the traditional ceremony. With all the aromas and sounds of coffee roasting nearby, it felt like a small piece of heaven on earth.

Being here with my family made me ache for Papa, though. He had loved spending time on this porch, discussing important matters with everyone assembled. I remembered the last time we were together on this porch. It was three and a half years ago during my holiday break. I closed my eyes tight, hoping I could visualize him here with me now. Nothing. I tried even harder, shutting my eyes tighter, but nothing was coming. In the past, whenever I was sitting out here for coffee, I had been able to see him clearly. Had too much time passed that his features were no longer visible to me? Was that really all it took for me to forget the most important man in my life, forget what he looked like, smelled like? NO! I knew I had to try harder, and as I thought that, I saw him. Sitting right next to me, holding his black coffee in one hand and playing a rock game with me using the other hand. He always had such great balance and it amazed me every time. I smiled at him, he smiled back, and I opened my eyes.

Having seen my Papa, I decided I would make a trip to where he was buried and spend some time with him. As my grandparents bid farewell to the family and retreated to their rooms for their afternoon naps, I tapped Yonatan's shoulder and asked him to go with me to visit my father's grave.

"Yonatan, come with me, please. I do not want to make a big deal out of the trip and everyone will want to go with me if I tell them, so let's just go together, you and I."

"*Eshi*, I have been wanting to go since I got here myself so yes, let's go. I'll drive though, I do not want the driver telling mama we went, or Yeshimebet to know that we went without them," he said.

We walked away from my house and towards Yonatan's brand new 1957 Mercedes Coupe.

"Wow, nice car, Yonatan. When did you get this and how come you did not tell me about it in your letters?"

"Papa had it waiting for me when I came back from school. It's nice, *Aydel?*" he said.

I rolled my eyes, and made a face that showed jealously and excitement at the same time. "Some of us get forced into marriage while others get new cars."

I was only half joking but I smiled at Yonatan to show that I meant well. I was happy for him; I knew how much he loved cars and this was the perfect one for him.

"*Esti*, let me be nice and open the door for you, *Mademoiselle* Bella."

"Oh, how nice. *Merci, Monsieur.*"

My French was always good; the many years of boarding school in Egypt and France had helped me learn many languages. Papa used to tell me that it was hard to talk secrets around me because I could understand just about every language he spoke. I had mastered Italian, French, Arabic, English, and, of course, Amharic. I also had a working level of Tigrinya, which was spoken in my father's homeland, Eritrea and Tigray, located in the northern region of Ethiopia. Of all the languages my father spoke, the only one I did not understand was Russian.

The drive to the cemetery at Kidest Selassie was beautiful that afternoon. The heat had gone down and people were still at work, which resulted in light traffic. Yonatan had the windows open, and I could feel the breeze hitting my face and hair. Once we reached the church, we drove past the gates and pulled into our usual parking space a few feet from Papa's grave. I hurried to cover my hair with my favorite scarf out of respect for the church and the dead. It was customary to cover up when on church grounds in Ethiopia. We walked to Papa's resting place and simply stood there looking at his statue for what felt like an eternity.

Whenever I thought about the dead, I used to imagine sadness and fear. However, losing Papa and spending time with him here changed that for me. Although I was heartbroken over losing my father, my time with him at the church was always uplifting and healing. His gravesite was done beautifully. Yeshimebet had a statue made in England that showed his handsome face with all his features. The writing on the gorgeous marble was in Amharic and French.

Blantangeta Lorenzo Kidane

"Loving Husband, Father, Legend. May your work always go on and may you finally get the peace you deserve."

"They sure did love each other," said Yonatan.

"I know, it was almost too good to be true. They were a perfect match, always enjoying each other, laughing, hugging, and dancing. They always supported each other. I can only wish that I will find that kind of love one day."

"You will, Bella. I know you will, and you probably will drive the man crazy, too," laughed Yonatan.

We wandered around the gravesites and looked at the other names buried there, many of whom we either knew or knew of. We found a bench that faced Papa's grave and sat there talking about him until the sun started to fade away.

"Did the thought ever occur to you that Papa is buried only steps away from where he worked so hard to make change?" I asked. "I think about that often. I wonder if he is still working diligently up in heaven as well. Sending messages, leading councils, fighting the good fight, whatever it may be."

Yonatan laughed at my thoughts and was about to make a comment when I looked at my watch and noticed the time.

"Oh my, it is getting late. I'm sure Emama will wonder where I went. I did not tell anyone before we left. Can you stay at our house tonight? I miss you. I want to talk about so many things that have happened to me since I last wrote to you and I have a surprise to tell you."

"Bella, I cannot tonight, as I made plans with Saba. Maybe afterwards I can come, although you know how Emama is about late guests. I will probably have the door locked on me again. How about we catch up tomorrow?"

It was now my turn to laugh and make a comment. "A date with the princess! Do tell me more about that. Sure, tomorrow works as well, but let me just tell you my surprise now while we are driving home. I applied to the school of law at Montpelier University in France, and I'm waiting on my acceptance letter now. I want to join you at law school, Yonatan, and go to the school that Papa attended as well."

"Bella, that is wonderful news. I am sure you will get in. I admire your determination, Bella Lorenzo. You are one tough lady."

"Why thank you, I think I am pretty tough as well."

We both laughed and enjoyed the ride home.

"Enjoy your date, cousin. Do not do anything that I would not do," I laughed as he dropped me off at home. "That would be pretty much nothing," he said as he started the car back up and left.

I entered the house to find Emama and Princess Maryam sitting in the living room whispering about something. I knew only too well that it had to be about my escape, but I did not want to barge in on their conversation, so I knocked on the door and asked if I could enter. They both smiled at me and

Emama said, "Of course, silly girl, come here and plan your adventure with us."

I walked towards both ladies and gave Emama a kiss on her forehead, then I hugged and gave Princess Maryam the traditional three kisses on her cheeks. Princess Maryam was beautiful, probably the most beautiful of the princesses. Tall and slender, she had high cheekbones, beautiful light brown eyes, caramel-colored skin, and long black curls that draped perfectly on her shoulders and back. She was also highly favored by her parents, and by Ethiopia in general. Extremely well-educated and active in women's rights, she played a big role in ensuring that Ethiopian women received proper education and could get jobs in the government and the private sector. She believed that women could have children and a career as well. A mother of two children, she was well into her thirties and juggled numerous responsibilities with grace. So many women looked up to her for inspiration and empowerment. Princess Maryam looked at me with kind eyes and said, "Yes, do sit with us. Let the planning process begin."

The Jubilee Palace *Addis Ababa*

CHAPTER 3

Planning an Escape to Asmara

I watched Emama talk to Princess Maryam in amazement. This woman always fought for what she believed was right and did not take no for an answer. It was a trait that I had attempted to master for years.

"Listen, Maryam. I need Bella's exit to be quiet and fast. The General is already asking why the wedding date has been postponed. Your father has done us a huge favor by postponing the wedding on Saba's request. This thankfully bought us more time, but I'm worried that General Kebede will somehow get the date pushed up. I have had people look into different ways to get Bella out of Addis, and it looks like driving her through Tigray would be the best way. She would go as a commoner, no titles, no positions, and no money on hand. I can get her fake documents with a new identity in order to leave the city, but once she is in Asmara, I want her to use her first and last name. I want her to build a life with the people knowing who she is. It would mean a lot to her father."

"Wait a minute, Emama. I do not intend to live there permanently, I want to come home at some point," I said. "I do not know my family there, I do not speak the language that well, and it's a small city from what Papa said. What am I supposed to do there?"

"Listen here, child. It's either that, or you can get married and have children with the old general, you pick."

"Asmara, here I come," I responded with a scared yet determined face.

"You'll love Asmara, Bella, trust me!" said Maryam. "Which part of the plan should I get involved with? I think it will be best if my part starts once she is in Asmara. I can and will take full responsibility for her. She can either stay with us at the palace, or I can help her get her own place in the city. What should I tell Father when the time comes, though?"

"I will work on what we will tell the emperor after Bella is gone. Sooner or later he will find out where she went, and unless we have a good plan in place for when that happens, he will command that she be brought back and there will be nothing we can do. So, ladies, this is where we all need to come together and get creative. I will do my best to get her out, but I need you two to come up with a plan of how we can keep Bella hidden, and then how we'll fight for her to stay there and away from the general once her location is revealed. This is especially important. We need to make it sound like the plan will benefit the country in some shape or form instead of making it about Bella and her freedom."

"What if I tell him that I needed her in Asmara with me for a short time to work on an education project I am starting and will send her back to Addis once it's complete?" said Princess Maryam.

"No, why would we hide her if she is on official business? It doesn't make sense. We need to come up with something very good; a deal where he has no option but to agree to it."

As I listened to Emama, I came up with a brilliant plan!

"I got it!" I exclaimed.

"I have a meeting with the emperor to discuss my wedding. I'll go to the meeting, talk to him about the details, and talk about how much I miss Papa and wish he could be here to witness the ceremony. Then I'll bring up how there is so much I do not know about myself and about his history and how I would love to learn more. Then, we'll leave it at that and I'll go to Asmara with no one knowing. When the emperor finds out I'm gone and starts to have me searched, Princess Maryam can then tell him that I needed to find out who I was, where I'm from, and make it emotional so that he can somehow sympathize. With that we can at the very least buy me more time."

"*Aye*, Bella, brilliant. You are brilliant, *Yene Lij.* This is exactly what we will do," said Emama, smiling broadly.

"What will happen when he orders you to come back?" asked Princess Maryam.

"I have a good feeling that somehow he will not ask for her return. The angels are speaking to me. Trust me, this will be good," said Emama.

We ended our secret meeting on a happy note and with a plan in place. Now, all we had to do was wait on my counterfeit travel documents and meet with the emperor before my escape could take place.

The next day I woke up early and headed to the palace to meet with Saba and hopefully find out what day I would be getting on the emperor's schedule. Tadesse, our family driver, took me on the scenic route because I wanted to experience the drive as many times as I could before I left for what might be an exceedingly long time. The palace guards knew the family car and opened the gates for Tadesse with a simple salute. The palace grounds were exquisite with all kinds of beautiful flowers, small exotic huts, and my favorite two animals that were always so welcoming— the emperor's pet lions, Mochuria and Mollua. They both grew up at the palace and I loved spending time with them. Where others were scared, I could see how powerful and yet tamed these creatures were. I was allowed to pet them and I never once felt frightened by them. Even when I was away in boarding school and came home, I remember how much love they showed me upon my arrival. Tadesse dropped me off by their stomping grounds so that I could say hello and spend a few minutes with them.

"You are a crazy child, Bella. They are not pets, they are lions," he would always say.

Not paying attention to his caution, I got out of the car and went to greet my old friends. They had aged since the last time I saw them. Mochuria's mane was changing color and he looked sad. "I know how you feel, my friend. It must be rough having all this privilege but still not being free to do as you please and go where you please. One day we will both be free." As I said the words, a powerful roar came out of his mouth and I smiled. He understood me!

I returned to the car feeling stronger and we drove another few minutes before arriving at the main palace doors. Saba was waiting for me by the main entrance.

"Lekay told me the guards called to say you were coming. I have so much to tell you! Yonatan and I spent time together, Bella, and we kissed," said Saba smiling. "It's not something I could tell you over the phone. I'm glad you came over today."

"*Anchi*, I want details — how, when, and how do you feel now? I need to know everything."

Saba laughed and I could tell that she was starting to blush. Was Saba in love with Yonatan? The thought alone made me smile and hug Saba tightly. Love was such a beautiful thing and the idea of having my two best friends together and in love made me beyond happy.

"Bella, I have yet to tell you the full story and you are already hugging me, wait till you hear the good parts. You remember the day of our party when I was talking to him? He told me stories about law school in France and I shared our stories from London."

"Wait, I hope you only told him your stories and did not include me in any of those escapades, because I was forced to be there," I said, laughing.

"Really, Bella, this is not about you, so do you want to hear the story or not?"

"I'm sorry, Saba, please go on."

"Thank you. Well, we talked and talked. And then I started to get pulled away by my mother to meet guests that came to congratulate and welcome us home, and since you were nowhere to be found, I had to deal with it all myself. He saw that I was getting busy and decided to leave me a note with Lekay, just telling me that we could continue our conversation over dinner in a few days and that he would call me. I did not think anything of it until he called and officially asked me out. I said yes, a part of me thinking it was just two friends, while the other part of me kept revisiting the conversation we had in London when you told me he liked me. I guess him officially asking me out on a date confirmed it, and I wanted to see what he would be like on a romantic level instead of just my goofy, smart friend. He came to pick me up, and luckily for us, everyone was busy with the new deal my father is working on. So I was able to slowly slip away. I only told Lekay and the guards where I would be."

"*Ende*, your guards did not come with you? I thought the deal was that you would have to have them with you at all times outside the palace gates."

"Yes, they were there. Sadly my father did not forget our bargain. Even though I begged Yonatan to lose them, he refused to do it. He said he respected my father and mother too much to try to disappear from the guards. Let me get to the good part. We drove for a while, but it felt like seconds, in his beautiful new car."

"He took me to this incredible Italian restaurant called Castelli in Piazza. I was shocked that I never knew about it before, but apparently it opened only months ago. Turns out it opened on Christmas Day. The ambiance was exceptional; there were different dining rooms, which gave it a homey, private feeling. All the rooms were dimly lit, and with candles on the table, it was very romantic. The restaurant is owned by the Castelli family, and they have been living here since the Italians came in the 1930s. Father would never approve of me eating at such an establishment, but they were such sweet people. The food was astonishing, even better than the pasta we ate in Rome or Milan. I ate saffron pasta while Yonatan had bistecca. They sat us in a secluded area of the restaurant so we could dine and talk freely. We talked for hours, laughing about old times, and discussing what we want for our future. He asked me a question that made me think of my life's choices. *What do I want to be remembered for?* I never thought about the future in that sense, or even the present for that matter. I'm always trying to have fun and enjoy the moment, which is great, but talking with him about his future and what he wanted to be remembered for made me think about my life as a whole. I think it's time I grew up. I need to take my role and possibilities as princess more seriously. I want to help people and build a legacy like Maryam is doing with the schools. I guess I just need to figure out what makes me happy and hold on to that."

"Saba, you have no idea how happy this makes me feel. I'm so proud of you, and I know that whatever it is you decide to do, you will be great at it. Better than great, in fact! You will thrive and make such a difference in this world."

"I hope so, Bella, I really hope so."

"Okay, what happened next? When and where does the kiss come into play?"

"Oh, I almost forgot the most important part. After we ate dinner and dessert, we stayed there and continued talking until they were closing for the night, then we got up to leave and he grabbed my hand to hold. He walked me to his car, opened the door for me, kissed my forehead, and closed the door. We did not say much to each other on the ride home, I guess we were both lost in our own thoughts and in the beautiful night. When we got home, he parked the car, opened my door, and held my hand as he walked me to the front steps. Then he kissed me goodnight in the sweetest and most loving way. It was a slow kiss. I think he meant to kiss my cheek, but I moved, making our lips touch. Bella, I had chills. I still have chills talking about it now. Something sparked in me that I never knew I had."

"I think that's what love is," I said.

"Is it? Am I in love with Yonatan? Oh Bella, I feel so happy. Should I call him? What will I say? How should I act when I see him again?"

"Slow down, Saba, let's take it day by day. Yes, call him but act normal. I am sure he is feeling the same way you are so there is no need to be nervous and act differently. He loves you for you and I believe he has loved you for quite some time."

We talked for hours. Saba was so excited that she kept repeating the story of her first date over and over again. Somewhere on her sixth storytelling episode, I brought up the meeting I was supposed to have with the emperor.

"Oh my, that was actually the main reason I wanted to see you this morning. Father wants to meet with you tomorrow. Are you ready?"

"Perfect! Yes, I'm readier than I'll ever be and confident too."

We continued to talk about Saba's date, and without realizing it, we spent all morning together. Suddenly it was lunch time.

I asked her if she wanted to come home with me for lunch with the incentive that Yonatan would be there. I could tell she wanted to see him again, but declined my proposal in order to spend time with her sister and nieces.

We said our goodbyes, and I rushed out the door and into my car to get home for lunch with my family and to tell Emama the news.

When I got to the house, Emama was not happy with me at all. "You missed our cooking session today, where were you?" was all she said to me. I knew my grandmother was not a woman to be trifled with and felt horrible for missing our time together, but did not see how I could have walked away from Saba either.

"I'm sorry, Emama. I went to see Saba, and we both lost track of time discussing her date with Yonatan, but I brought great news with me."

"It is great for you to miss our time together?"

"It is, I promise. Saba told me that the emperor will meet with me tomorrow to discuss my wedding. It looks like our plan will start sooner than later."

"That is indeed wonderful news. Okay, you and I must go over what you will say later this afternoon. No more leaving the house today, madam. I need to spend all the time I can with you. This old lady's days are numbered, and if you are going to leave me again, I want to be spending every day with you until then, especially our cooking sessions. Promise me, Bella, no more going out until after lunch." I promised and gave her a light kiss on her forehead. Some days she was so fierce, and then on days like today, she seemed so fragile.

Lunch was divine, and with each bite, I regretted not being able to witness Emama instruct the maids on how to make the different meals. My family gathered and prayed before hearing what the day's special would be — all Ethiopian dishes —, Doro Wot, Tibs, Yebeg Alicha Wot, and tomato salad. Seeing everyone so happy together and enjoying their mid-day meal made me smile, although I was also feeling sad. This tradition was probably going to be the hardest to leave behind. Just as I got lost in my thoughts, Yonatan and I caught each other's eyes and I gave him my "I know what you did" smile. He automatically caught on, winked, and shrugged at the thought that his baby cousin had already heard all the details. As lunch was wrapping up and the family was moving outside for our daily coffee ritual, Yonatan caught up to me and whispered,

"I know you know, so what do you think? Do I have a chance with the beautiful princess?"

"What are your intentions with my best friend, monsieur?" I said in a joking manner.

"Bella, be serious. I'm being serious with you. What did she say?"

"I cannot share that with you. She confided in me and knew I would never divulge her secrets, but I will tell you that she cares for you. Whatever you said to her really made her think about her life, and for that she is grateful. I think you have a chance, Yonatan. Just be yourself, though! You are a wonderful man, and she would be lucky to have you."

"Thank you, Bella!"

"So, when are you going to see her again?"

"I called her right before coming here. I want to take her out for a picnic tomorrow during the day, either early morning or around sunset. I plan on going to Entoto, the view is breathtaking. What do you think?"

"I love that idea. She will love it! Good job, Yonatan."

I noticed Emama looking at us chatting and I smiled at her. I wondered if our family would be okay with Yonatan being with the princess, and how Saba's family would take the news. Yonatan was my father's nephew, so at least they weren't blood relatives. I could tell Emama had a thing or two to say, but would hold herself back until her opinion was asked for by Yonatan. I wondered what that opinion would be, but I had my own relationships to worry about.

"Yonatan, you should talk to Emama about Saba, and get her blessing before you do anything else. You will need her support if you want to get anywhere with the imperial family. Go to her first, but not today. I have a date with her and I do not want you to mess it up for me," I said jokingly.

He told me he would talk to her tomorrow afternoon. Emama got up and said her goodbyes to everyone as she headed to her room for the daily nap. Ababa got up right behind her and followed suit. I knew I would have to wait until later in the afternoon to discuss my upcoming meeting with the emperor.

It felt like hours passed before Emama woke up from her nap and had me summoned to her quarters. I immediately got up and dashed to her room so that we could talk about our plans. As I entered her room, I was startled by how fragile she had become. She had lost weight, but it wasn't just that; she looked old and that was something I thought would never happen. Emama must have read my mind because she interpreted my thoughts and said:

"I am okay. A little wrinkle here and there will not hurt your strong Emama. Stop worrying."

"How did you know I was worrying?"

"I can see it in your face. You tend to lift your brows when you're stressed or worried and there is a facial expression you make, which I do not think you should be doing at all, if you ask me."

I knew there was no winning this debate and let it go.

"Come now, help your Emama get to the gardens for my afternoon tea."

With that I got up to help place her in the wheelchair and push her outside. Once Berhana set up the tea and left, I began sharing the details of my morning with Saba.

"The emperor has requested we meet tomorrow. Emama, I'm nervous but excited at the same time. I feel like this will push up our timeline and get the wheels turning for our plan. Can I practice my speech with you?"

"Speech? Start our plan? Bella, this is not one of those mystery books you read or a game. This is your life on the line here. You need to grow up, child, and take this very seriously. You need to be alert. VERY alert! Pay attention to his demeanor, the way he talks to you, what kinds of words he uses. All of this will be very important information for us to gather. I have known the emperor for a very long time and can sense when he knows something is not right. We do not want him to feel like that at all. We want him to think that you are simply nervous and have questions about the wedding.

"Very well, what do you think I should say? I wrote out a speech, but it only referenced that I declined the marriage," I said.

"Had you gone into the palace with that speech, you would have placed the emperor on edge, and he most likely would have pushed your wedding date up again. You must be very calm, speak out of wisdom and not fear or anger. You must be gentle and ladylike, submissive even: that is what he wants. Speak from the heart but do not share everything, only the parts that you know he wants to hear. His people will seem like they care and want only what is the best for you, but understand that is just an illusion to get you exactly where they want you."

"Okay, but now I'm very nervous!"

"Do not be nervous, think of this as a play. You are an actor in a play and this is your starring moment. Play your part to the best of your ability. Before you can be the best actress though, you must learn all about that character, right? How she talks and walks, her mannerisms and demeanor. Then you learn how to relate to your audience because at the end of the day, it's them that you will have to please. If they love you, you will continue working, if not, you will become history after one show. Therefore, since we already know what kind of character you need to be, you can easily bring that piece together. This leaves us with your audience. I have about four hours to groom you for this life-changing performance."

I listened very carefully to every word that came out of Emama's mouth. We spent the entire afternoon practicing the script, and how to deliver it un-der extreme pressure. It made me think of what military training must be like: intense and exhilarating. I knew my life depended on this meeting and I was determined to make it work no matter what situations arose. By around the fifth hour, we heard Berhana come into the garden to announce that dinner was served and asked if Emama needed help going back inside the house.

"No, my granddaughter will take me."

"*Eshi*, everyone is waiting for you, Emama."

"I'm coming, I'm coming. Give us five minutes," she said.

"You are ready, *Yene Lij.* You will do great tomorrow. I will do my Rosary tonight and tomorrow as well. The Virgin Mary and all the angels will stand by you tomorrow or else!" she said, waving her finger at the sky to show the angels she meant business.

After dinner, I wished everyone good night and had excused myself when Emama called me back and asked me to help take her to her room. Everyone immediately jumped in to help, and she simply ridiculed them for not hearing her ask me.

"I want my grandchild to take me. If I needed your help, I would have asked for it."

I laughed and started walking Emama to her quarters. There, she handed me a silver box. In it was a beautiful gold necklace with a blue sapphire pendant. I knew this necklace, and had seen her wear it on special occasions.

"I want you to have this necklace Bella. I have been saving it for you and I think now is the perfect time to give it to you. You are starting a new chapter of your life and I know this will always give you great luck in whatever you do. Always remember how much you are loved, darling."

"Thank you so much, Emama. I do not know what to say other than thank you. I promise I'll wear it forever," I hugged and kissed her cheeks before saying good night and retiring to my bedroom.

"Go to sleep, child," she called after me. "You have an important day ahead of you tomorrow."

The next day I woke up with knots in my stomach. I wanted today to go perfectly and knew that my future depended on this one meeting. In my dressing room, I started picking out my most business-like attire. I wanted to look professional and youthful at the same time so that the emperor would take me seriously while also seeing the child in me. My main goal for the meeting was to remind the emperor how much of my father I had yet to learn about, and how much I missed him. Most importantly though, I was hoping to touch his soft side. In doing that, I would be able to buy myself more time and maybe, just maybe, he would see the mistake in this marriage proposal and even free me from having to go away. I knew this was a long shot, but it was still worth a try.

The vanity desk in my room held all my secrets, all my dreams, and my daily journal. I opened it to write down how I was feeling and poured myself into the pages. Apart from the gardens and our family kitchen, these pages were my greatest joy. After writing for a while, I gave myself a long stare. I looked like a grownup in a black pencil skirt, sheer Dior blouse, little makeup and my newly gifted necklace, plus a pair of pearl earrings that Papa had bought me for my 13th birthday. I was ready, or at least as ready as I would ever be.

"You are great, Bella. You will achieve greatness. You are great," I said, right before walking from my room into the main hallway. I reached the main door before realizing that I had forgotten my heels.

As I dashed out the door, this time with my full attire together, I heard Tadesse telling Berhana that he was outside waiting to take me. He stopped halfway through the conversation as soon as he saw me.

"Weizerit, today you look like a Weziro," Tadesse teased me playfully, commenting on my transformation from a brash, young, unmarried woman to someone who looked mature and poised to face any battle.

"Thank you, Tadesse, I need to look like a Weziro today. I have an important meeting. Pray for me, please."

We drove out the gates and onto the main road heading straight for the palace. I started to think about my own strength, my ability to stand strong and keep pushing. Whenever life threw obstacles in my way, I always managed to dodge them and keep going.

"This should be my life's motto," I thought. "Whatever happens, I will never stop pushing through, I will never GIVE UP." With those thoughts I stepped out of the car, said goodbye to Tadesse, and walked into the palace. I was informed that the emperor would meet me in his main office, which was in the next building. Upon arrival, I was ushered into the waiting area and told to sit there while the emperor finished his weekly morning meeting with the generals. Generals!

My body cringed at the sound of the word. Did this mean that General Kebede would be there? I prayed I would not run into him. Just as all these thoughts floated into my mind, I heard a group of men ascend from one of the rooms behind me.

"Lord, please do not let him be here. Please, Lord, please!"

Moments later, Emperor Haile Selassie emerged and greeted me as an uncle would greet his niece.

"Bella, *Yene Lij*, come let us talk," he said, ushering me into his grand office. He was wearing a black suit with two of his medals attached to his suit pocket. His beard was trimmed while his mustache looked like it had grown a bit since the last time I saw him. Although his warm brown eyes and quick smile were approachable, for obvious reasons I was intimidated and very guarded. Sensing my tension, he called his secretary from his desk and had her close the door behind her. Then he took a deep breath, relaxed in his seat, looked me in my eyes, and asked the important question:

"Tell me, what is it that makes you so nervous that you need to come and speak with me directly?"

There it was. He could see I was nervous and was asking me the one question Emama had warned me about. This was how he was going to reel me in and make me share my thoughts. This was him sounding concerned when he actually wasn't. Or was he? I was suddenly confused. His face seemed so sincere and it was a simple question and who was I to lie to the Emperor of Ethiopia? But who was I not to lie? I did not want to marry an old general, and lying was my only way out. I started to get a headache with all the talking that was going on in my head.

"Your Highness, thank you so much for taking this meeting. I know you are very busy. I needed to talk to you because, while I am incredibly grateful for the opportunity to marry General Kebede, and I cannot wait to be his wife, I feel like there is so much I need to learn about myself. I am young. I do not truly know who I am yet. I miss Papa very much and he was the one who used to answer these questions for me. I feel confused, Your Highness. I do not know how I can be a good wife while I am still confused about life."

"My child, I feel like this is more of a conversation for Saba or Maryam or even the queen. Unfortunately, I'm not the best when it comes to sensitive topics, but I can share with you the type of man your father was. He saved my life on more than one occasion. He was smart. Smarter than anyone I have ever met, and funny too. He knew how to work with people of all races and ages, and could make anyone believe what it was he wanted them to believe. Bella, your father was an honorable man. Now is this really what you wanted to talk to me about?"

I started crying as the words describing Papa left the emperor's mouth. I missed him so much.

"My sincere apologies, Your Highness. I do not know what has come over me."

"It is understandable, dear, grief is never an easy task to uphold, especially at such a young age. You are strong, Bella, and he is watching over you. Everything will be just fine."

"Is he watching over me? I feel as though if he were here, I would not be so confused."

"There will always be doubt in our hearts, there will always be questions we ask ourselves. What is important is what we do with those feelings. The strong will deal with it and move on, while the weak will allow confusion and fear to build up in them."

I knew that the longer I stayed in this meeting, the more I would be inclined to tell him that I did not want to marry General Kebede. I thought I was strong, stronger than my circumstances, but hearing the emperor talk about my father, being in his office, just talking to him took all the strength I had. The meeting could only get worse from here.

"Bella, I can see you are in pain. Did you come to talk to me about your father, yourself, or General Kebede? I'm confused, my child, and very busy. I can see you are confused too. I want what is best for you, and marrying General Kebede is exactly that. He is a wise man and will be good for you. He comes from an outstanding family and is of royal blood. If you are worried about love, please know that the queen and I were in an arranged marriage and we learned to love each other. Your parents' marriage was also arranged, as was that of your grandparents. It's what we do, Bella. This is how we keep the power and prestige amongst us."

I knew better than to argue with the emperor. I remembered what Emama had told me: "Do not share what is in your heart!" So, I nodded my head to show him that I agreed.

"You are right, Your Majesty. I will learn to love General Kebede and will be ready to marry him when the time comes."

"Take these few months to get yourself together, spend time with your family, and learn as much as you can about your father. That will do you some good. The wedding will take place in September after the new year." With that comment, the meeting was over. Now I knew what I had to do. As I walked out of the office, my tears dried, and a smile came to my face. I was ready to leave all of this behind and start a new life.

Castelli Restaurant *Addis Ababa*

CHAPTER 4

Learning about Eritrea and Ethiopia

The drive home was quiet. Tadesse attempted to start different conversations with me, but I was in my own world. What would Asmara be like? What would my family be like? I meant to ask Yonatan about it as well. Then I remembered that my trip was a secret I could not share with anyone. This meant that Saba could not know, that Yeshimebet would not know. I wondered how worried my family and friends would be once I left.

Before I knew it, Tadesse was parked outside our home where Emama was sitting on the front porch waiting for me.

"*Yene Lij*, you look stunning. How was the meeting? Tell me everything," Emama said.

"I'm not proud but my performance was decent enough. I did not disclose anything about our plan but he could tell I was scared. I believe I even managed to confuse him because he asked me twice what my purpose for the meeting was. I began crying, however, the second he talked about Papa."

"Bella, come here. Give your Emama a hug. *Ayzosh*, do not be sad. You look too beautiful to be sad in this ensemble. At the very least, take off the Dior." Emama was only joking with me but I knew her well enough to know that she half meant it.

We hugged and talked for a while, I described the entire meeting, withholding no details, and Emama expressed how proud she was of me. I had not derailed the plan in any way at all. Rather I had given us more time. This was a good thing, yet I could not stop thinking about how I could have done better.

"*Beka beka beka,* stop! *Ende.* What's done is done and you did a good job. Maybe you should become an actress," Emama said, joking again. "Come, let's make lunch. I had Berhana tell the staff to start without us today and I want to oversee their work. Change your clothes and meet me in the kitchen." I did as I was told, and as I was walking into the house, I heard her call my name and tell me she loved me.

"I love you too, Emama, more than you can ever know!"

At lunch, the family was all together, sharing stories of the day. Hearing them laugh and joke made me forget about my own troubles. Yeshimebet, who was talking about her day at the University of Addis Ababa, went on and on about the freshman English classes she taught. I listened with pride to my beautiful stepmother. She was the kindest, most loving woman I knew. She always had a way of making everyone feel important and wanted. These were the traits I knew my father loved so much, and it was what made her an excellent mother, wife, friend, daughter, and now a teacher as well. Her students knew she had their best interest at heart; she listened to their concerns and wrote her curriculum based on their English language needs instead of what the dean or university wanted her to teach. This made her superiors and some peers upset, but she did not care. She said her job was to elevate the students and make sure they learned how to use proper English grammar in their writing and speaking. Now that the Allies had won the war, English would become the common language in our part of the world.

"So, had the Germans won, would you be teaching German and not English in your classes, Aunty?" said Yonatan's little sister Marta.

"Yes and no, *Yene Mar.* Had the Germans won, maybe the rest of Africa would be learning how to speak German and probably even Italian, instead of English. However, we have a close relationship with the British monarchy, and that in itself would have probably kept English in most of our schools and curriculums. But who knows."

"Oh, I love the Italian language. Papa speaks it and it sounds so beautiful. I wish I could learn that instead of English."

"Hush, child. I speak Italian because in Eritrea we were colonized by the Italians. I was forced to speak it. You, on the other hand, are being given an opportunity to choose. Be grateful!" said Uncle Mikael.

"Is that why you have Italian names, Papa?"

"If you must know, yes. That is why my brother Lorenzo and I have Italian names. We went to a missionary school in Keren that was run by Italian priests, and they changed our names from Mebhratu and Fisseha to Lorenzo and Mikael. We were too young to understand."

"If you like, you could change your name back now, right? asked Marta. I loved how specific Marta's questions were. These were questions I had always wanted to ask.

Ababa sensed Mikael's frustration, so he answered Marta's question on Mikael's behalf.

"Changing your name is never that easy, *Yene Lij*. It takes time, and your uncle and father have built a legacy with the names they were given as children."

"But Ababa, if it reminds them of colonial days…" Marta clearly had more to say but was silenced by Ababa.

As soon as lunch was over, I headed to my room while the rest of the family went outside for our ritual coffee ceremony. I could not get our family conversation on names out of my head. I wondered why Papa had given me an Italian name when he was forced into his. I hoped going to Asmara would answer many of my questions. I could go back to my roots, explore where I was from, and meet other parts of my family as well. I wrote about my thoughts in my journal and managed to somehow take an afternoon nap.

What felt like minutes but was indeed hours instead, I was awaken by the sound of my name being called from somewhere outside my bedroom window. I looked out to see and hear Berhana yelling my name and asking me to have tea with Emama in the gardens. I closed my windows, fixed my dress, and headed out to meet them. Afternoon tea time always included homemade cookies or pastries and sometimes, depending on the season, we had fruit as well. Blackberries, oranges, and even peaches were all grown in Emama's garden.

"Hello there, sleepy girl. I trust you rested well, because we have a lot of work to do now."

I responded with a nod and asked if there was anything I could do at that moment.

"My contact, who will provide the counterfeit documents, called this morning and told me that they are working on the final touches for your identification papers. Our lunch conversation gave me an idea, and I changed your name on the passport. He said we should have the final products in hand in two weeks. This is perfect timing for us. We need to start arranging your transportation and make sure you have cash in the different cities on your route. I will start contacting people I know and trust in the cities you will be passing through so that they can provide you with accommodations. I do not want you to travel with cash on hand. Remember, you will be a different person, with a different name and family. Do not speak unless spoken to and never share too much with anyone until you reach Eritrea."

"Yes, Emama. What is this name change you made, though?"

"You will see when you get your passport. It is a surprise."

"*Eshi*, is there anything I can do in the meantime?"

"Yes, we need to start by getting you ready for the drive to Asmara. I want you to be familiar with the different cities you will be driving through, to know and understand the route. That way no one can take advantage of you. Who do you think can help with teaching you and will keep these lessons a secret?"

"How about Tadesse?" I asked.

"No, no, no, Tadesse is loyal to Ababa and will turn his back on us the first chance he gets. We need someone who will stay loyal to us and owes me favors, someone who will take our secret to the grave if needed. This person needs to be knowledgeable and wily as well. Think, Bella. Who should we ask?"

Different people came to mind, but no one that was knowledgeable on the different cities in Ethiopia. I saw Berhana approaching us with more food, when the most obvious person came to my mind. "You know what, Emama? What about Berhana's husband, Marcos? He is the driver for Uncle Mikael and should know the drive through Tigray well enough. We should ask him. You got him that job, thus making him in your debt. Not to mention, he works for my uncle and therefore his loyalties will stay with him. I have known Marcos since I was a little girl. I am positive he will not mind assisting me now."

"Great work, Bella, you are always so wise! He will be the perfect person. I will discuss the matter with Berhana first. She raised you and will be happy to help us. I'll have her talk to Marcos and set up a time for you to meet with them at their home. He can teach you the roads and give you history on each city you will pass through, and then I will have him find us a driver that we can trust."

"Perfect!" I said, just as Berhana set down extra biscuits for us.

I had a good feeling about this plan. Berhana and her husband were like family to me, and I knew they would help me in any way possible. We continued to drink our tea and eat biscuits until we were called inside to get ready for dinner.

The next morning, I was awakened by a shake from Berhana.

"Marcos said he will help you. Bella, *Yene Lij*, I will be very sad to see you go, but I know it is for the best. I will pray for you every day. Promise me that you will never forget me, that you will write to me and tell me all about your new life, just like you did when you were away at school. I will have my children read me the letters. We love reading your words."

I hugged Berhana as tears fell down my face.

"Of course! I will write to you often, I promise. Thank you, Berhana. Thank you for trusting me and loving me as though I were your child."

"You are my child. I will always protect you. Now, I promised Emama that I will not speak of this to anyone but Marcos, so your lessons will take place at my home while I take the children to church on Sundays. This way we will not be home to hear your plan, and most of the neighborhood will be gone as well. You will have from 7 a.m. to roughly 10:30 a.m. for the lessons. You have to be out of the neighborhood by 10:45 at the latest. Do not have Tadesse bring you. Take a taxi. Wear comfortable clothes and a scarf, and keep a hat on always. I do not want people to recognize you. We will start your lessons this Sunday. Do you want me to pick out the clothes for you on Saturday?"

"Yes, please. Just so I know what is right to wear."

"I will have your clothes laid out for you on Saturday afternoon. Remember to take a taxi, *Eshi*. We will talk some more on Saturday but just in case, I wanted to discuss it all with you today. Emama is already aware of the plan as well."

"Thank you again, Berhana. Thank you so very much!"

It was Friday morning, which meant I had two days before my first lesson was to start. I was excited and nervous at the same time.

"Berhana, where is Emama right now?"

"She is in the living room doing her Rosary."

"*Eshi*, I'm going to go pray with her."

"Go, go! They had not started when I left them."

"Them? Who is praying with her?"

"Yeshimebet is here today and wanted to pray. Go now. Change out of your pajamas later."

I grabbed my favorite rosary and dashed out. By the time I got to the living room, they were already on the second decade. I chimed in, looking at Yeshimebet's fingers to see exactly where they were.

"Hail Mary, full of grace. The Lord is with thee. Blessed art thou amongst women, and blessed is the fruit of thy womb, Jesus.

Holy Mary, Mother of God. Pray for us sinners, now and at the hour of our death."

We repeated the Hail Mary prayer over and over again, and included an Our Father, Glory Be, and the Ave Maria song once the second decade was over. I prayed for safe travels and for my new life. I prayed for love, happiness, and abundance. I prayed for forgiveness because I would be missing Mass to attend these classes with Marcos. Emama, on the other hand, was praying for me to gain wisdom and heart. Yeshimebet prayed for her students, for them to be brave and seek knowledge. She prayed for us, her family, for Papa's soul, and lastly, for my upcoming marriage. Three quite different prayers, three different women. Yet we were all strong in our faith.

By Saturday, I was extremely focused on my trip and spent the day at my uncle's house, talking to Mikael and Yonatan about Asmara, Keren, and other cities in Eritrea. Uncle Mikael was proud and happy that I was curious about his hometown and different cities, while Yonatan was skeptical.

"Why all the questions, Bella? Are you planning a trip?"

"I just want to know."

"What are your intentions with the information that Ababa is giving you?" he asked.

"What? What do you mean, 'my intentions'? Can't a daughter ask about her father's homeland?" I was starting to get mad, feeling like he did not trust me, and that hurt.

"Of course she can. But you've never shown interest in Eritrea before, apart from it being where your father came from. Now you are asking about our family, the land, Asmara, the culture, and so on. Something seems a little off here."

"Yonatan, you are not a lawyer yet, and if you were, I would tell you what Yeshimebet used to tell Papa all the time — 'stop bringing your work home'.' With that, I thanked my uncle and walked away. I could hear Yonatan calling my name as I stormed out of the house and into my car with Tadesse. He was still calling me as we left their compound. What right did he have to question me? I can ask any question I want, anytime I want. Who did he think he was? Was he right, though? My conversations about Eritrea had only been in passing with Papa. I did not have the same drive and passion for the country the way he did. So, did that make me less Eritrean? No, I would not let Yonatan, or anyone else for that matter, make me feel that way. Regardless of where I grew up, how I grew up, regardless of everything, I AM WHAT I AM.

I got home still upset, but proud of my actions as well. I knew these types of questions would come up more and more, especially when I moved to Asmara, so maybe this was God's way of preparing me for what was to come. Maybe this is why God had placed this struggle in front of me. I needed to experience life on my own in order to reach my fullest potential. The thought made me shake my head. Why could it not be easier? All these thoughts, all these conversations in my head all of the time! I rushed to my room to start recording it in my diary.

As I entered my room, I saw Berhana going through my closets with a look of dismay. "Bella, where did all your home clothes from last summer go?"

She was clearly without luck trying to find something for me to wear to her house the next day.

"Yeshimebet took those a while ago. She gave them to the girls at Princess Maryam's school," I responded.

Berhana shook her head, shocked at herself for forgetting. Minutes later, she pulled out a pair of my black travel pants and a large pullover sweater from the closet. She looked closer and saw how nice the sweater was, then folded it before putting it back in my closet.

"How about this?" Berhana pulled out a green sweater that had "CIAO" written on it.

"The color is kind of obnoxious, but it might do. I haven't worn it in years, so no one would suspect it was me coming into your neighborhood. I'll also wear a hat and my travel boots."

"*Eshi*, perfect. I will not be home tomorrow when you get there, but Marcos will be waiting for you. He has a map ready for you and will meet you outside our gate by the main road. I want him to make sure no one is nearby before letting you into the property. This way we stay clear of prying eyes."

"Thank you again, Berhana. I do not know what I would do without you."

"Everything will be fine," she said, and walked out of my room.

Dinner was short as not many of my family members were around for the

full meal. Yonatan was there, which annoyed me, so I asked to be excused earlier in the evening and went to my room to write and just be alone to think for
a couple of minutes. Then I heard a knock on the door. I opened it to Emama
in her wheelchair with no one pushing her. She saw my facial expression and
blurted out,

"I am very capable of pushing myself, dear. I just choose to let all of you
push me around, because I enjoy seeing you all suffer a little."

"Emama, you are very funny. I'll remember this next time you tell me you
need help though, especially from the gardens."

"Young lady, you're my favorite grandchild but do not test me."

I smiled at her. She was so strong, so beautiful and full of grace. She was
everything I wanted to be as a woman, a mother, a friend, and a fighter.

"Listen, I want to talk to you about Yonatan. He came by right before dinner today and told me about the princess. I blessed him, although I am not too
thrilled about it. I can see that he is happy with Saba and that makes me smile.
I did warn him of the life he will be walking into if he makes this relationship
official. There is no turning back from that kind of life."

"That is wonderful news, Emama. I know Yonatan loves her. He has for
some time now, and Saba is falling for him as well. It is only a matter of time
before things get serious. I think they will get married."

"That's nice, but we talked about other things as well. He mentioned that
you were at their house today asking about Eritrea and your father's family. He
was concerned because you were defensive and stormed off, and that is not like
you at all."

"It has always been like me to stand up for myself."

"How are you standing up for yourself in this situation?" Emama asked.

"Emama, are you taking his side on this matter? He acted suspicious, as if
I were a criminal, when the fact of the matter is all I did was ask about Eritrea.
I do not see the harm in it at all, and for the record, I do not like that he came
here to tattle on me. What kind of man runs to someone's grandmother to talk
about a little disagreement?"

"Listen here, young lady. I will not have you talking to me in that tone of voice. He came not to complain, but to check on you. He did not run to me to tell on you or blame you for anything; he came out of concern. He knows you very well and felt that something was wrong. I would have appreciated it if my cousins wanted the best for me and came to tell my family when they sensed something was amiss. It would have saved me from so much trouble when I was younger. You know your grandmother was a feisty woman, just like you. All that aside, you need to apologize for your actions today and adjust your entitled attitude. You do not want to draw attention to yourself right now."

I opened my mouth to defend myself, and she shut me down almost immediately. "No. I will not have it. You hear me, Bella? I will not have it. Make sure you make peace, Annabella Lorenzo. Do you hear me? Make peace!"

"Yes, Emama, and I am sorry if I have offended you in any way. I love you."

She accepted my apology and asked me to help her get to her room. "You have drained all the energy out of this old lady." She winked, and I smiled as I turned her wheelchair around and took her down the hall to her quarters.

The next day I woke up ready for my very first lesson on the history and geography of Eritrea and Ethiopia. I had never snuck out of my house before and it made me uncomfortable. I was scared that Ababa or one of my aunts or uncles would catch me tiptoeing out of the house and then I would have to answer a million questions. God blessed me that day because no one was awake as I headed out, not even our gardener Mekonnen.

I got a taxi about two blocks from our house. The ride to Berhana's neighborhood was short, but tiring at the same time. I was always driven to her house and automatically assumed it would the same 15-minute drive in the taxi. Little did I know that taxis did not go into her neighborhood very often and had to take a circuitous route.

Marcos was waiting for me at the entrance of his neighborhood, and we walked together in silence. It had been so long since I last saw him, and now I noticed distinctive lines on his face that showed how much he had aged. He was tall and had broad shoulders. Once a soldier in the war against fascist Italy, Marcos had fought bravely to defend Ethiopia against colonization. He had always fascinated me. With his fair skin and brown curly hair, he looked more like the Indians who taught at Princess Maryam's school than an Ethiopian soldier.

We arrived at Marcos' house, and I could tell he was uneasy about having me there alone without his wife and family. I grew up spending many Sundays there with them but somehow, now that I was an adult, it made him uncomfortable.

"Would you like some water or tea, Weizerit Bella?"

"No, thank you, and please, Marcos, you know me. Call me Bella." He laughed.

"Okay, let's get started. Berhana tells me that you will be traveling by car to Asmara and she wants you to know the different places you will be visiting along the way. The drive will take you roughly three days. I will review all the cities you will pass through and the ones you will most likely spend the night in. Emama has directed me to ensure you have accommodations in each city, and I am looking for a trusted driver for you as well."

"*Eshi*, thank you very much, Marcos."

"Do not thank me yet! Save it for when you arrive safely in Asmara."

He left the tiny room in their hut for a couple of minutes, which gave me time to look around at their home. Their one room home was made of sticks and mud, and while small, was always filled with love and joy. I could still smell the same scents of onions mixed with different spices from my childhood, which brought back memories of eating injera together on a plate with Berhana's children, or playing card games in the corner so we were not in the way of the grownups. As a child I had spent so much time here, and always considered it a treat. Biniam, their oldest son and my childhood crush, died from influenza when we were twelve years old. At that time I stopped coming to the house, and yet it had not changed much apart from feeling a lot smaller. The sitting chairs were still the same, although the blue shade had now become gray and the little table in the middle of the room was missing a leg. The window cracks had gotten bigger over the years, but the portrait of Marcos in his military uniform was still standing in the center of the one concrete wall that held the hut together.

Marcos came in, moved the three-legged table and placed a large map of Ethiopia on the floor. "This will help us get familiar with the different cities and give you an idea of the route you will take. I wish I could take you myself, but given the situation, it is best I find you a trusted driver."

His index finger landed on a section of the map that showed Addis Ababa, and looking directly at me, he showed me the path I was to take. There were curves that meant mountains and different landmarks, some of which I had never noticed before, along the map. "Ultimately, the goal is to get you here with little to no commotion," he said, pointing to Asmara.

"You will leave Addis early in the morning and drive all day to Dessie in the Wollo region. There will be security checks along the way, so make sure you study your documents well. The only city where you will possibly make a stop before reaching Dessie will be Debre Sina, a beautiful town where you can stop for fresh water and food. I will arrange housing for you in Dessa with a friend who served in the military with me. It will not be what you are used to, but at least I know you will be safe. The next morning, you will drive through Woldiya to Mekelle. All cities before Mekelle will speak Amharic. Mekelle is the capital city of Tigray and the people there speak Tigrinya. But their accent is different from your father's, so you might not understand. Anywhere you go, speak only when spoken to, say very little, and stay away from people as much as you can. There are many who work for the emperor in all the cities, and they might recognize you once word gets out that you are missing. If that happens, you will not only have to worry about soldiers and the emperor, but also about the people who dislike your father for his work with the emperor."

As Marcos was talking, I could not help but think about my parents. All those years ago, Papa left my mother alone in a church and promised her he would come back. He told her to stay quiet and speak only when spoken to.

Was my fate going to be the same?

"Pay attention. This is not a joke, Bella. You need to understand the routes. Stop daydreaming."

"Marcos, thank you, but I think it's enough for one day. It's almost 10:45 and Berhana asked me to be out of the house before she came home with the children."

"Yes, yes. I lost track of time. I will walk you out and around the corner. From there you should be fine to walk alone to the main road and get a taxi. We only have next Sunday left so I want you to take the map and study the route I showed you so far. Be careful with the map. Do not let people see you with it. Next week we'll talk about the cities after Mekelle, and I will have the name of your driver as well."

I thanked Marcos again, and we both walked out of the hut and onto the main road. I could see him from a distance, watching me get into a blue and white community taxi that would take me to Piazza, the busy shopping area in one of the oldest parts of the city. From there, I would have to change taxis to get home.

Piazza was home to all my favorite gold shops, boutiques, and most importantly, the Catholic cathedral that my family attended. I decided to take a small risk and go to church while Mass was still going on. Although I would not be able to take Communion or even enter the church out of fear of facing my family, it was worth sitting outside and being near the house of God on a Sunday morning. Once I got to the main gate of the church, I saw that it was unusually packed with people I had never seen before. Had I never noticed the crowds that had to stand outside to hear Mass? It shocked me how little I knew about what was happening outside of my comfortable life. There were beggars asking for money, little boys pickpocketing and getting caught, and people selling all kinds of goods outside the main gate. In all the years that I had been coming to this church I had never noticed any of them. I felt humbled and small. In God's eyes we were all the same, these people and I, yet how had I been so lucky? Or was it I who was at a loss? These people looked happy, even the mothers and their children begging for money. They seemed genuinely content, yet I had everything and was so far from happiness. Maybe I was the one missing out on life and running away from it.

I left the cathedral before Mass was officially over and hurried home. This time I caught a smaller, yellow taxi sedan that took me all the way to the main road about two blocks from my house. I ran all the way home and made it with only minutes to spare. Just as I was changing my clothes, I heard Tadesse honking the horn and Mekonnen running to the main gate to open the doors for the rest of my family, who were returning from Mass. I ran into the bathroom and washed my face to make it look like I was just waking up. Mission accomplished!

Sunday brunch was being served in the gardens. For some reason that day, everyone was talking about the homily our priest had given with regard to John 1:4. The verse was about love coming from God and how His love is made perfect in us and because of that we should not be afraid of anything. Where His love is, there is never fear because His love takes that fear away for us. That is the beauty of being His child. As my uncle was talking more about the verse and how beautifully our priest gave the homily, I kept thinking about my own life. My faith had always been strong. Now more than ever, I felt God near me, pulling me in the direction He wanted for my life. Why else was I going through everything happening to me these days? It had to be for something bigger that He was preparing me for. He needed me to be strong, smart, and ready to obey His will. I would not be afraid of this journey. I would accept this and everything else that God had coming my way because His love was in me, and He would never hurt me. I knew I felt that, so now I just had to sit and watch for what He had planned for me next. I exhaled a big loud breath as everyone turned to look at me.

"Annabella, where were you this morning? I did not see you at church with us," said Ababa.

"Oh, I, um."

"She was feeling unwell, so I let her sleep in," interjected Emama. I smiled at her, and she gave me a wink.

"Very well. I hope you are feeling better now."

Emama quickly changed the subject and all attention went back to the homily. I looked up to see Yonatan staring right at me with a knowing look.

As family members started to leave, I told Emama I would be spending the day with Saba and went to look for Tadesse so I could get a ride to the palace. Two steps out of the garden, Yonatan was waiting for me by the main door to the house.

"Listen, Bella, I know something is going on with you. I just do not know what it is and while I am genuinely concerned, I do not want to bother you with my nosiness."

"At least we agree on one thing. You, my dear friend and cousin, are very nosy. If this is part of what being a lawyer means, I will be a horrible lawyer and you will be a great one."

"Funny, funny. But seriously, I am just worried. I hope you know I always have your best welfare at heart. I just want you to be happy and safe. You did not look like you were either when I saw you last."

"I'm fine. Everything is fine. Listen, I am on my way to visit Saba so I cannot talk much. If you are here to apologize, then the apology is accepted."

He smiled at the mention of Saba's name and laughed when I took his apology without him formally apologizing to me. His laugh always made me smile, even when I was upset with him. This was the part of our relationship that I loved and would miss dearly.

"Would you like a ride to the palace?"

"That would be great. Do you mind if we make a stop to visit Papa first, though?"

At Kidest Selassie Church, there was a funeral taking place and the roads in and out of the area were jammed. We ended up not spending time with Papa, but instead drove straight to the palace to meet with Saba. I had Yonatan drop me off at the Lion's Den for a visit with my animal friends, Mochuria and Mollua, and told him I would walk to the palace from there. I wanted to give the two lovebirds some time alone.

"No, thank you. I think I am better off seeing the lions with you."

"Are you scared to be alone with your princess?" I teased.

"Not scared, just wise. I spent time with her on Friday and Saturday. I do not want the staff, and even worse her family, thinking anything is going on between us without me formally discussing it with her parents."

"I see." My attention quickly shifted to Mochuria and Mollua, who were sitting in the corner of their den soaking up the sun. They looked so peaceful just lying there. They both saw me and came to the corner to greet me with a powerful roar. Their trainer came running at the sound of their roars and shook his head at me.

"Daughter of Belantageta Lorenzo, every time you come here, they roar. What do you do to them? I cannot get them to move."

"They just need love."

"Love? Who needs love when you have power?" he said, shaking his head and walking away.

Yonatan and I got back in the car and drove to the palace where Saba was waiting for us by the door.

"Why is it that every time the guards call to announce you are here, it takes you forever to come to the door? Are you walking from the gate?"

"Hello to you too, princess. I went to go visit the lions."

"What about him? Hi Yonatan. I am very glad you came too. How are you?"

"I'll answer for him. He was scared to come see you without me."

"I never said that," Yonatan said, embarrassed by my comment.

"What is on the agenda for today, my friends? Should we go have lunch somewhere, or stay on the grounds and have a picnic?"

"A picnic sounds great. If only we were back in London, at Harrod's for our weekly cappuccino date."

"Our cappuccino here in Addis Ababa is way better than anything you can have at Harrods," Yonatan boasted. "Do not forget, Ethiopian coffee is the best in the world. Let me take you both to this great place in Piazza."

"What about our picnic?" I said.

"The picnic can wait for another day, Bella," Saba replied." That's the beauty of living in Addis. The weather, my dear, will always be nice."

We drove into Piazza and took refuge in a corner table secluded from the rest of the café. Yonatan placed our orders for us and within minutes, delicious pastries were on our table, along with three hot and perfectly made cappuccinos. I decided to try their puff pastry first, and agreed almost instantly with Yonatan that these treats and coffee were the best I had ever had. Golden color on the outside and creamy on the inside. Every bite was joy bursting in my mouth.

"Saba, this should be our weekly spot," I said, and instantly wished I had not. I was leaving the city and did not know when I would be back. Yet here I was making plans with my best friend. My best friend, who would be crushed when she found out I left without saying goodbye or sharing my plans.

"I agree, Bella. We can even have someone pick it up for us and bring it to the palace or your house. Although the coffee would probably get cold by that time."

"We'll make it work somehow."

We left after two hours of laughing and enjoying great desserts and coffee. We decided to take the scenic route back to the palace. Addis was such a beautiful city, with its many gardens and magnificent architecture. I especially loved Piazza! It always reminded me of the times when Papa would bring me shopping for gold when I got good grades at school. Other kids would ask for toys or new clothes; I, on the other hand, always wanted jewelry.

"Yonatan, park the car here right now, please."

"What, what is wrong? Are you okay? Annabella Lorenzo, if you are sick and throw up in this car, I will kill you!"

"*Zim Bel!* Just park the car, *Esti.* I want to say hello to Ato Hagos and his wife and see if they have any new pieces."

"You want to see them or their handsome son?" teased Saba.

"They have a son? Oh yeah, what was his name again — Behailu? Oh yes, let's say hello to him, too." I smiled while both Yonatan and Saba rolled their eyes. I had forgotten about Behailu until we came to his neighborhood, but it would be nice to see him.

"The last time I was here, Papa bought me a necklace and had my initials engraved on it. I have so many wonderful memories of walking these streets with him on Sundays."

We found Ato Hagos alone in his shop. He had sad news for us. His beautiful wife had passed away four months ago and Behailu had left shortly afterwards to go to America for school. Ato Hagos looked sad, tired, and defeated.

"Princess Saba, it's an honor to have you in my store. Please come in, have a seat," said Ato Hagos.

"Annabella, Yonatan, how are you both? How are your families? I miss seeing you and your father in here, Annabella. We lost a hero when your father died. Come, *Esti*, let's find something fit for that beautiful long neck of yours. I have the perfect piece in mind. Behailu made it just before his mother died, just before he went away." Ato Hagos was obviously not happy that his son had left the country. As he went in search of the necklace, I had a moment to look around the shop. There were many beautiful new pieces that I had never seen before, very grand with gold and diamonds. I wondered who Ato Hagos's new goldsmith was and made a point to compliment him because the pieces were exquisite.

Ato Hagos came back to the room with one of the most beautiful pendants I had ever seen. It was cross- shaped and attached to a thick gold necklace and could be worn as a choker as well. When I looked at the details more closely, I could see other Ethiopian crosses woven into the intricate design. The pendent was huge, almost the size of my hand and each corner was embellished with ruby studs. I was mesmerized at first sight and asked for the price. "This is not for sale, Annabella, I want you to have it. Think of it as a gift from your father."

"Oh no, Ato Hagos, I could never do that. This is probably worth a fortune. Please tell me. I'll have Emama or Yeshimebet send Tadesse with money for you."

"Please do not insult me. Your father was my friend, my best customer, and more than that, he inspired me. My family left Eritrea because of his story and came here for a better life. I would not be here if it weren't for him. This is yours and I will not hear another word about it."

"Thank you. Thank you so much," I said as I hugged him, and tears came to my eyes. I looked up at him and he was crying too. I do not know if the tears were for me, or for his own loss, but I could tell that giving me this necklace gave him peace.

We said our goodbyes and left the store. I remembered my question from earlier and ran back into the store alone.

"Ato Yohanes, who is your new goldsmith? He is amazing. Do not ever let him leave."

"I already have. It was Behailu," he said sadly.

"Behailu did this?!" I asked, shocked.

"He learned from the best. We taught him everything we knew, his mother and I. What good did it do me? I lost them both."

"He'll come home. They always do."

I gave him one more hug, thanked him again, and left the store. God had truly sent me there for a reason. I looked up to the sky and smiled knowing Papa and God were in this together, gifting me a goodbye present from my favorite jeweler and his son, my childhood friend and crush. Wearing my beautiful new pendant, I was dropped off at home by Yonatan and Saba.

The week after that flew by and before I knew it, it was Saturday evening and I was prepping for my Sunday lesson with Marcos, the last lesson before my trip. I had spent the week studying the map as instructed and felt confident in my knowledge of the route. I thought of maybe taking just one more look at the map, but quickly changed my mind after looking outside and seeing it was already dark. I had used the garden bungalow to study, and turning on the lights in the bungalow at this hour would attract unnecessary attention. Instead, I laid out my clothes and went to bed, thinking of the big day ahead of me.

On Sunday morning, I got up early, got dressed, and tip-toed out of the house to not wake anyone. The front gate wasn't locked with a chain as it normally was every night. I thanked God and Emama and quietly left my home. On the main street, I got into one of the white and blue community taxis and went to Piazza to catch a different taxi to Marcos and Berhana's house. As promised, Marcos was at the corner of his street waiting for me and signaled for me as soon as I got out of the taxi. We walked to his house together in silence. Once inside his home, he asked for the map and laid it on the table for us to discuss right away.

"Did you study the map?

"Yes."

"From Addis to Mekelle, or the entire journey?"

"The whole route, but let's go over Mekelle to Asmara, and then go over the entire thing one more time to be sure."

"Good idea. So, as I said last week, Mekelle is in Ethiopia, but it will be the first city where you will start to hear Tigrinya, your native Eritrean dialect. The dialect is much different than your father's Tigrinya, however, so there will be words and phrases that you will not understand. The people of Tigray will know that you are Eritrean once you start to speak, especially in Mekelle. Therefore, I urge you to not speak Tigrinya. Stick to your Amharic and do not speak unless spoken to. You will stay the night in Mekelle with one of Emama's good friends. The driver will have the address and they will be expecting you. From there, early in the morning you will leave and drive to..."

"Adigrat, through the mountains."

"Yes, good, *gobez* Bella. Now, from Mekelle to Adigrat is roughly 150 kilometers, and the roads are usually empty except for trucks bringing fish or salt from Massawa and taking coffee and grains back. Those drivers are often reckless, so you will have to stay alert along with your driver. He will know what to do. Adigrat borders Eritrea, but it will be easier for you to enter through Zelambessa, which is about 50 kilometers north. The Italians left it unfortified and the town is practically abandoned. Most of the villagers moved away during the occupation, and the official border is still in question, so there will be very few soldiers. It's the perfect place to enter Eritrea. Once you are in Eritrea, you will continue through Senafe, Adi Keih, and Decemhare before reaching Asmara. The total drive time from Mekelle to Asmara will be about nine hours. Your father, Ato Lorenzo, may God rest his soul, was from Adi Keih. Ato Mikael once had me drive to the house they were both born in. I will have the driver take you past there as well. Once you get to Asmara, Princess Maryam will take you in and from there you will be under her care. I do not know of the plan past getting you to Asmara."

"Well, we shall take everything step by step. Thank you again, Marcos," I said. "This has been extremely helpful. Do we have time to go through the entire plan one more time?"

"Yes, of course. Now, from the beginning…"

We went through the plan once more in detail and finished right on time. I put my hat and scarf back on and hurried off, afraid that Berhana would be back with the kids and that people in the neighborhood might see me. In the event I got caught, the last thing I wanted was to get Marcos and his family in trouble. Going against the emperor was considered treason and they would be drastically punished for helping me. They knew that and yet still decided to help me. The love I felt for both of them and for their family was deep. We had been through everything together since I was a child. Death, birth, remarriages, betrayals, sadness, and happiness. All of it.

I rushed out and got a taxi to take me straight home. Once safe at home I took a shower and put my pajamas back on before my family came back from church. I did not join them in the gardens that day. Instead, I closed my door and stayed to myself, thinking, writing, and daydreaming about my trip and my new life in Asmara. Yonatan came to check on me, and Saba called to see if I was okay, but I could not bring myself to join them on our very new Sunday ritual in Piazza. I knew I was leaving and I hated lying to them, to all the people I loved. I stayed alone in my room, thinking about all that I was about to explore and endure. I thought about what my life would be like a year from now, five years from now, and that thought kept me calm and focused even though I was about to lose everything I loved.

Mollua the Lion *Addis Ababa*

CHAPTER 5

Weizerit Membrahtu

"*Anchi Lij,* if you do not open this door, so help me God, I will have Tadesse or Mekonnen break it down and you will be left without a door." It was Emama who finally got me to open my bedroom doors around 5 p.m. that evening. Once I let her in, she pretended everything was okay.

"Nice to see you alive and well. How are you, my child? You look fine. Might I ask why you have been hiding in this room for an entire day?"

"I am sorry, Emama. I wanted time alone to think and did not feel like talking to anyone or doing anything."

"Well, are we not a tad bit rude today? Bella, these are your friends, your family. What do you think you will gain by ignoring everyone?"

"What option do I have but to ignore them? I cannot tell them what I am doing. I cannot share my deepest secrets with them. How can I spend time with them right now, hearing them laugh, when I truly have nothing to laugh about, hearing them make plans, when I cannot?"

"Are you listening to yourself?" Emama asked in annoyance. "Annabella Lorenzo, in all my years raising you, I have never heard you be so selfish. Do you know how many people are putting their lives at risk to help you? Do you understand how much people love you and would do anything for you? Do you know that while you spent your day doing God knows what in here, Yonatan was out there thinking there is something wrong with your health? Saba wanted to bring in their family doctor. While you are in here complaining about how bad your life is, people are out there worried about you. Shame on you! I raised you better than this. Your father and mother raised you better than this. If for one second you think you will leave this house and go to Asmara with that attitude, you are gravely mistaken! If you think you are a victim in this situation, you are naive. You are never, ever a victim. In anything life throws your way, you must always be a survivor, a conqueror. Do you hear me, Annabella?

Hearing her explain my actions in that light made me feel even more ashamed. I could barely look her in the eyes as I responded: "Yes, Emama. I guess I was so busy thinking about my own worries that I forgot to be grateful for my blessings. Thank you for reminding me. I'll call Yonatan and Saba in the morning." Still not able to look her in the eyes, she accepted my apology and took my face in her hands so that our eyes could meet.

"You are stronger than your circumstances, *Yene Lij.* Always remember that." She kissed both my cheeks and told me she had something for me. Moments later, she pulled out a little gray book with two lions and a crown on it. I recognized the emperor's stamp and knew it was my new passport.

"It's finally here," I whispered.

"Yes, it is finally here," Said Emama with satisfaction. "Your journey begins on Wednesday. Marcos found a very suitable driver and I know his family, so he will serve us well. Marcos told me that you are ready for the trip, and you know the cities and destination points from here to Asmara. I have all the houses lined up where you will stay, and money has been dropped off for their efforts and for any of your needs. You will leave bright and early on Wednesday, before the rest of the house wakes up. I'll have Berhana pack a few things for you and take them with her on Tuesday evening. Just in case anyone sees you leaving, you'll be empty-handed."

"Emama, why do I feel so nervous?"

"That's normal, *Yene Lij.* This is new for you, and it will be scary. Continue to pray and think about what would happen if you stayed in this city. The risk outweighs your current situation. That is why even I, as sad as I am to see you go, am happy you are leaving."

"What will you tell Yonatan, Saba, and the rest of the family?"

"Do not worry about that. You just worry about staying safe and getting to Asmara."

"Emama, I cannot thank you enough."

I gave my grandmother a big hug and held on to her tight. I knew I would not be receiving these types of hugs for a while and wanted to remember this moment for as long as I could.

"Wait, I have yet to show you the best part. Look inside your passport. Beautiful picture, but more than that, look at your name."

I opened the passport that looked identical to the one I already had, but without all the stamps. And the name was different; I was now Weizerit Membrahtu.

I remembered the story my father had told me years prior about my original birth name Weizerit and how he changed it after I came to live with him. I never knew nor imagined her knowing that story though.

"Interesting name — why did you pick it?"

"You do not remember our conversation with your uncle and the family?"

"I remember. Yes, yes. I remember! Membrahtu was Lorenzo's Eritrean name, his birth name. Oh Emama, this means so much to me. How can Weizerit be my first name though? It means 'Miss.' Will it confuse people if I get stopped?"

"That's the name you were given at birth. It is part of your identity, regardless of what society tries to do to take it away." She gave me a long stare to ensure I fully comprehended what she said.

"I like it. It suits me. Weizerit."

We looked at each other and laughed the honest, familiar, loving laugh that only we shared together. It was our way of telling one another that everything would be all right.

"Emama, what will happen when I get to Asmara? Should I keep this name?"

"That's up to you. I like it, and if you want a new identity, this would be the way to do it. But I feel that the people of Eritrea should know who you are, Bella. Who your father was, and what he was trying to accomplish should never be forgotten. His legacy should continue through you and your children. It's your duty to make sure that his story gets told through generations. So, go to Asmara, meet your family and your people, and start a life with them. Let them get to know the beautiful, smart, loving child that you are and in you they will see your father again."

"Marcos told me that he will arrange for the driver to take me past the house where Papa was born. I cannot wait to see that house and his village."

"What a great idea. You'll have to write and tell me all about it once you are all settled in and some time has passed. Keep writing in your journal every day. It is one of your greatest gifts, and it will keep your memory fresh so you can share everything with me later. I will miss you greatly, *Yene Lij*."

For the first time, I saw tears forming in her eyes. I could tell that she wanted this adventure and freedom for me, but that she was hurting at the thought of seeing me go.

"I will miss you, Emama. Even words cannot explain how much. I promise to write in my journal every day and to write you lots of letters describing my journey. I'll have a telegram sent to you once Princess Maryam tells me it is all right to do so."

The next morning, I woke up early to pack my bags so that Berhana could give them to Princess Maryam when she next went to Asmara. I went through Papa's old souvenirs and decided to leave most of it in Addis. I did not know what my new life would bring me, and I did not feel comfortable taking it. What I did take was his favorite pen, the one he used at the League of Nations and to sign official documents. He used to tell me that although it was his business pen, he loved it most because it was the one he had used to write to me while I was away at boarding school. Holding it in my hands, I closed my eyes and tried to visualize him sitting at his desk and writing me that last letter:

My dearest Bella,

Why are you not behaving at school? Are you bored with the lessons? Your grades are impeccable, but while knowledge is power, my daughter, your behavior must always show grace and harmony. Have a positive look on life, and that mentality will push you forward through life. Everyone will not always see things the way you do, as the world is full of people with different mindsets. For example, when I was in Russia, some people thought I was the hired help instead of the ambassador because of the color of my skin, and even here in Paris it is the same thing. But I never showed them any kind of ill behavior. Do you know why? Well, it is because I know who I am and what I am about. How others see me is their concern, however. I will not do anything that I am not proud of, and I expect nothing less from you. Life can be hard sometimes, Bella. You more than anyone know and understand that, but we must keep pushing and stay positive. I know you will graduate in a few months and will probably go off to London or Paris. I am beyond proud of you, but please, I do not want to receive any more telegrams from your school with bad news about your behavior.

Love You Always,
Papa

I kept this letter close to me always, and his words had a big effect on how I viewed the world and my behavior towards people. This letter had changed me. I could tell he was hurt with my actions, but he did not want to punish me over a telegram; he instead wanted me to understand how my actions affected him and how they would affect me if I continued to be disrespectful. Papa died not too long after this letter was sent.

I opened some old photo albums and went through pictures that told his story. There were many different events with dignitaries, travels with Yeshime-bet and I, and dozens of family portraits. They were all there. He wanted to be a family man, that I knew, but his life would not allow it. His work was important to him and to the thousands of people who counted on him. I remembered a story that Emama used to tell me about how he dressed as a woman to get in and out of Ethiopia during the Italian invasion, and how he worked tirelessly to return the emperor to the throne. It was all meaningful and very important work, but now he was gone. How harsh life could be sometimes. All that effort and commitment and now he was gone. It was now my turn to pick up the pieces and continue on fighting for what I believed to be true, just as he did years prior.

As I was glancing at the different photos, I found one photo of us in Cairo. I must have been ten or eleven years old. He was taking me back to boarding school after a summer in Addis with Emama. I looked miserable, and he appeared so proud standing next to me. I remembered that day as though it were yesterday and decided to take that picture with me on my journey. I closed the album and left to find Emama for our daily morning Rosary. She was in the living room, sitting on her favorite chair with a beautiful statue of Our Lady of Lourdes that she had bought in France. There was incense in the air and I could hear the rest of the family getting ready to start their day, each leaving the house for different reasons. It was just me and Emama praying that day and she decided to start a Novena for my safe journey to Asmara. We started it together and she made me promise to continue it every morning for the next nine days. We prayed in silence for what felt like a very long time, both of us lost in our own thoughts as usual. When I opened my eyes, I was surprised to see hers already open and waiting for me to finish.

"Let us get lunch started."

"But Emama, everyone just left. It is a little too early for lunch now."

"I said start, not finish. In life you must always be prepared, and what better time to prepare than now. Come, my child, let us go. Today we will be making linguine al pesto. I want to make the pasta from scratch and that will take time. So, come on, '*Andiamo*' as the Italians would say. Should we add beef or chicken to the menu? I want to do lamb instead. I will have Mekonnen start the wood fire and grill the sheep there." She was always one to start and finish her own conversations, even when they involved questions.

"Emama, that sounds delicious," I said.

"Yes, it does, and for dessert we will do a tiramisu to complete our Italian theme. Come, let us get started. You can make the pasta with Berhana while I make sure the pesto is done right, and Mekonnen can work on the meat. I'll have the cook start the tiramisu, since that takes time."

She was always in charge, always knew just what to do, how to lead. I watched her every move, and even though she was getting older, she was still as graceful as ever. We worked in the kitchen, all six of us following her orders, learning from her and wanting to make her proud. She treated everyone in her kitchen equally, from her own granddaughter to the young maid who was hired yesterday.

By noon the entire family was assembled in our dining room enjoying a delicious meal. I looked at Yonatan and smiled, watching him as he ate and spoke to my uncle about the new world powers; how Ethiopia was positioned in the right place to push Emperor Haile Selassie's vision for a united Africa. "Father, more and more of our African leaders are understanding the power of our unity, hence they want to build the Organization of African Unity and have it housed right here in Addis Ababa. We are leading other nations to new ways of thinking, with growth, prosperity, and unity for all nations. This is what our emperor wants for the future of Ethiopia, and Africa as a whole," Yonatan said proudly while the rest of us listened to him. He reminded me so much of Papa. I, for one, thought it was a great idea and something Papa had worked hard for. That was what had initially pulled Yonatan in that direction as well. Papa, however, saw a side of power that Yonatan had yet to see. Yonatan had so much to learn and experience in his own time. I thought about him marrying Saba, wondering how his views would change, or even if they would change at all. I wondered if I would still be a part of their world after leaving Addis. Would I be able to attend the wedding and have a close relationship with them? I prayed they would forgive me, because I did not have the option of saying goodbye to them. I had already decided that I would just leave and write them each a letter from Asmara.

CHAPTER 6

Leaving Addis Ababa

The days went by quickly and before I knew it, it was Wednesday morning, August 3rd, 1957. Early morning, I walked past Emama's room and kissed the door, whispered "I love you," and quietly passed through the living room, dining room, front door, and finally out the main gate towards a waiting car with a driver named Kasahun who I had met the day before. We said our hushed hellos and started our journey. I thought of making small talk with him, becoming friends maybe, but then again, I did not want new friends. I did not want to talk. I felt ashamed, like I was committing a crime, even though that crime was trying to save my own life. With a heavy heart, sitting in the back seat of Kasahun's car looking out the window, I tried as best I could to take in the early morning stillness and the peace that came with it. We drove out of Addis Ababa with no problems and the scenery was breathtaking. For as long as the eye could see there was green and lush vegetation everywhere, but at the very edge, I could see only high mountains. In all my years of living in Ethiopia, we had only traveled out of Addis south to Debre Zeyit on family vacations. A couple of times, Papa took me to see my mother's town of Harar. Along the way we would go to Dire Dawa and visit Kulubi St. Gabriel Church. This was Papa's favorite place in all of Ethiopia. He met my mother at this church while both were there on a pilgrimage. Neither of them were Orthodox Christians, yet both were full of love for the Archangel Gabriel. I remember Papa praying for hours whenever we went there, while I took time to enjoy the beauty of the church.

North of Addis Ababa was just as beautiful as the south but seemed more peaceful and quieter. We passed through villages where I saw people of all shades, shapes, and looks. All were proud Ethiopians. After a few hours we arrived in Debre Birhan, and I was charmed by the small town. The weather was beautiful and clear, and I felt like I could reach out and touch the sun. Kasahun and I had the windows rolled down to enjoy the fresh, crisp air. In the city, there was always a bit of pollution, but here, just outside Addis, I felt like I was in a completely different country. There were the scenic mountains and abundant farms and greenery, with children playing and chasing the car. Laughter, joy, and happiness. I took it all in, smiling and breathing big sighs of relief. With each sigh, my heavy heart felt more and more at ease. I was beginning a great adventure, and it felt wonderful.

Some hours after that, we arrived in a different yet also beautiful town called Debre Sina. Kasahun drove us to a small neighborhood restaurant he knew that claimed to have the best dishes in the area. I ordered tibs, my favorite Ethiopian dish, while he got the key wot. Then for the first time since we started our journey together, he spoke to me.

"Are you tired and hungry?"

"Yes, I am both."

"You will love the food here, Weizerit. It is the best. The owner's son is my friend, and the mother cooks everything herself."

"Oh, please call me…" I stopped myself mid-sentence realizing that Marcos probably told him I was Weizerit Membrahtu, just as my passport showed.

"Great," I said instead. "I love home-cooked meals, even restaurant versions."

Our eyes met from across the small table, and I smiled. He smiled back and quickly looked away.

Kasahun was right about our meal. The food was outstanding, and I enjoyed every bite. Our food came on one plate but was separated to two different sides. He offered me some of his key wot, which I declined while eating my tibs and enjoying every bite. I must have been famished because I never looked up to notice my surroundings or offer him the tibs on my side of our plate. As I looked up to apologize, he said, "At our home, we always share our meals together."

"You could have easily taken a bite from my side of the plate," I replied, slightly embarrassed.

"I did not want any. Thank you for the late offer though. I will keep that in mind next time we eat."

I wondered why he would tell me about sharing his meals at home if he did not want some of my food. Was this his way of small talk? I did not think it was wise to share anything about my family, so I let it go.

The journey from Debre Sina to Dessie was long. Marcos had warned me of military stations and stops along the way. At around five that first evening, we encountered our first military checkpoint. My hands started to sweat and I could feel my heart racing. They asked us for our identification, and we showed them our documents.

"*Wedate nachu?*" the officer asked, which meant "*where are you going?*" in Amharic.

"*Wede Tigray,*" Kasahun calmly replied, indicating we were headed towards Tigray.

"*Lemen Godaye,*" *For what purpose?* the officer asked.

Kasahun explained that we were going to see family, and after what felt like an eternity, the officer looked back at us, aggressively waved his hand, and told the other officers on the far end of the dirt road to lift the steel bar and allow us passage.

I wondered if Kasahun had given him cash with his documents as a bribe to allow us through. Whatever the case was, I thanked God that things had gone smoothly in our first encounter with the military.

"Kasahun, would it be better for me to sit upfront? It might cause less questions if we were thought to be travel companions."

"Does sitting in the back mean we are not traveling together?" he said, while clearly laughing at my naivety. For the first time I noticed how attractive and genuine his smile was. He had white teeth and beautiful brown eyes.

"*Uff,* never mind," I said, laughing back. I caught myself and stopped almost immediately. I was not here to be friends with this man, even if he was handsome.

"I am joking with you. Yes, come sit up front. Let's get to know each other. If we are going to pretend we are family, I should know who Weizerit is."

"I can say the same for you," I said, sitting next to him now in the front seat. "How about I get to know you first? Who is Kasahun, what is your last name? Where is your village? Do you have siblings? What are your dreams? Have you always been a driver? Are you married? Do you have a girlfriend? Oh, sorry you do not have to answer the last two, that's none of my business." I blushed and he laughed a sincere laugh before answering.

"Well, all of those questions are none of your business, but since we are getting to know each other, I will answer them. My name is Kasahun Gebremichael. I am from a small village in Eritrea called Hibo. Well, really my family is from there. I was born and raised in Addis Ababa and have never gone to Eritrea before; this will be my first time. I have two younger sisters and I work to help my parents pay for their schooling. I believe I am 24 years old, but you did not ask for that information. No, I am not married. I thought I had a girlfriend, but she recently told me she did not want to be with me anymore, so I guess this makes me a single man now."

"What did you do for her to tell you that?" I asked.

"It is nothing I did or did not do. It has more to deal with what she wants from me. She wants to be taken care of, and right now I am focused on my sisters' education so I cannot give her money and things the way she deserves. I asked her to be patient with me, but she could not. She breaks up with me quite often in this manner and then comes back after some time. I am not too concerned."

"That is horrible. Why would you want to be with someone like that?"

"She makes me laugh, among other things."

We both smiled. I understood what he meant by "other things."

"Have you ever been to Eritrea?" He asked.

"No, this will be my first time. My father was Eritrean. He died roughly three years ago and I want to learn more about him from his people."

"I see. So, tell me more about you."

"Well, my name is, um, … Weizerit Mebrahtu."

"That part I know."

"There is not much to say about myself. I love to read, I love history, I like to travel, and I love my family and friends. Above that there is nothing of interest to include."

"I do not think that is true, but *eshi*. Where have you traveled to? Do you have siblings? What are your dreams? Are you married? Let me ask you the same questions you asked me." He smiled at me, and I blushed again. He was handsome without a doubt and from where I was sitting, I could notice his beautiful brown eyes, bright smile, and muscles as he moved the steering wheel.

"Hello, *ende*, Weizerit."

"Huh, what — sorry, what did you say?"

"Well, I was asking you the questions you asked me and then you went silent for a moment or two, like you were thinking of the perfect answer, or the perfect lie. Which one was it?"

"I do not lie. But to answer your, I mean my, questions — since you are lazy and do not want to think of questions yourself — yes, I have traveled. I have gone to Diradawa and Harar."

"No, I do not have any siblings, although my cousins all grew up with me. I dream of … that is a great question. I do not dream of the future a great deal."

"Now I know you are lying because no woman has ever asked me that question, and for you to ask it, you would have had to feel it for yourself or at least understand what it means to dream. Therefore, let us try a different response," he said.

"Are you always this annoying? Is this why your girlfriend left you?" I started laughing.

"Yes, pretty much always."

"Okay, fine, you win. My dream is to one day run the Ministry of Foreign Affairs."

"What?! Weizerit, come on. Just tell me the truth."

"I am being honest. That is my dream. I want to represent Ethiopia to the world. I want to work towards making Africa strong and creating an Africa where we all work together against colonization."

"Sounds interesting."

"Sounds interesting? Interesting? You ask me what I dream about and that is your response? Typical Ethiopian man. All you see in us women is what is on the outside: our beauty, our bodies. Did it ever occur to you that women are more than something to look at? We have brains just like men. In fact, we are smarter than most men."

"*Ende*, all I said was sounds interesting and that is because it is indeed interesting."

"You know what? I do not remember you telling me what your dreams are, so I am not answering any other questions until I hear your answer."

"Well, if you must know, I wanted to be a pilot. I wanted to fly planes and see different countries, learn about different people and their cultures. But like I told you before, I work to help my parents put my sisters through school."

"Why do you talk about being a pilot like it is in the past?"

"Dreaming is for dreamers. I live in the real world and in this world, we have to work hard just to survive."

"Thank you for sharing with me. I hope one day your dreams will come true. Have you asked what it would take? Did you know that Ethiopian Airlines actually trains their pilots from within?"

"Well, are you the head of Ethiopian Airlines?"

"No."

"I did not think so. Tell me why they would want me. I am not educated. I do not come from a rich family, and I have no skills in flying. I have never even been on a plane or even near one, apart from seeing them take off and land from the fields by the airport. What do I have to offer them?"

"Well, how do you know if you have not tried?"

"Okay, enough about me. Have you tried to become Minister of Foreign Affairs?"

"No, but I will. You just watch. Nothing is going to hold me back."

"Well, when you become the Minister, I will become a pilot."

"Deal."

Suddenly he stopped the car, and I felt my heart start to race. We were in the middle of nowhere and although it was still daylight, I could see that sunset would soon be upon us.

"Are you okay? Is the car okay? Why did you abruptly stop?"

Kasahun laughed and put his hand out. I gave him the same look Emama always gave me when I was doing something crazy.

"Excuse me, but this is no time to play. Why did you stop?"

"I am giving you my hand. Let us shake on it."

"Shake on what?"

"On our deal. You become Minister and I become a pilot." Right then and there, I smiled and gave him my hand. That was my first pact with a man, and it was done in the middle of nowhere with the sun setting in front of us.

"Where are we anyway?" I asked, trying to change the subject.

"About an hour away from Dessie. You will be staying at Ato Zerihun's house."

"Yes, I know. And where will you be?"

"I will spend the night in the car right outside. We will leave for Mekelle first thing tomorrow morning."

I was sad that our talk would have to be interrupted in an hour, but then thought of all the hours from Dese to Mekelle and then to Asmara. We had plenty of time together.

When we arrived in Dese, Kasahun walked me into Ato Zerihun's home, introduced me to his wife Weizero Beletish, then walked away without even a backward glance. I felt suddenly alone and unwanted, as though I was a burden to this family.

"You will sleep here," she said, pointing to the barnyard where their sheep were snuggled in for the night.

"Excuse me, what?"

"You will stay here tonight and be gone before the sun rises tomorrow morning. I will not deal with yet another mouth to feed," she said with a mean look in her eyes.

I started to say that under no circumstances would I sleep in these conditions and quickly realized that there was no point, and I should be grateful. It was either sleep with the sheep or go back and marry the general.

"Okay, may I please have a blanket to keep me warm?"

"The sheep will keep you warm," and with that Weizro Beletish turned and walked back into her home.

That night I did not sleep at all. I wondered if my parents had to endure such circumstances when traveling to St. Thomas Church. Did my pregnant mother ever have to sleep in a barn with sheep? Then I thought of the birth of Jesus. If Mary could do this while pregnant, then I had no reason to complain.

It was extremely dark in the barn, thus not allowing me time to write in my journal. I pulled my rosary from my pocket and let my prayers and thoughts drift to Kasahun, Saba, Yonatan, Yeshimebet, Emama, and the rest of my family. I wondered if they were looking for me by now. I'm sure Ababa would be calling on everyone to find me, which meant I had to be extra careful going forward. I wondered if Kasahun knew exactly who I was and was just playing along. I prayed that I could trust him.

Somewhere between my sixth Holy Rosary and thoughts of my years in London, I heard Kasahun calling softly for me from the main gate. Wait! Did this man know that I would be sleeping in the barn the whole night? Oh, I was livid. I grabbed my bag and ran out, ready to show my anger, but the darkness outside caught me off guard. It was pitch black and I could hear hyenas howling nearby.

"Call my name again. I cannot see anything."

"Follow my voice. Be mindful of the rocks."

"I cannot see the rocks!"

"Just be careful."

I felt something solid and cold. Was it a wall or the gate?

"Kasahun, I think I am at the gate, but I cannot feel the knob. Can you turn on the car lights please, so I can see what I am doing?"

"No! The lights will wake the whole neighborhood. Just keep moving your hands across the gate, you will get there."

I did as I was told and finally found the knob. Thank you, God!

I pulled the handle and was free.

"Okay, I'm out, where are you?"

"I parked about ten steps from the gate, hold the wall and continue following my voice."

I counted each step and made it to the car.

"That was scary. Did you hear the hyenas?"

"Yes, but that is normal for these parts. They will not eat you."

"You could have told me that last night. Speaking of which, did you know I would be sleeping in a barn?"

"Yes. That way it is much easier for you to get out in the morning without pulling attention towards yourself. Why? Did you have a problem sleeping in the barn?"

I wanted to scream, *YES, of course I did.*

"No, no, not at all. It was quite lovely."

"Beletish mentioned that you seemed unhappy and asked for a blanket."

"Unhappy? Me? She must have mistaken my gratitude for something else. I am tired, however. If you do not mind, I would like to sleep for a bit now."

"Oh, so the sheep were a problem?"

"Leave me alone," I laughed.

Hours must have gone by before I woke up. We were stopped at yet another checkpoint in Weldiya. Marcos had given me enough information about the town for me to feel confident in knowing exactly where we were, given certain landmarks like the Weldiya Gabriel Church. Kasahun was just coming back to the car when I woke up.

"Good morning, or should I say good afternoon?" he said, smiling at me.

"Good morning. I cannot believe I slept all the way to Weldiya."

"Have you been here before?"

"No, but I know my cities," I smiled.

He was starting the car at this point.

"Why were we parked?"

"Marcos left us cash and instructions here instead of Mekelle. He said things could get tricky along the city borders."

"What does that mean?"

"I do not know. I am just the messenger."

I thought of maybe telling him who I was at this point. Marcos must have had a reason to leave me money and instructions here instead of Mekelle. Was the border closed? Were there military personnel waiting to take me back?

"I got some bread for you. You must be hungry."

"Thank you. I am."

The drive from Weldiya to Mekelle wound through the mountains and the air was very dry. It almost felt like we were in a different country when compared to the greenery of Debre Berhan. We drove past little villages occasionally, but for the most part there was clear land and nothing for the eye to see but hills upon hills upon hills. Then with the sun beaming at me, I saw something that looked like a military truck and the closer we got to it, the more I was convinced that it was another check point. That was the last thing I needed right now. Something did not feel right. All the knots in my stomach were coming back and I felt like throwing up.

"Kasahun, I do not feel so well."

"What is wrong? You were fine just a moment ago. Is it the curvy road? Maybe it is the higher altitude. That happens to a lot of people."

"I do not know, but I think I am going to vomit." I opened the door, and even before the car came to a full stop, I threw up the bread and everything else I had eaten the day before right on the road.

Great! Now, I felt bad, probably looked horrible, and still felt very scared. Kasahun had parked the car on the side of the road, and two soldiers came running to see what the problem was.

"Why are you parked here? What is the problem?" they asked.

"*Selam*, greetings to you. It is my cousin. She does not feel well and had a small accident. Do not worry, it came from the mouth, nothing else." Kasahun thought this was funny. My life was on the line, and he thought it was the time for jokes.

"Does she need water? *Selam*, my sister, what exactly happened? Are you pregnant?"

"No, I am not pregnant, I do not know what is wrong. It came out of nowhere. Maybe it is what I ate yesterday."

"Okay. Are you feeling better now?"

"Yes, thank you."

"Where are you two heading?"

"Mekelle, to see family," said Kasahun. I did not respond at all. Emama and Marcos had made it clear that I was to be silent and follow his lead.

"Okay, where is your family located? What neighborhood?"

Kasahun opened his mouth to say something when the other soldier, who was taller and covered in scars and bruises stopped him and said, "No, let her answer."

"Me?" I looked straight at Kasahun. Oh, dear God. I did not know where we were going. I barely knew the roads into the city, let alone the roads in the city. I thought quickly and responded with: "Our family lives in the middle of the city. Not too far from the castle." Lord, I thought, please let there be a castle somewhere in the city.

"Great, can we catch a ride? Our truck broke down."

"Sure, come on in." Kasahun and I both smiled at them, both of us in relief of what could have been a disaster. I thanked God for the love of castles the Ethiopian people had. I thought again about telling Kasahun who I really was, because if something like today happened again, I needed to know what I should do. I could hear him and the two soldiers talking and laughing about nothing of great importance. Their mere existence in this car was a threat to me, and yet this man was joking with them. I decided that once we arrived in Mekelle, I would tell Kasahun who I was, and then also inform him how annoying he was.

"So, what are your names? We are supposed to be asking for identification, but your cousin's illness made us forget."

"My name is Kasahun and she is Weizerit. She does not say much. Are you both stationed in Mekelle?"

"Yes, and we usually do not come out this far, but we received urgent orders to find the granddaughter of one of the Ras's (Dukes). Apparently, she has been kidnapped or something. The military is on high alert."

"High alert to find one woman?"

"Well, she was supposed to marry General Kebede, so not only is she top priority, but as of right now she is our only priority."

So that was the story Emama decided to go with. I could feel my stomach-turning upside down again. I was pretending to sleep and because I had just been sick, no one seemed to think anything of it.

"Have you two seen any royals around this area?"

"No. But what do they look like? I have only seen the royal family in the newspaper."

"She is young and apparently incredibly beautiful. She is the daughter of Lorenzo Kidane. That is pretty much all we know right now. I doubt she would come this way though, and even if she was kidnapped, which I personally do not believe is the case, there is nothing this way north but dry lands. A woman like that would not be able to survive up here. But, an order is an order, so here we are, playing *akukulu* (hide and seek) with some royal pain."

"What is her name?"

"It is some foreign name, Bella, Anna, one of those or maybe both. Anna-bella. Yes, Annabella Lorenzo Kidane, that's it! You know, I do not understand why these people have foreign names. We lose our culture this way. The emperor thinks he is educating our people by sending them outside the country, but he is changing our culture when he does that. Now, these people think they are different and want to embrace the western cultures, when they are just like us but with more money."

At this point they were feeding off each other. One would make a comment about upper class Ethiopians and the other would add his thoughts and they went back and forth all the way to Mekelle. I could hear Kasahun saying his goodbyes when he dropped them in front of their camp.

"Thank you, Kasahun. If you are in town for a while, we will invite you to tea or coffee."

"*Eshi,* thank you and you are most welcome for the ride. Glad I can be of service."

As we drove away, Kasahun said, "Wake up Annabella, or Bella or Anna, or whatever your name is."

Though his tone gave away how livid he was, I ignored him.

"Wake up right now or I swear I will return you to those soldiers myself. I want to know everything, and I want to know why you and Marcos did not tell me. I have a family in Addis. I have a life. What was Marcos thinking?"

I pretended to wake up and said, "I do not know what you are talking about."

"Do not play the fool with me. I swear I will turn this car around."

I could tell he was angry. Very very, angry. Even when he was upset, though, he still looked so handsome. I guessed I would not be telling him how annoying he was after all. I knew if I told him the truth there would be no coming back from it, and that made me nervous. What if he took me back himself, or worse, told the soldiers who I was? Why was General Kebede sending the entire military to look for me, or was that Ababa's doing? No, this had to have come from the general. Only he would have the power and desire to want me back this badly. My family and the emperor would have handled things much differently.

"Do you hear me, Weizerit or Annabella or whoever you are? I want to know who you are and what this is all about. I knew there was something wrong with this contract. A beautiful, smart girl just wanting to see her family? It made no sense and we left in the middle of the night. You are always watching your back and asking too many questions. How could I have been so stupid? Tell me the whole story now."

"The whole story? That might take a long time."
"Well, we have plenty of time, so tell away."

I took a deep breath and sighed heavily, trying to convey that what I was about to tell him meant life and death to me. I described for him a clear picture of my entire life from start to finish. He listened while driving and I could tell he was interested in everything I had to say. He nodded at me, added small oneword comments here and there, but never interrupted me as I spoke of my family. I told him about Papa, traveling overseas for boarding school, and never having a home other than what Yeshimebet's family gave me. Never meeting any of Papa's family apart from my Uncle Mikael. Lastly, I told him about my arranged wedding to General Kebede and how my grandfather approved it and not me. I told him how I meant to talk to the emperor about it and how my grandmother made me back down and play smart instead. I wanted to sound strong to Kasahun, yet obedient as well. I wanted to explain my life in ways that he could understand or relate to, so I did not seem like a spoiled rich child. I wanted him to like me the way I liked him, I guess. Yet, however much I tried to make my life seem humble and boring, the words told another story. Here was this girl who grew up in luxury with royals, had traveled the world and received a brilliant education, and now, when asked to settle down and create a beautiful home for herself with a powerful man, she apparently sees herself as too good for it. As I told my story, I found myself apologizing for my actions. Somewhere between me telling him the plans I created with Emama and Princess Maryam, and then my meeting with the emperor, I stopped and said, "You know what, Kasahun? I am proud of myself! I took action for my life, and I wish every woman could do the same. No man has the right to decide whom I marry and what I do with my life. It's my life."

"I agree," he said.

"And furthermore, I will not be judged by you or anyone else for that matter. Wait, what did you say?"

"I agree." He said it again, this time with a smile.

"Oh, oh, well okay. I thought you were about to tell me I was a spoiled brat who needed to get over herself and then drop me off on the side of the road. Speaking of which, should we not have arrived at someone's house by now?"

"We passed your planned accommodations a while ago. I did not have the heart to stop you while you were talking. And honestly, I was scared that if I left you somewhere without hearing the entire story, I would probably never come back for you. I am glad I heard your story. First and foremost, my condolences; your father was a great man. He was a legend in our house. Second, I feel honored that Marcos would trust you to me, but I wish he had told me the truth so I could be better prepared. What would have happened if we got caught at one of the city borders?"

"I understand, and I am sorry for keeping the truth from you. I was told never to share anything with anyone, that it was safer that way for everyone. I have learned my lesson with you and I trust you now. I am also grateful that we have not had much trouble so far."

"True, and pray that we do not run into any trouble at the town borders going forward. Now, where should we stay tonight? I do not feel safe traveling at night, and I do not want to park the car just anywhere in case soldiers pass through."

By this time, it was already well past sundown, and we could see stars brightly shining in the sky next to a full moon. The temperature outside was chilly and refreshing, and I felt like rolling the windows down and putting my head out to enjoy the breeze on my face. I had no idea what we would do, no plan really, yet I felt safe with Kasahun. Safe and free. It was a relief that he knew my true story. It was safe to be myself with him, to finally talk to him about my troubles, maybe even safe to fall in love with him. I wondered what would happen if I did fall for him. Maybe it was already happening. I was intrigued by his strong demeanor, character, and looks. He seemed like such a well-rounded man, but as I had learned early on in life, looks can be deceiving. I trusted my family and friends, and where had that gotten me? A wedding to a man I did not know nor love, out of comfort for everyone else but me. I trusted the emperor when he blessed my need to receive higher education, and where had that gotten me? I was smart and with a degree, yet running away from the only home I ever knew.

We drove in circles, staying within city borders so we would not pass by any police or the soldiers stationed on the outskirts of Mekelle. News had traveled far already, which meant that everyone was on high alert to find me. I knew our luck earlier with the two soldiers was a gift from God, and I did not want to test that luck again if at all possible. Around the third or fourth circle of what seemed like a small town I spotted a huge willow tree under the light of a full moon that looked tucked away off the main street. The tree was in between an open field on the left and a schoolyard on the right.

"Kasahun, look at that willow tree. It is the perfect place to hide the car for the night."

"Have you gone mad? It's right by a school. What will happen when the teachers come to work tomorrow morning?"

"We will be long gone before that. Plus, the branches are long and thick enough to hide us from plain sight."

"You are indeed crazy." He laughed and started driving towards the tree.

The branches were extremely heavy and looked thicker and thicker as we drove closer to the tree.

"Do you know how to drive?"

"Me?"

"Yes, you. Do you see anyone else here?"

"Okay, look. No one gets sarcastic with me other than me."

He laughed at me, which made me think about what I had just said, and that made me laugh with him. He really knew how to get under my skin, but he did it in such a cute and funny way, I could not help but laugh. I liked this man. Yes, I liked him a lot.

"Well, do you?"

"No, I do not. But I am a fast learner. What do you have in mind?"

"Well, you obviously will not be able to pull the branches aside yourself, so I was going to have you drive the car while I made a path for it.

"Kasahun, honestly I think you are overthinking. Your vehicle will be fine. It does not need you to baby it."

"First of all, my car is a boy. Please refer to him as Lijay. Lijay is not an 'it.' Simple objects are referred as 'it,' and, my friend, this car is not a simple object."

"*Weyne*, you and Yonatan would have been best friends." I laughed and he looked at me seriously.

"Who is Yonatan? Is he your boyfriend?" I laughed some more. He looked even more serious. At this point, something inside me clicked. Men were such easy creatures to read and very possessive. This man clearly liked me. He liked me so much that he was jealous of the mere fact that I mentioned another man's name.

"Wait a minute. Why do you care so much about who Yonatan is?"

"I do not. So, are we going to park Lijay under this tree or what?"

"No, no, no. My friend, you are not going to change this subject."

"*Anchi Lij,* if we get caught out here we will both go to jail! You will be returned to your lover, or husband-to-be, or whatever the case is, and I will probably be put to death or at the very least beaten up pretty badly. So yes, we are going to change the subject. Now, how will we get this car through these branches?"

"Yonatan — I mean Kasahun," I said, smiling. I was loving this!

"How about we just test what it, I mean Lijay, will do if we simply and slowly drive him through. You know what, we can search for a weak link. Yes, we studied this exact strategy in one of my classes last year - finding the weakest link. It is the best method for militaries to infiltrate enemy lines. Wait here."

I got out of the car and walked around the giant willow tree. The branches were mostly pretty thick, and I circled around it, feeling each individual branch. I smiled knowing that Kasahun had a soft spot for me. I wondered if he had liked me from the start, and then a thought hit me — what if he liked me only because he now knew who I was? Emama had always warned me about

men and their desires for women with ranking titles. I wished I had sensed
Kasahun's feelings prior to him finding out who I was.

Damn it. Each branch I grabbed was sturdier than the one before. The air
was getting colder, and the brightness of the full moon was being blotted out
by clouds. My time was limited, and things got worse quickly. A group of seem-
ingly drunken men were singing loudly and walking towards the tree. I could
hide but what about Kasahun? If I went back to warn him, I would get us both
caught, and yelling for him would be even worse. Ultimately, I went through
the branches whispering his name.

"Kasahun, Kasahun… come here!" I could not see much while inside the
canopy of branches and I tripped a couple of times, finally getting his attention.

"Weizerit, where are you? Do I hear men singing? Are you okay?"

"Come here now!" I whispered as loudly as I could. "Leave the car, we will
come back for it. There are drunk men coming your way. Follow my voice. I'm
inside the tree branches."

"Are you crazy? You're definitely crazy! If we leave the car, they will find it
and come looking for the driver or worse, try to steal it."

"These men are definitely drunk. Just come, or they might start something and bring unwanted attention to the both of us."

I could hear their voices getting louder and louder.

He refused to leave his vehicle and instead urged me to return so that
we could drive away, but there was no time for that. The voices had gotten
extremely loud. I climbed up the tree to try and get a glimpse of exactly what
we were dealing with. All the years of climbing trees at our house and at the
palace finally paid off. I got to the third level of branches before I could spot
three drunken men in uniform. Soldiers. Great. This was exactly what we did
not need. Lucky for us, the soldiers were so drunk they probably could not
even remember their own names, but this was still going to be a problem. I
could not see Kasahun nor his vehicle from where I was standing, but I knew
that the soldiers would pass him any moment now. I did the only thing I knew

with certainty that would help us. I prayed.

"Lord, I know I am asking for a lot here. I know I am dealing with a hard-headed fool, but Father Lord, I think I like the fool. No, I know I like him. So please, please save him for me, for his family, for the girlfriend he left back in Addis even though she does not deserve him and broke up with him already. Save him, Lord, please. Amen."

The singing stopped. I closed my eyes to pray again harder and then I heard the soldiers talking amongst one another:

"What is this car doing here in the middle of the night?"

"I do not know, but who cares, our shift ended at nine. I want to go meet my Makeda, hurry up."

"Exactly, if we take this car, we will get there faster and back too. Then in the morning, we can leave it somewhere and go home."

"Lord, please do something. PLEASE!" I kept praying.

"No! I do not want to be killed or sent away because of you idiots. It is bad enough we are sneaking out to meet women and have had a bit too much alcohol. If the colonel finds out he will have our necks because of this. What if this car belongs to one of the dignitaries? Look, the tags are from Addis. So, no, no way. Now shut up and walk faster so we can see the women and be back home before we get into any trouble."

I liked that soldier. *Yes, go see your lady friends and walk away*, I thought. "Thank you, Lord. You are always on my side," I said in a whisper while looking up at the skies, although all I could see were branches.

I watched the three soldiers walk away and turn the corner before I climbed down the tree and looked for an opening to get to Kasahun. As I pulled through the branches, I noticed an opening with branches that were not as thick. The perfect place for the car to drive through. "Thank you again Lord!" I did not want to lose this entrance and it was too dark for me to walk away from it and bring Kasahun back, so I called out for him instead. "Kasahun! Kasahun! I found a way in." I called again and again before he answered, asking where exactly I was. "Inside the tree," I responded. "Follow my voice and drive to me. There is room to hide the car here."

He turned on the car lights and I saw how close he was. I had him turn them off as soon as he got to the tree, where he pushed through the branches without a scratch. It was quiet and dark in our tree shelter. Finally, we could rest and sleep for a couple of hours at the very least. I figured I would ask him more questions about his feelings in the morning, but at this point, I was happy he was alive, that we had gotten this far, and that we were together.

Kasahun jumped out of the car and came straight for me in the darkness. With both arms, he pulled me into a tight embrace. It felt good, yet I could not determine if this was a friendly hug or something more.

"I cannot breathe," I whispered.

"Thank God you are okay. I am okay. We made it safely. I was scared. I saw my life flash before me: my family, my friends, you."

"Me?"

"Yes, you. Marcos gave me a mission and I intend to complete it."

"Right. I am your mission. How come your girlfriend's face did not appear instead of mine? What's her name by the way?"

He gave me a confused look before saying, "Oh, Lemlem, you mean. I told you already. She broke up with me."

"No, you said she always did that, and that she would be back."

"Why do you care about Lemlem anyway?"

"I do not care. I am always curious, but right now I am cold. Can we go inside the car please?"

He let go of me, and we both crawled into the back seat in order to sleep. I never thought my first night with any man would be in the back of a car, but the cold air and the fact that we only had one blanket to share outweighed any thoughts I had of what my first night alone with a man would look like. "Good night," I said, but sleep was the last thing on my mind at that point. I wanted to know more about Lemlem without sounding like I cared.

"Kasahun?"

"Hmm."

"Are you awake?"

"I am now. Are you okay?"

"Why did you get upset when I brought up Yonatan? Please tell me."

"Weizerit or Annabella or whatever your name is… just sleep. It's late and we have to leave early in the morning. Please, we must sleep."

"No, please tell me."

I heard him begin to snore. How rude! I could not see his face, but I knew he was not sleeping. How could he? I figured this was his way of keeping me quiet, and in all honesty, having this discussion would be better in the morning. That way, I could gauge his expression when I questioned him. I finally dozed off thinking about how I would bring it up again.

"Weizerit, wake up. Annabella, wake up. *Anchi (meaning girl)*, wake up."

"I have a name. Do not call me *anchi*."

"Apparently you have more than one."

"You may call me Bella."

"Yet another name."

"That is what my friends and family call me."

I opened my eyes and stretched, then noticed that he was looking straight at me.

"What? Do I have something on my face? Oh Lord, please tell me I did not drool."

He chuckled softly, flashing that beautiful smile.

"No, you have nothing on your face. We must leave before the sun comes up and the streets start to get busy. Help me drive the car out of this tree, please."

I nodded and got up to help. Once I was out of the car, I looked around and saw just how beautiful and big the willow tree really was.

"The coast is clear," I said and he navigated admirably out of the tree. We were both extremely hungry and stopped at a local café to get breakfast. I realized I had not eaten anything but a piece of bread since the day before. I was famished and dirty and probably quite unattractive, having recently slept in a barn and the back of a car. In Tigrinya, my father's language, I asked the lady behind the counter if there was a washroom I could use.

"You must be from Asmara?" she asked.

"How can you tell?" Kasahun replied.

"Well, your accent gives you away. Yours more than hers." She smiled at us and told me I could use her house to clean up. As I walked away, I could hear her asking Kasahun why we were in Mekelle.

It felt wonderful to freshen up. It was hard to believe I had only been away from home for two nights. I missed coffee more than anything. Coffee and a warm bath in my tub with my favorite soap from Harrods. Laughing at my own thoughts, I daydreamed about my last visit to Harrods. It was so recent yet felt like a different era. Adventures in London had nothing on those in northern Ethiopia.

I brushed my hair and cleaned myself as best I could. When I went back to the front of the café, I found Kasahun ordering us breakfast in a dialect that was extremely hard for me to understand.

"I know that's Tigrinya, but I barely recognize it."

"I have some friends that are from here and their parents only speak to them in this dialect. I spent so much time here growing up, I guess I picked it up along the way."

"What did you tell the lady we were doing in Mekelle? Please tell me you ordered coffee, I'm dying for good coffee."

Kasahun laughed. "Yes, they are about to start the traditional ceremony now. While we wait, tell me more about your life — your real life."

I smiled. "Well, there is not much to tell apart from what I already told you."

"Who is Yonatan?"

"Oh, we are back on that subject, again are we? Who do you think he is?"

"Well, if my memory serves me right, you are supposed to marry a general. Is it Kebede? Yes, General Kebede… so Yonatan must be an old lover, or a new one. Maybe someone you met at your university. Someone smart like you."

I was going to have fun with this conversation. "Yonatan is smart, very smart. He is studying to be a lawyer at the same university my father went to in the south of France. We grew up together and my father became his mentor. If you want to know more, you must first tell me why you got so serious when his name came up."

"I saw how relaxed your face got when you said his name, I guess. Or maybe it was that you compared me to him. Honestly, I do not know what to tell you, Weizerit."

"Bella. Please call me Bella."

"Right. Sorry, it might take a while getting used to a foreign name on an Ethiopian woman.

"So, I am Bella, and for the record, Yonatan is my cousin. Our fathers are brothers and yes, you remind me a lot of him."

His face flushed red in embarrassment.

"You just made me answer all those questions and go through that for a cousin." He laughed and added, "You really are something else, Bella Lorenzo."

His voice lowered when he saw the waiter coming with our food. I smelled the roasting coffee and our food before I turned around to see the waiter. Every sip of my coffee brought me joy. Every bite of my firfir made me close my eyes and enjoy paradise. It was that good. "Either you both are very hungry or my food is very good," said our hostess.

"Both!" I replied. We had cleaned our plates in minutes. Emama would have scolded me if I ever displayed such bad manners at home.

"Are you still hungry?" Kasahun asked me.

"I am good for now. I could go for a nice piece of cake but mostly I am satisfied. Will we stop again before we reach our destination?"

"Yes, Marcos has two more stops for us with specific instructions for each, but we will get to Asmara before nightfall tonight."

The drive to Adigrat was exactly 150 kilometers, just as Marcos had said. We did not talk much, each lost in our own thoughts. There was not much to see apart from mountains and a few small villages. We stopped in a neighborhood right off the main city road in Adigrat to pick up one of the packages from Marcos that I believe had money and documents in it.

"I wonder how Marcos got all these packages together," I asked Kasahun.

"The old soldiers stick together. I see it with my father as well. They stand up for each other, they help each other out. They say that is how they defeated the Italians in the Battle of Adwa, and why the Italian military could not colonize Ethiopia the second time around as well. Sadly, this new generation of soldiers are not built like that. Now everyone only thinks for themselves," he said.

I nodded and he changed subject.

"Look, we are almost at the border now. We're heading to a place called…"

"Zelambassa — right?" I asked, reviewing the route in my mind.

"Yes, are you sure you have never been this far north in Ethiopia?"

I nodded my head, "I'm a quick learner though. Cities and far off places fascinate me. Even small villages fascinate me. A new place is a new place."

Zelambassa was even smaller than Adigrat, and just as Marcos had predicted, the border was wide open, which made the crossing from Ethiopia into Eritrea surprisingly simple. From my lessons with Marcos, I pictured the border crossing process to be more dramatic, that it would involve running and hiding. There were no signs saying we had even entered Eritrean territory, no soldiers barricading the road, nothing that signified you were in a different city, let alone a different state.

I was sitting in the front seat beside Kasahun, and he could see the surprised look on my face as he told me we were now in Eritrea. "I thought you would be happy. The worst part is over."

"Is it though? You misunderstand my joy. I am simply shocked at how easy that was," I said.

"It would have been quite different had we made this little commute while the Italians were still occupying Eritrea. Now that Eritrea is a federalized state of Ethiopia, it is easy to travel in and out of both places. Marcos was right to pick this town as the entry point, though, as it is one of the only ones that is not guarded."

"Why are the other points still guarded?"

"Who knows? Politics is ugly, my friend, but you already know that."

I nodded in response. Oh, if only he knew.

"What are you thinking about right now?" He stopped the car abruptly for the third time since we met and looked directly at my eyes. I could tell he wanted an immediate response. "I'm thinking about many things, while also thinking about nothing. Is that even possible?"

"*Anchi.* Do not play games."

I opened the car door to get out, breathe in the air of this new place, and answer his question. He came out shortly after me

"Well, I am thinking about the dangers of politics and how many innocent people suffer at the hands of a few. I am also thinking of what my father would say to me if he were here. We always planned to make this trip together. He wanted to show me his land and his people. He wanted me to know and love where I was from, and he also wanted me to be educated and free. He told me that education was the key to freedom. He said I had to lead myself first before I could lead anyone else. I wish he were here now. So many things would be different."

CHAPTER 7

When the Driver Becomes the Lover

First, I felt his arms come around from behind me, then I turned, and our lips touched. It wasn't exactly the kiss I had imagined, but I was happy. Happy doesn't quite put my feelings into words, but I cannot think of any other way to describe it. Overwhelmed perhaps. I had been kissed plenty of times before but there was something different about this, about the way he held me tight and guided my body. As I felt my limbs melting in his arms, I heard a child laughing and quickly became conscious of our surroundings. I opened my eyes to see three young children laughing and wrapping their arms around their own bodies, imitating what we were doing. Kasahun and I looked at each other and laughed. He then opened the front passenger door for me, closed it, and went to get in the driver's seat. For a while we were both quiet, and then he reached for my hand and clasped it tightly.

"Bella, I know our worlds are quite different and that a man like me would never be able to give you the life that you deserve, but I want you to know that in these few days you have given me such hope and the desire to want more for myself. Thank you!"

"Happy to be of service," I said, smiling. "Kasahun, you are a wonderful man and I would be honored to be courted by you. I do not care about money and status. I do care about mindset and the drive to achieve. My father and grandmother always taught me that if you desire more for yourself and are willing to work hard, success will always occur. You, my darling, will be successful. Look at how far Papa got in his career; he came from nothing and at his highest level he was the Foreign Minister of Ethiopia."

Kasahun was smiling at me.

"Speaking of your father, this is his town — Adi Keih. Should we ask around and see where he was born or if his family is still here?"

I told him the little I knew about his remaining family and that his parents had died several years prior. We parked the car on a main road and started exploring on foot so that we could get our bearings in the small town. As we were walking, I noticed a school that had Papa's name on it.

"Look, Kasahun, they've named a school after him. Do you think they will let us in? I wonder if he knew about it. I think he would have told me if he did."

We crossed the street and walked towards the school where a guard was sitting by the gate with a big stick in his hands.

"What do you want?" he frowned.

I remembered Emama telling me that it would be safe to use my real identity in Eritrea and decided to tell the man who I truly was. "*Selam*. My name is Annabella Lorenzo, my father's name is written on your school, and I would love to see it." I used the best Tigrinya I could gather up and it worked.

"*Besemame*. Bella! Bella is home! Have you visited your family? Have you seen your cousins? Yes, yes, please come and see what is built in your father's name. How we are cherishing Ayaye Lorenzo in a way that he would be so proud of. We are educating our own people. We are not waiting for the Italians or other white people to teach us. Your father lives in our hearts and in this school. And who is this handsome man? Is this your husband? A fine couple you are. We never got to see your mother and we were all sad when we heard she died, but we also heard that Ayaye Lorenzo's new wife is a gracious woman and that she was raising you as her own. We were all happy. We begged your father to send you here to us, but he was never able. I knew your father when he was just a young shepherd. He was always begging for books and wanting to teach himself how to do everything. That is why those Italian missionaries took him off to Keren to teach him. They saw something in him. They knew he was destined for greatness. Oh, so many stories, but come, come inside. Everyone, look who has come home finally! Here is Bella Lorenzo."

I walked onto the school grounds and immediately felt Papa all around me. I felt like I had been there before, maybe in my dreams where I see and talk to him, maybe in photos, but somehow, I had experienced this school before.

There was one building with maybe seven or eight classrooms. Each had roughly 20 desk tables that could fit a maximum of three students. There was a large chalkboard at the head of each classroom next to the teacher's desk. I opened one of the shared classroom textbooks and saw that the students were learning different levels of math. Other books I explored covered science, geography, English, and even Tigrinya, which I was incredibly happy about. The kids would learn how to read and write in their own language, something I was never taught. The school had done well; the people of Adi-Keih all contributed what little they had and built it right. I wondered if Yeshimebet knew about it and whether she had sent any money for them. They taught children from first grade all the way to eighth. From there students went to high schools in Asmara or Keren. The first batch of graduated students were now in different universities around the world. Their foundation written on the wall was based on my father's view of education: Educate one, Educate all!

"Papa would have been proud and honored at what you have accomplished here," I told the headmistress, who was pleased to welcome me into the building.

"Well, your father led by example and now it is our turn to do the same. So, what finally brings you home? How long will you be staying?"

Excellent questions that I had no way of answering. I practiced a tactic

I had recently learned from Kasahun that seemed to work wonders for him. I responded to her questions with my own set of questions on funding and diverged the conversation as best I could. I glanced at him and smiled with a wink.

"Well, everything we have here is funded by the people of our town who already have very little. We also have some help from one or two Eritrean dignitaries who were close with your father. Oh, and your uncle is a big part of the process. For example, the idea for this building came from him. He said it was something your father had wanted to do for a while and never got the chance. He sent us plans for a school your father had designed only months before he passed away." Was Papa planning to create this for the people and never got a chance to tell me? I started wondering about other things that were left unsaid before he passed away. And why did Uncle Mikael not tell me about all this himself?

"You are doing a wonderful job. I would love to be a part of it somehow. I can come back and visit often, maybe even teach once or twice a week depending on whether I can get a car to bring me here from Asmara."

"So, you will be staying in Eritrea then. Oh, thank you, Lord, thank you!" she said, clapping her hands together and looking up to the sky. Papa meant so much to these people that they wanted me here without even knowing me! Emama was right to have me come here, and she was even more right to have me use my name in Eritrea. These people wanted their son back and somehow, I could give them that.

September 2019

"No way our diva grandmother falls in love with the driver! Way to go, Grams
— way to go!" My grandchildren hooted and cheered. "Does Kasahun move to
Asmara with you?" I laughed at their questions and how well they knew me. "I
do not want to spoil the story for you. Just listen patiently and you will know."

CHAPTER 8

Family

We left Papa's school and continued touring other areas of Adi Keih. I felt a sense of belonging there, a feeling I had not experienced for a very long time. Even without Papa there with me physically, I felt his presence in everything I saw. I imagined him herding his sheep on the same street or playing with his friends as a young boy.

"I want to see where he grew up, Kasahun. I need to see it."

"Of course you do. They have a school named after him, so therefore I am sure the people will know where his family resides," he said and with no hesitation, he pushed me to ask the first person we saw for information on Papa's family.

It was a woman carrying a baby on her back and rushing to go somewhere.

"*Selam, Yigreta*! Hello, my apologies. I'm looking for the home of Lorenzo Kidane. Can you help me, please?" I said in my best Tigrinya. It sounded a bit messy, but still surprisingly good. She smiled at me and asked whose daughter I was.

"Your face — there is something about your face that looks familiar." She said.

I smiled back and even blushed a little. "I am his daughter. The daughter of Lorenzo Kidane." The words coming out of my mouth felt so powerful!

"*Ewey Ewey Ewey!* No wonder I recognized you! You look so much like his family." With her child clinging to her back with his legs, she opened her arms to embrace me. Then she looked down and I could see sadness in her face.

"My condolences. Your father was an honest man. His family is brave. You come from a long line of brave people. Be proud! Always be proud! Your grandparents have a house down this street. Go down the hill and turn left at the red gate. The house will be on your right. There is a lot of property there. Your father and uncle kept buying up pieces of land for your grandparents, but they never came to do anything with it, so the house sits the same. Your grandmother, God bless her soul, used to complain all the time about how they sent her money, but they never came home. Oh, she was so happy when she found out you were born and your cousins too. How is your uncle? Do you keep in touch with him? How are his children, his family?"

So many questions, so much information. My father had kept ties with his family and never told me. I wondered why.

"Your relatives now live on the property. They will be happy to meet you. The person who takes care of it is Moges. He is your father's first cousin on his father's side. Such a wonderful family, just wonderful. Bless you all." She hurried away, still praising Papa's entire family.

"Well, that was easy enough," I told Kasahun, beaming with pride from having a whole conversation in Tigrinya and hearing great things about my family.

"Beginner's luck," he teased me. "Let's try another person, just to see what happens."

I laughed and refused his offer, eager to meet my relatives.

"Bella. We can go, but I have to remind you that we need to get back on the road shortly. They are expecting you in Asmara by nightfall, and I do not want more police and soldiers on the lookout for us than there already are now."

"I know. I know. I promise it will be a short stay. I need this, though."

It hit me then that my time with Kasahun was coming to an end. He would return to Addis and I would stay in Asmara for a while at the very least. What would happen to us? Was there even an 'us'? I became sad all of a sudden. I missed him already.

"Are you okay? What's wrong?" he asked.

"Nothing, I am fine. A little nervous about meeting my family for the first time, but fine nonetheless."

"Women," he laughed. "One minute you are laughing and joyful and the next you are close to crying. I'll never understand you."

"Oh, shut up," I said, laughing.

"Okay, we are at the red gate. Did she say turn left or right?" He looked at me.

"Umm, I think she said left. Why were you not paying attention? Let me ask someone just to be sure. She said Papa's cousin Moges was watching over the house."

We confirmed the directions and walked a few more blocks before we came to the property. At first, I did not see anything but trees and grass, then I noticed a small home that looked almost identical to Emama's garden bungalow except that it was made with mostly mud. There were windows on each side of the house. I had seen houses like this before in Addis and lots on the way to Eritrea but was a bit surprised that this humble abode was where my father grew up. Although the fields surrounding the home were vast, the house itself was very old and looked like it was not well cared for.

As I kept walking towards the house, a man came out who looked identical to Papa, making me stop in my tracks, speechless. All I could do was stare at him. My mouth opened to say something but words would not come out.

The man looked confused and asked who we were.

Kasahun gave me a nudge. "Speak up, Bella."

I opened my mouth to speak for the second time and again words would not come out. How was this possible? He had Papa's chin, the same eyes, com-

plexion, height, and even the same gentle frown as my father. "Papa" was all I
could say.

"I'm sorry, sir. Are you Moges?" asked Kasahun.

"Yes. Who are you? What can I help you with? Is she okay?"

I grabbed his hand and shook it. "Hello. My name is Bella. Annabella Lorenzo. I am the daughter of Lorenzo Kidane. You look just like him. Only your
voice is a little different. Well, that and your handshake. Papa always shook
hands extra-firmly. I never knew you existed!"

I was about to gush more about Papa when Moges interrupted.

"Lorenzo Kidane's daughter. *Besemame. Besemame.* You look so much like
your grandmother. Bella, oh Bella! Welcome home! Come, come meet your
family."

He called his wife and their three boys from the fields, and they all looked
like me. I could see features of Papa, Uncle Mikael, and Yonatan in each of the
children.

"Please come inside. My wife will make you and your husband coffee,"
Moges said.

"Thank you! Kasahun is my friend and sadly, we must be going. We are
expected in Asmara. I will be staying there for quite some time, so if it is okay
with you, I would love to come back and visit."

"Please, please do. You should at least come inside and see where your
father was born. My uncle had this hut built the day he found out his wife was
expecting. Both of his boys were born right here. Your grandfather wanted
something different for his children and he knew how smart they were, so
he sent them both to school in Keren with the priests. People thought he was
crazy, but they were wrong!"

"Do you know why Papa never came back here?" I asked Moges.

"I do not know. No one does. They sent money quite often. In fact, your
uncle still does. They sent letters and pictures of you children, but they never
came back to visit. For a while we all believed it was because of the Italians, but
then the Italians left, and your grandparents died, and I guess they just never

felt the need to return home. That is a different story though. You are here now, and you are your father's daughter. You being here means he is here, he is home at last."

We walked inside the small hut and I could sense Papa's presence. "Where did he sleep?" I asked Moges.

"In that corner. He wrote things down over there as well. Come look."

On the wall in small letters I saw Papa's messy childhood handwriting. He had written out his name in bold letters: Membrahtu Kidane. This was his name before he went to the missionary school and became Lorenzo Kidane. I smiled and told Moges and his sons that he only wrote like that when he was in a hurry and that his handwriting had thankfully gotten much better over the years.

"I wish I could stay, but I promise to come back often and visit. Thank you for allowing me into your home."

"This is your home, Annabella. Come back soon, please."

Kasahun and I walked back to his car in silence. "Will you be back?" Kasahun asked as we began the drive to Asmara.

"Of course! Why would I not? These are my people, my family."

"Well, your father never returned, why is that? Also, you have people and family in Addis as well. What is your plan?"

I could tell this was not just about my family. He was asking for my plans for his own sake as well. I could pretend that he was simply asking to be polite or I could entertain the idea that he wanted a future with me in it.

"Why are you asking?" I asked, intrigued to hear his answer.

"I have taught you well, Bella! I see you keep using my trick of answering a question with a question. Admirable, but please just answer the question."

"Well, I do not know what my plans are. Honestly, I do not even know what tomorrow will bring. For right now, all I know is that I do not want to

marry the general, so here I am in a car with you in Eritrea. Once I get through
this part, then I can focus on my dreams and plans again."

"What are your dreams?"

"I want to study law like my father and cousin Yonatan. I want to marry
for love and start my own family. Most importantly I would like to continue my
father's work in some form."

"A wise woman once told me you can do anything you put your mind to."
He pulled my hand into his, giving it a gentle kiss. Our hands fit together so
perfectly, it amazed me. How was it that I had only met him three days ago?
It felt like I had known him for years. He was easy to talk to, he listened to my
thoughts, tended to my needs, and seemed to genuinely care for me. I did not
feel the weight of who I was or where I came from. I found it easy to be myself
and it was liberating! That was what I wanted in a relationship. Maybe that was
why God put the two of us together on this journey. It was for me to learn to
value myself and my independence, and to know what to expect going forward
in any relationship with a man. At that moment, looking at him, I knew we
probably would not be together. His life was in Addis, while mine was here for
now. For me to ask him to stay would be wrong. His family needed him more
than I did. If our paths ever crossed again, I would take it as a sign that we were
meant to be.

On the drive from Adi-Keih to Asmara, we passed many beautiful villages
amidst exquisite scenery. Kasahun held my hand the entire way, even when I
fell asleep with my head resting on his shoulder. He woke me up gently once
we entered Asmara. It was nothing like Addis! If anything, it reminded of the
little Italian towns that Saba and I visited when we were at King's College. The
city was modern, clean, and vibrant. The people I saw on the streets were well
dressed and the storefronts looked prosperous. There were beautiful villas and
palm trees that made me feel as though I was at the beach on vacation. I
opened my window to enjoy the balmy, fragrant breezes. I felt excited, but then
quickly realized my arrival meant saying goodbye to Kasahun. At the palace
gates he let go of my hand, and that simple gesture told me it was over. Whatever we had started, whatever it had been or meant to us, it was now over. We

were back in the real world and in that world, I was being dropped off at the palace by my driver.

"Name! Pass! Who are you here to see?" said the guard at the gate. Growing up in Addis, I was used to seeing guards at palace gates, and even though these men wore the same uniform, they were very different from the guards I was used to seeing. I could see Kasahun was nervous as well and gave my new name and counterfeit documents to the guard without hesitation.

At once the guard gave me a salute and told me the princess had been waiting for my arrival.

"You are late. Please enter. Only you. You can walk to the residential quarters."

"Walk? I would prefer to stay in my vehicle." I was not ready to say goodbye just yet.

"My orders are to allow only you into the compound. Your driver will have to leave."

Kasahun's face changed at the guard's comment. "It is okay. Go, Bella."

Everything was happening so fast that without thinking, I told the guard to notify the princess of my safe arrival and that I would return to the palace shortly. Both the guard and Kasahun could not believe what they were hearing.

"Excuse me. What did you say?" the guard said, with a puzzled look on his face. "You want me to do what?"

"You're excused. My Tigrinya is not the best, so let me repeat myself in Amharic. Tell the princess that I will be back this evening. Thank you and goodbye," I said, as Kasahun backed away from the main gate.

"I loved that! Who did he think he was, or more importantly, who did he think I was?" I was laughing, but when I looked at him, I saw Kasahun wasn't.

"What you did back there was beyond stupid, Bella. The princess is risking her life for you. Hell, we all are, and you think it is a game. What were you thinking, telling the guard that you will be back like that? You are a guest in their home. It is not just a home, it is a palace. The palace."

I was offended at best and appalled at worse. "Excuse me, I was trying to stand up for you. I talked to him the way he talked to you. I thought you would be proud of me for speaking up. And you do not have to tell me the risk that Princess Maryam is taking for me, because I already know and understand it."

"Well, you sure are not acting like you do, and for the record, let it be known that I did not ask you to stand up for me. I can handle myself just fine. I do not need you or anyone else feeling sorry for me or doing me any favors."

Instantly, I realized what he was doing. He wanted me to be upset and leave with no regrets. "Kasahun, it doesn't have to be this way. I care for you, but I have made peace with the fact that our time is not now. You have your family back in Addis, and I must figure things out for myself here in Asmara. If we are meant to be, then God will make it happen some way or another." As I was talking to him, I noticed the lines on his face slowly disappear and he reached for my hand again.

"I'll never forget you, Annabella Lorenzo. Everything we talked about, I will work on. You have made me a new man, a dreamer, because you believed in my dreams with me. I will not let you down."

"I know you will not! I hope to be on your very first flight one day soon. You must keep in touch. I look forward to hearing about your many adventures."

"Sure, just give me the palace's phone number and mailing address!" he said, laughing.

I told him how serious I was and that if he wanted to keep in touch, he would find a way.

"That reminds me. You know all the stops we made to pick up money? Well, here you go. My instructions were to give you this envelope upon arriving in Asmara. Your grandmother wants you to have this for your new life," he said.

I was shocked; there was an enormous amount of money in that envelope. I should have known Emama would do something like that. She always thought three steps ahead of everyone else.

I wanted Kasahun to have the money. He needed it more than I did and would be able to start a new life for himself with it.

"You take it. It will help get you into flight school and pay for your sister's education as well," I said.

"What? Annabella, I cannot accept this. Have you lost your mind? This is a lot of money. It will help you start your new life here."

"I know, Kasahun, but you risked your life to save mine, and this is the least I can do. I need to do things on my own going forward. I need to experience life for what it is, and this money just keeps me tied to my family and everything they stand for. My grandmother will understand, and besides, no one has to know that I gave this money to you. I will not say anything if you do not." I smiled at him.

"Thank you. Thank you very much. You are an angel, my angel." He hugged and kissed me, and I could feel my body melting in his arms. After a while he let go, kissed my forehead, and told me it was time. I agreed and even though I was sad, I was okay. God placed him in my life to show me that love can happen for me.

He dropped me off at the palace gates, and I got out of the car with all the grace I could muster. I looked back after a few steps and saw him parked at the gate, waiting for me to look at him. I could hear the guard aggressively telling him to move on, but he was focused only on me. Our eyes met. He smiled, gave a nod, and I knew he was telling me that everything was going to be fine.

The Governor's Mansion *Asmara*

CHAPTER 9

Early Days in Asmara

Princess Maryam was waiting for me at the front door. "Is everything all right, Bella? The guards mentioned you came earlier and left," she said with a concerned face. We embraced and then walked into the palace, which was magnificent. Built by the Italians, it had served as the first governor's palace in the late 1890s. The architecture was classic Italian renaissance, with modern touches. The entrance hall was made entirely of Italian marble and was furnished to perfection. I could not stop admiring all the exquisite details as she led me to a sitting room.

"I will show you to your quarters shortly. First, let us sit and talk," she said, leading me to two arm chairs in a sitting room that faced a powerful and breathtaking painting showcasing Ethiopian history through many generations. As we took our seats, I heard children's voices yelling from somewhere in the background. "The children do not know you are here and will be pleased to see you. I worry that their innocence can harm us." I immediately noticed the concerned look on her face and began to worry as she continued to tell me that she had received information that General Kebede had tasked the entire military to find and bring me back to Addis Ababa. "Our guards have strict orders from me not to notify anyone of your presence here, but I do not know how long we can keep this a secret. We need a plan, Bella. I have been thinking that we should telegram the emperor and let him know that you are here with me. We could casually tell him, since I have not received anything from him or his office yet in reference to you. I can say that you are safely in my custody and will stay with me for some time to help with the children, or something along those lines."

"Princess Maryam, thank you for everything you have done and are continuing to do, but with all due respect, I doubt that will work. I agree we should let it be known that I am here, but unless we make it seem as though my being here is helping the country somehow, I believe the emperor will demand I return immediately. At that point, there will be nothing we can do about it."

"I do not know what else we can do. I am positive Father has people here who report everything to him. He is very thorough, as you know. What if I sent you to Yemen, and then Europe from there?" She must have seen the look of dismay on my face because she quickly corrected herself, with her hands in the air adding, "You belong here. I know, I know. Let us discuss this further in the morning. It is late and you must be exhausted from your journey." She rose from her chair to personally show me my new living quarters. As we walked together I noticed that we were heading away from the main living quarters and heading south of the palace.

"Princess?"

"Yes, Bella?"

"Why are you doing this for me? You are risking a great deal. Your father's anger, your husband's, even your own life. Why?"

She looked at me, smiling. "Your grandmother must not have told you my story. That woman always keeps a secret."

"Told me what?" I asked.

"Nothing. It is not important, and we will have plenty of time to discuss stories, but for right now I want you to know that I am helping you because it is the right thing to do. You deserve the right to live your life as you see fit. Besides, that old general has no business pushing the military around the way he does and demanding that things be done just to his liking. Who does he think he is?" She smiled at me, and we both laughed.

"He is also decidedly ugly and has bad teeth," I added. "But Princess, I have known you all my life and I know you mostly follow the rules, so please just tell me."

She gazed into my eyes for a while before speaking again.

"You are just like him, you know. Your father. It is remarkable. Nothing gets past you. Well, if you must know, I am helping you because long ago, I myself was forced into marriage, not with Dawit, but like you, with an older, much older aristocrat who believed that using his fist was the best way to be obeyed by his wife."

"What? When? How come we never knew?"

"Sweet child, there is so much you all do not know. This was decades ago. I was seen as an object instead of a person. If it was not for your grandmother who fought for me and convinced my mother to do the same, my life story would be quite different." She gave me time to process the information she had just shared. "So, from one strong woman to another, it is my duty to help you in any way possible. I want you to find love, Bella. You deserve to be happy, and free to live the way you want to live, not the way our society tells you to."

"What happened to the man you were supposed to marry?"

"Well, from what I heard, he was shipped somewhere far away."

"I'm happy you were able to get away, Princess. I hope my story will have a similar ending. Thank you for sharing this with me. Good night." We hugged and she left. I was alone in a room in a land that was my home, yet I did not know it at all. I looked around and noticed how beautiful the room was, with Persian rugs and silks from Damascus. There were three large floor-to-ceiling windows, which meant that when the curtains were opened during the day, one could probably see most of the town from the bed. On the right side of the bed were built-in cupboards and to the left was the bathroom. I could probably stay here in hiding very comfortably. I started to think about Kasahun and his drive back to Addis Ababa. I thought of Emama, Saba, and my family back home. Even though I was exhausted, I stayed up late into the night thinking about my options. How on earth was I going to convince the emperor to let me stay here? What would Papa have told me to do? Would he have done as he was told? Maybe, but when he believed in something, he always fought for it. I had to do the same — fight for what I believed in. My staying in Asmara and away from General Kebede was something I strongly believed in. Hearing Princess Maryam share her story with me inspired me even more to push through with my own fight and come up with a solution that would not only benefit myself, but countless other women who were more than likely experiencing the same fatal predicament. This was not just about my problems anymore. It was about saving a generation of women — my generation and hopefully all the generations that would come after me. I had to come up with a way to appeal to the emperor's heart. I would make him understand. I fell asleep looking across from my bed into the night sky, grateful to be in Asmara and free.

The next morning, I woke up to a light knock on the door from Princess Maryam and two ladies who brought me trays of food.

"Are we expecting more people?" I asked the princess, who gave me a confused look before understanding that she had brought too much food. She laughed, "Well, I did not know how hungry you would be after the drive, so I brought you a little of everything."

"I see. Thank you very much."

"Your clothes are all hanging in the closets and there are fresh towels in the bathroom. Your grandmother did not think you would need too much, so she sent only one suitcase. I can have someone go shopping for you if you like."

I opened the closet to see my favorite belongings hanging neatly. "This is perfect, thank you again. Thank you so much for everything. I was thinking last night, and I know this will sound crazy, but I genuinely believe that the only way we will win your father over is by telling the truth and appealing to his heart. It is either that or killing the general, and I for one do not want to go to jail for murder." She did not find my joke very funny but gave me a little smile, nonetheless.

"How exactly do you envision this happening?" Maryam said. "More importantly, when do you envision this happening? We need to make sure the timing is perfect. If we catch him at a good time, he might just listen and agree. We will need allies within the court; Father always requests counsel from the people he trusts most. My mother will help us. We cannot count on your grandfather. Dawit and my brother Addisu are a possibility. We will have to get both men on our side before going to Father with anything. Give me until the end of the week to talk to them. But Bella, I hope you know how risky this plan is. If they decide not to help us, they will tell General Kebede where you are. Are you sure this is the route you want to take? I do not have any other ideas besides Yemen, and this seems even riskier."

"Yes. I honestly do not see any other options. I cannot live in hiding forever. I have a good feeling about this. I know it is risky, but it just might work."

"Very well. I will start working on Dawit today and then focus on my brother. In the meantime, you will have to stay hidden here just to be safe. I will be back later in the afternoon, hopefully with good news. Oh, and one more thing. I saw this and thought you might like it for your new adventure." It was a shiny, thick, new journal; exactly what I needed.

"Thank you. Thank you very much! I will start writing in it today. Once this is all behind us, I want to start helping other women like us who are facing the same challenges."

"Help them how?" asked Maryam.

"I haven't thought that far ahead yet, but I want to do more for them, help them escape, provide funding, shelter, and education. I do not know, but doing nothing is not going to work for me."

"Your drive never ceases to amaze me. First things first though. Let us work on saving you."

After three days in a car with no shower and barely anything to eat, everything on the trays Maryam brought looked great. I enjoyed fried eggs, firfir, and the ful fava beans that were one of Emama's specialties and one of my favorite things for breakfast. There was also tea with small fried treats, oranges, bananas, and cactus fruit. I ate enough to make up for the last few days of hunger. The two ladies who came with Maryam earlier cleared the trays and opened the curtains before they left. I could see the entire city from my windows, and even though there was a beautiful long balcony within my reach, I stayed indoors out of fear of being seen. No wonder Maryam liked it so much here; it had the feeling of a European city while still being very much African. I could see why everyone called it The Little Rome: "*La Piccola Roma.*"

As I looked out the window, I wrote about what I observed on the streets; how people dressed and walked; how lovers held hands and hung around the park in front of the palace; how mothers grabbed their children's hands and rushed them to school; how people stood in orderly lines for the buses or taxis, and how different the cars were as well. They were mostly Italian and painted in the most vibrant colors. I noticed how the workers started cleaning the roads at the crack of dawn every day before the streets became busy with people. One thing I noticed and admired was that traffic was light – people mostly rode on bicycles. Asmara was alive and thriving, and even though I knew the people here had gone through much pain with colonization, I could not see it from my window. I wondered what Papa would think if he saw it today. Would he be happy that the Italians left? Would he be happy that the British and Americans had come instead, or that Ethiopia was involved in Eritrea now as well? I thought of ways he would have phrased what was happening in Eritrea today: "One colonizer moves out while another moves in. Different name, same story." At the end of the day, were we truly free? My head began to hurt from all the questions and doubts I was having, and I knew it was time to take a break from the journal.

I had not bathed in three days, so after breakfast and the journal, the first thing I did was draw a hot bath. Looking around, one could easily notice that the bathroom was designed by an Italian, full of brightly colored tiles and marble. I wished Saba were here to share these moments with me, laugh about something silly, or tell me about her relationship with Yonatan while I told her about Kasahun. Not sure if I would ever see him again, I let my thoughts drift to him while I soaked in the tub. Sweat was dripping down my face from the heat of the water, my hair was wet from being washed, and I was dozing off when I heard the maids knocking and entering my room, calling out my name and requesting permission to enter. They asked for my dirty laundry, but I was embarrassed to give them the filthy clothes I had been wearing throughout my trip.

"I can wash these myself, please do not bother,"

I insisted. One maid must have understood how I felt, because she smiled at me and said, "Do not worry, the kids' clothes get very, very dirty. We are used to this. We will wash it and bring it back as good as new."

Once they left, I got dressed. Emama had made sure my favorite pants and shirt were packed, and I could not wait to get into some clean clothes. I settled in at the desk and did some more writing in my journal. I made a note to ask the princess for books so I could read in my spare time. I loved reading books on history and political movements. There was so much power in people gathering to protest against injustice. I had seen it on so many occasions across Africa, and heard firsthand how Papa had gathered hundreds and thousands of people to fight the Italians when they occupied Ethiopia from 1936 until 1941. I wish I had been old enough to see him at work.

That afternoon Princess Maryam entered my room, followed by her husband Ras Dawit. She had a smile on her face and with a great deal of excitement said:

"Well, that was easy. Dawit is fully committed and promises that even if Father demands your return, he will ensure your safe travels out of Eritrea. This is great news, Bella! GREAT news!" She was holding my hands and looking at Dawit to get his confirmation.

"That is wonderful news. Thank you so much, Ras Dawit. I know you are both risking a great deal by helping me, and it is something I do not take for granted."

"Nonsense, child," Dawit said. He held his wife's hands in his own and looked at me. "We almost did not get the chance to be together because of an arranged marriage, so anything I, we, can do to help, we will do."

"Now, I will start working on bringing my brother on board and if that happens, we can start planning how to talk to Father about you staying here," said Maryam.

"Not if, when," corrected Ras Dawit.

"You are right. When that happens. It will take some time though. I will send him a telegram in the morning urging him to come and visit."

There was a knock on the door that startled me. Ras Dawit had guests who had arrived and were requesting his presence in the living room.

"Thank you. I will be right down," he told the butler and turned to us. "Ladies, I must leave. Bella, welcome to Asmara. You will love it here. Do have someone take you out and show you around our beautiful city. If you like riding horses, there are stables not too far from here and the kids would gladly go with you."

Then he looked at the princess and said, "My love, I have to take this meeting, but afterwards, if you need assistance on the telegram for your brother, I can draft something with you." He then gave her a kiss on the forehead, said goodbye one more time, and left the room.

"I hope you two become the next emperor and queen of Ethiopia. You make such a wonderful team," I said.

"Oh Bella, I do not want that title, even if it came with all the riches in the world. No, I am perfectly happy right here doing what I enjoy: raising my children, loving my husband, and ensuring that girls in Ethiopia receive an education."

"That is exactly why you will make the perfect queen," I told her, smiling. "So now that Ras Dawit knows I am here and approves of it, I would love to see the children. What time do their lessons end?"

Princess Maryam had decided to do things differently in Asmara and send them to a local private school instead of setting up a classroom and tutors in the palace. The children attended an Italian school run by Catholic nuns. I knew the emperor would be outraged if he knew, but she chose to do it regardless, which made me respect her even more. "I love that they are learning with other children, not just the children of other royals or aristocrats but normal children from normal families.

"I love that too. Can I go pick them up with the driver, or are you picking up the children yourself these days?" I smiled at her and she laughed.

"No, the driver fetches them and sometimes I go with him. We can go together this afternoon. They will be very happy to see you. Before we pick up the kids though, how about we go for a walk in the city and have lunch at my favorite little bistro downtown. We can walk to the children's school afterwards and have our driver meet us there."

The palace was located in the heart of the city and across the street from the governor's main office. Everything seemed so close and convenient, and I wondered why anyone would need to drive a car here. As we walked, people recognized Maryam and graciously nodded, but she did not walk with a security detail around her as she did in Addis or whenever she traveled. Saba would have loved it here, not just for the city, but the freedom from her royal duties. I could imagine her thriving and happy in Asmara. The city was even more beautiful than it had appeared from my windows at the palace. There was an elegant opera house called Cinema Asmara on the main road, flanked by lively restaurants and bars. On one street I saw all kinds of stores and boutiques. On another I noticed hair salons, barber shops, and small inns that were called "*Albergo*," which meant hotel in Italian. We walked past Our Lady of the Rosary Church, and I counted eight magnificent big bells in one bell tower, making the church seem even more grand. A little way past the cathedral was the university. Down the street from the university was the fish market, and further down I could see the fresh market as well. As we reached the end of the main street, I saw a large open space. The princess mentioned that they were going to build a stadium there big enough to fit the population of the entire city, which she said was about 100,000 people.

Princess Maryam's favorite restaurant was called Alba Bistro. It was situated right off the main road by the post office. The place reminded me so much of my favorite café at Harrods back in London, except this one had much more of an Italian feel.

We walked in and everyone knew Maryam. The head waiter greeted us warmly and took us to what must have been her favorite table, for which she thanked him greatly. It was then that I noticed him. The most handsome man I had ever seen. Tall, clean-shaven, and well-dressed, he looked like he belonged in a magazine. He was having lunch with two other men, one white (probably Italian or British) and another who looked either Eritrean, Ethiopian, or maybe even Sudanese. The other two men continued talking, and while he was quiet, his eyes locked on mine. I gasped for air, smiled at him, and turned to ask the princess who he was.

"I do not know him, but Bella, this is not the time to be looking for attention. You have enough to worry about as it is. Addisu responded to my telegram and is coming to Asmara early next week. Let us focus on him for now and find love later.

"You are right. I must focus on Prince Addisu. Papa was always fond of him and told me on many occasions that he was very smart. Do you think he will side with us?"

Princess Maryam felt that it could go either way. Addisu was indeed very smart and modern, but he was also very loyal to the emperor and the nation. He would do what he felt was right for the greater good. Our argument had to be focused on the marriage not being a good match, and how I was more valuable as a free woman to the future of our nation. Everything we would tell him had to lead to building a better Ethiopia.

As we were talking about different ideas and methods of persuading Prince Addisu, I kept sensing the handsome man staring at me. Every time I glanced his way, he smiled. It was very forward and direct and I liked it. I thought of the men I had dated in England; no one had ever simply stared at me before. I knew I would see this man again; it was only a matter of time before he would find a way to contact me. My thoughts were confirmed when we asked for our bill and were told that the gentleman had paid it. Maryam laughed and said, "Not even a day in Asmara, and you already have admirers, Bella. Saba would be proud." I turned to look at the man again to thank him, but he was gone. I asked the waiter for his name and was told he was Daniel Kahassay. We walked out joking about it and got in the family car to pick up the kids from school.

Makada and Zewditu were eight and six years old, Princess Maryam's pride and joy. They were both born in Addis but had lived in France, England, and now Eritrea. The last time I saw the girls was in Addis during my graduation party. They had grown a lot since then! The two were in third and first grade at school and already spoke fluent Italian. Both were beyond excited to see me. They wanted to know why I was in town, for how long, if Saba and Yonatan were with me, and what I had brought them from Addis. I promised to answer all their questions as soon as we got home.

As the days passed, I spent much of my time alone in my room or walking in the city, while my late afternoons were spent playing and talking with Makada and Zewditu. In the evening we all went for a walk, which was customary. Once the kids went to bed, the prince and princess sat down with me and we finished discussing what we would say and do when Addisu arrived from Addis Ababa. I thought things were going well, until Maryam brought up Saba and my family.

"I did not want to say anything, but I feel it is best that you know, and that you hear it from me sooner rather than later, Bella. Saba has been calling me more and more since your departure. She often phones to check if I have had any word on you, and to give me reports of any developments in your case. She is terribly worried and does not think for one minute that you planned an escape. She believes you were either kidnapped, like General Kebede is saying, or that something else has happened to you. She tells me that your family is also very worried, but that Ababa is angry and thinks you ran away. She called today while you were out with the kids and informed me that your grandmother has had a heart attack and is in critical condition. The doctors do not know if she will recover."

She said more but at some point, her words became mute to me and the room started to spin and go dark. No. Not my grandmother. Not Emama. I felt hot and could not breathe, could not speak, could not cry. The next thing I knew I was on my bed with doctors surrounding me. "What happened?" I asked the princess, and found out that I had fainted and hit my head on the coffee table.

"How do you feel?" a doctor asked in Tigrinya, and I told him I was okay, but had a bad headache. I looked at the princess and thought to ask her if I had been dreaming about Emama being sick, but the look on her face told me otherwise. With tears streaming down my face, for the first time in a while, I felt scared! "Bella, she is not dead, stop this. She needs you to be strong. God works miracles," she said, which is what everyone says in those situations.

"So, what exactly happened? I need details."

She told me that Emama had not been feeling well two days ago, had complained of a tightness in her chest, and felt light-headed. By that evening she asked for a doctor and within minutes of that, she had a heart attack. She explained further that Emama had the best care and the doctors were doing everything they could for her, but that it did not look very promising. Her organs were not responding accordingly and her brain was not functioning at full capacity.

Listening to the princess, I realized that the reason why she was nervous to tell me the news was because she knew I would want to go home. She was right; I wanted and needed to go home. "How fast can I get back to Addis?" I asked.

"Wait, Bella. We do not know exactly what is happening, and do you honestly think she would want you back in Addis given everything she did to get you out?"

I told her that did not matter! Nothing mattered apart from me being with Emama and telling her how much I loved her. I was not able to do that with Papa, and I would not let the same thing happen with Emama. "Please, Bella, let's just think about this," said Maryam. "Addisu will be here in two days, and then hopefully you will no longer have to be in hiding. Let us pray and be optimistic instead of jumping to conclusions and fearing the worst."

She was right. We said good night and I stayed in bed. From the bedside table, I pulled out the rosary that Yeshimebet had given me and did my Hail Mary prayers, starting a Novena on Emama's behalf. This reminded me even more of her and all the prayers we had shared over the years. She was such a faithful Catholic, such a devoted Christian, and knowing that gave me relief. On my last decade, I looked up and saw my new journal on the writing desk. I finished praying and started writing down all the thoughts that were running through my head. Should I head back to Addis? Would Emama welcome me back or be disappointed? Would Kasahun drive me? I had yet to even hear from Kasahun.

I knew Princess Maryam was right that Emama would not want me to come back, but would I be able to live with myself if anything happened to her and I was not there to say goodbye? I knew that returning to Addis would mean marrying General Kebede, but Emama meant more to me than anyone in the world. The more I wrote, the more clarity I had. I had to persevere! I had to create a life for myself in Eritrea, because that was what Emama wanted for me and that is what I wanted for myself. I could hear Emama's voice saying: *Do not dare come back here! You hear me? You run and you run as fast as you can. Create the life you want. Create a life you choose for yourself! Be your own woman. Be proud and fierce!* I fell asleep with a fierce smile on my face.

The next day, I decided to take a walk through the city. I needed fresh air and wanted to attend Mass and pray for Emama. "Should I come with you or have one of the housekeepers go with you? You are not familiar with the city just yet," Princess Maryam offered. I graciously rejected the offer and jokingly said, "I'm sure someone can help me get back to the palace." I wore my walking shoes, trousers and a simple shirt that I used when traveling. I had secretly come to love this simple way of dressing, although I would never dare share that with anyone back home. That was the beauty of being in this new place. I could reinvent who I was as a woman. I could dress and speak the way I wanted. Here in Asmara I was free to be me, and I loved that feeling. But who exactly was I? In a matter of mere weeks, I had gone from being told exactly who I was, to finding out that my father had a different birth name, and that he left home and never went back, and then I had fallen for a man I barely knew. Saba and Yonatan would be shocked if I told them all of this.

I walked for a while before I reached the cathedral and went in to pray. I entered the heavy doors and took a seat by the altar. The church was as beautiful on the inside as it was on the outside. The altar was massive and built entirely of marble with two large stained-glass windows on either side, which brought in plenty of colorful light. I knelt in front of Our Lady and prayed to her in the words Emama had taught me. I recited the same verses repeatedly, each time with more passion and desperation than the time before. I made promises that I knew would be hard to keep, but I made them anyway with the intent of keeping them when Emama was healed. The more I prayed, the more comfortable I became in my decision to stay. It was as though Our Lady was speaking to me through my fears, calming them, keeping them quiet, and ultimately chasing them away. I walked out of the church feeling confident in my decision, and in the fact that Emama would be okay.

I left the church feeling free and at peace with my decision to stay. Taking advantage of the beautiful weather, I decided to have a cappuccino outside at a little café on the main road opposite Cinema Asmara where the sun was beaming on the patio tables. I wished I had brought my journal; this would be the perfect place to sit and write.

There was much to write about. I closed my eyes to soak up the sunlight and let my thoughts wander. Papa's dreams of working towards a better and stronger Africa were still very important to me, but fighting for that in a politi-

cal way seemed less urgent to me now. Instead, I had thoughts of business opportunities, teaching, writing, and other ways to bring value to people's lives.
Seeing where Papa was born and raised, seeing the school that his people had
built in his honor, identifying myself as Eritrean, and living amongst my people
was changing me. I liked this newly evolved version of me, I liked her a great
deal. I felt free and hopeful!

Church of Our Lady of the Rosary also known as Cathedral *Asmara*

CHAPTER 10

Meeting Him and Losing Her

Two sips into my cappuccino and a thousand miles away in my thoughts, the sun that was shining on my face abruptly disappeared. I looked up and saw him. The intriguing and handsome man who had paid my bill at Alba the other day. Quickly composing myself I said,

"Hello! You are blocking my sunlight."

"Am I? My apologies, but you have been occupying my thoughts and therefore blocking my sunlight since the day I saw you at Alba with the princess. Seeing you here today is most definitely fate. May I join you?"

He did not wait for me to answer, but simply pulled up a chair and took a seat next to me. I liked and admired his confidence, although it could easily come off as a bit too much. He gave me his hand and introduced himself: "I am Daniel Kahassay." When I told him my name, he repeated it in an Italian accent and kissed his fingertips, as if he was complimenting the chef. He told me he was a banker in the city. I could tell he was successful by the way he dressed, his impeccable grooming, and expensive cologne. He was wearing a three-piece suit, like the ones I had seen on fashionable men in London.

He gushed about my beauty, telling me that my parents had made a good decision when they decided to call me Bella since I was incredibly beautiful. I could not help but laugh, and to his dismay, could not stop. With every gesture he made, I continued to laugh, and his expression changed from happiness to confusion and hurt. His need to make me feel special was hilarious to me, and I told him that in the kindest way possible after regaining some composure.

"Do these lines work for you?" I asked.

"What lines? I am being sincere and your laughter is quite rude. Honestly, I am offended."

"Why, because I do not fall for your words the way other ladies do? I am not like other women, Ato Daniel."

"I see. What are you like? And, please call me Daniel. Just Daniel."

We were interrupted by a waitress who clearly knew Daniel and asked him if he wanted his usual drink. He nodded yes and I could feel her look back to stare at me as she walked away.

"You are quite the ladies' man. That poor waitress is killing me in her thoughts right now."

"Do not change the subject. What are you like?" He asked again.

I gave him a confused look and he said, "Well, you said you were not like other women, so what are you like?"

"Excuse me, but I was taught not to share private information with people whom I do not know."

He smiled and said, "Okay, I can wait. In the meantime, I will tell you everything about myself so that you can get to know me." He told me that he was born and raised in Asmara and that his family was from the south of Eritrea, from a province called Serae. He did not know much about his village apart from the fact that his family owned land and that his father still had family there. He was a city kid, and I could clearly see that in him. He had never traveled out of Eritrea but knew that living in Asmara was like being in Italy. I told him he was right.

"Ah, so you are a traveler?" He asked.

"Maybe, or I could just be into books and have read a great deal on Italy."

"Where is your accent from?"

"What accent?"

"Well, I know you are not from Asmara. I would have seen you before, and you were with the princess which tells me that you are either royalty or working for the royal family. Either way I know you are not from here. Plus, everyone knows everyone here and I am from here and do not know you. Therefore, I ask again, where is your accent from? Are you from Addis? What brings you to Asmara?"

I smiled, apologized again, and told him I would not share personal information with people I did not know.

"Aye, Bella, Bella, you are not going to make this easy on me. However, I have a strong feeling that getting to know you will be well worth the work, therefore I will continue to seek you out. For now, though, I must get back to work. I hope you have a wonderful day." He got up, took my hand in his, kissed it, and walked away. Just like that he was gone. I watched him walk away and not once did he look back. The man was so full of himself it was amusing. I turned to see the waitress and smiled, asking her for the check. She said, "Signore Daniel paid the bill already."

"How? I just watched him walk away."

She laughed again and said, "You must not be from around here. Signore Daniel has an account here. Everything gets paid at the end of the month. All guests included."

"But I was not his guest. He came and sat with me, which technically makes him my guest. May I please have my bill?" She laughed again and said, "Yes, of course, Signora. Wait here, I'll bring it right out for you."

I paid for both our drinks, left the waitress a generous tip, and asked her to let Daniel know that the bill was paid for by Bella the next time she saw him. I wanted to be sure that he knew that I paid for my own cappuccino. I left feeling proud, independent, and a bit lost as well. I needed to find my way back to the palace and resume planning my meeting with the prince.

Before we knew it, Prince Addisu's arrival day came. The palace was prepared, the staff were well informed, and the entire family was ready for him. Even the children knew exactly what they were supposed to say.

When I saw the soldiers, guards, and house attendants all lined up at the entrance, I knew the prince had arrived. The gates opened and a black Mercedes pulled in. Everyone waiting bowed their head for the prince. Princess Maryam had asked me to stay in my room until I was called for. She wanted to greet her brother, talk to him about home for a while, and give him time to rest before discussing my matters.

I used the time alone in my room to write in my journal. Even though so much was happening downstairs, even though Emama was sick and I was hundreds of miles away from her, what I really wanted to write about was Daniel. I was intrigued. Kasahun also came to mind, and I thought perhaps God put Kasahun in my life to prepare me for other relationships. Through Kasahun, I saw that I could be with someone who was not raised in royalty or riches and still be happy. I pictured Ababa's face at that thought and laughed. I realized that my time with Kasahun was short and sweet, but I felt a connection there and I knew better than to think God was not behind that with His own plan.

There was a knock on the door. It was time! I nodded at the housekeeper who came to get me, said a quick Hail Mary, and walked with my head held high to fight for my future.

The second Prince Addisu saw me, his face froze. He looked at his sister in confusion, then turned to his brother-in-law and asked: "What did you do? Do you know the damage you have created? I will tell you, you have committed treason. Everyone is looking for Annabella. How could you put the family in this position? We are doing what is best for her."

"With all due respect, Your Highness," I spoke at last. "How can everyone know what is best for me without asking for my input in the matter?"

The princess spoke next. "Bella, calm down, Addisu means well. Addisu, listen to Bella before you jump to conclusions."

"Prince Addisu," I said. "I know you love me and want the best for me. I know everyone does. Do you remember, though, what my father was like, how he fought hard for the importance of education alongside the emperor — your father? Remember how he fought to get the Italians out of Ethiopia?"

He interrupted me with, "Yes, and what does that have to do with you?"

"Shush, Addisu, let the girl speak," responded Ras Dawit.

"It has everything to do with me. I am my father's daughter. His struggles run in my veins. I want education, I want freedom, and I want the chance to determine my own future, even though I am a woman. We all deserve that, do we not? Imagine if your daughters or your sisters were thrown into prison and told to stay there for the rest of their lives. That is exactly what marrying General Kebede would be like for me."

"Nonsense! You cannot tell the future. You might have these feelings now, but they will change. This is our tradition, Annabella. We all went through the same thing."

"Addisu, remember my story," said Maryam. "Remember my struggle. I was not much younger than Bella. You fought with me. You protected me. All this child is asking for is the same chance. She deserves to have a life that she determines for herself."

"Yes, and that is what I do not like about this. Let's say we all fight for Bella? Then what? What happens to our future, to our traditions? Will planned marriages just go away completely? What are we really sacrificing here?"

"Addisu, please. This is not about Ethiopia, this is about a child."

"She is not a child and it is always about Ethiopia! Everything we do as leaders has to be about our country as a whole. Have you forgotten your place, Maryam? Has being away from us made you forget your loyalties?"

"Addisu, she is a child and you are being a hypocrite. Her father is gone. All she wants is a chance at a life that he himself would have wanted for her. You knew Belantageta Lorenzo, he was a forward-thinking man and I thought you were too. What has gotten into you?" Princess Maryam hugged her brother and begged him to show me mercy. Only after seeing the princess embrace her brother did I dare kneel at his feet and beg him to be in my favor.

He was very serious and told me he would think about it, and for right now, he would not say anything about my whereabouts. He would stay for the week as promised. Princess Maryam looked at me and winked; our work was for the most part complete. Now I just had to show him that I could help Ethiopia on a greater level by living in Asmara as a single woman than I could as the general's wife. I had a feeling though, that something was bothering the prince and I knew it was not my situation alone.

As the days passed, I spent more and more time with the princess and her family. I helped the girls with homework at their insistence, even though they had a perfectly able tutor. I worked on education and empowerment projects for women with the princess. Every day she kept me informed on Emama's condition. She remained in a coma, but the doctors were hopeful.

Prince Addisu and I spent time getting to know Asmara together. He was fascinated by the city's infrastructure and organization. He wrote notes to take home on different projects they could undertake to modernize Addis. I shared my ideas on how to best move forward with modernizing the city without displacing or harming the residents.

"Your ideas are outstanding, Annabella. We need more people like you in parliament."

I smiled at him and responded with, "Your Highness, if I return home, sadly it will be to become a general's wife, not a parliamentarian. My talents will be wasted stuck in a house directing staff."

"You do not know that for sure. The general is known to be modern and might accept you working outside of the home."

I rolled my eyes. We both knew that this wasn't true.

"Do you know who you are, Prince Addisu?" I asked.

"What do you mean? What kind of question is that? Of course, I know who I am, I am the royal prince of Ethiopia. I am the son of kings."

I shook my head and quickly rephrased my question. "Yes, of course you are the royal prince. I meant, who are you without the titles, without the prestige? What do you like? What makes you happy? We have been conditioned to believe that happiness only comes with our grand titles and legacies. I often think of what Papa thought about while he was dying. Did he question his decisions and the life he had lived? Was he proud of himself and his choices? Did he regret anything?"

I looked up to see Addisu staring at me as I talked. His expression softened and he said, "You know, no one has ever asked me that before or even dared to talk of such matters in my presence. Years ago, as a student in London, I too had different dreams. I wanted to travel the world and meet new people. I wanted to open businesses in different countries, exporting coffee and importing goods. But I was told to grow up and come home, to focus on my duties as prince. I allowed those dreams to slowly diminish and disappear as my role as prince took over." He closed his eyes and for a moment I thought he might cry.

"Are you alright?" I asked finally.

"Yes, yes. I'm fine. Annabella, you have reminded me of my youth, of a time when my dreams were boundless. The more time I spend with you and see you for who you truly are, I believe more and more in what you are doing for yourself. Every person, regardless of their sex, has a right to their own freedom. Who are we to tell them what they can and cannot be? I will help you

in any way possible. Not just for your sake, but for the good of Ethiopia as a
whole. Women everywhere should have the freedom to choose to become who
they were meant to be. That decision should be based on their own beliefs,
not those of the men in their family. Our culture and traditions are centuries
old, so this philosophy will take some years to instill in our people. I want you
to spearhead the project. Work with Maryam and bring our women into a new
era. I fully believe this will create a better Ethiopia for our children and grandchildren. That is why I came on this trip; I see it now. I had been troubled for
weeks about something that I could not quite put my finger on. I kept thinking
it was politics as usual. Now I see that all along it was women's rights."

I was beyond shocked. I wanted to hug him, but that was against all proto-
col, so I gave him my biggest and brightest smile instead. "On behalf of women
all over Ethiopia, I want to thank you very much, Your Highness! Thank you!
Thank you! Thank you!"

"Do not thank me yet. There is still work to be done. We must deal with
my father and that will not be easy. He wants to keep General Kebede as a close
ally, and unfortunately, this was the most suitable way."

"I am the most suitable way? Does my life mean nothing?" I was in utter
disgust.

"It does sound rather horrible now that I say it out loud," Addisu responded. "We are a work in progress, Annabella. You will have to be patient. Things
will not happen overnight."

The prince kept his word. Upon arriving back in Addis, he worked diligently with Ras Dawit to try and end my marriage proposal without letting anyone know where I was. As the weeks passed, Princess Maryam was still my main
source of news for all matters concerning my case and my family.

One Friday morning on December 10th, 1957, we were in the palace sun-
room drinking tea. I had been in Asmara for roughly four months and had fall-
en in love with the city and my work with the princess. It finally felt as though
my life had meaning, and even though I utterly missed Saba, Yonatan, Emama,

and the rest of my family, I was happy in Asmara.

A phone call came from Ras Dawit, who had gone to Addis Ababa two weeks prior to meet with parliament and get updates on my situation from Prince Addisu. Maryam walked to her office to take the call and I followed. From the office door, I could see Princess Maryam's face beam with joy as she smiled at me, nodding her head. They had done it! Ras Dawit and the prince had somehow convinced the emperor to revoke my marriage arrangement. I began to jump up and down in my joy, until I noticed the princess' face change. "No, no, no!" she kept repeating. She looked me straight in the eyes and I knew it was Emama. There was no need for her to confirm it, my heart already knew it and I felt heavy, so very heavy. I screamed repeatedly, "*Abai Mearay, Abai Mearay (my sweet grandmother),*" as I rocked back and forth. Princess Maryam pulled me into her arms and held me tight.

When the children came home from school hours later, we tried to compose ourselves. I asked Maryam if she knew any details of Emama's death and when the funeral would be held. The princess had me take the girls outside so she could call her husband in Addis and get more information. We found out that Emama had awoken from her coma and simply said: "It is done." She died moments later. Her last words were "IT IS DONE." As sad as I was, I smiled at that. Leave it to my Emama to make a dramatic exit.

The funeral was planned for December 15th, and I knew I had to be in attendance regardless of the issues it would cause with my family. I would not be able to live with myself knowing that I did not see her off the proper way. I knew Ababa and the entire family would need to be there through their anger. Family was everything to us, and we would need each other immensely in the days to come.

When I brought up my decision to Maryam, she said, "It is up to you, Bella. I do not see why not since Father has rejected your marriage arrangement. However, we will be exposing your location and who knows what could happen. You should sleep on it, and we can talk in the morning."

"I do not need to sleep on it. I have a good feeling that everything will work out the way it is meant to be. I need to say goodbye to Emama. I owe her so much."

"Okay, then it is settled. I will call Dawit in the morning and have him notify the palace and your family of our arrival. If we are ever going to face the truth, now is the time."

Cinema Asmara *Asmara*

September 2019

"Wow, that is so sad about your grandmother, and you did not get to see her before she died," said Gabriella, my eldest grandchild. "Yes, but who is this guy that had you at hello, Grams?" said Bilen. My grandchildren were more interested in the story about meeting Daniel then they were about my freedom. "He sounds amazing. Is this our Grandpa Daniel or another Daniel?" asked Segan. They were all blushing and laughing.

"I will neither confirm nor deny anything just yet. I want you all to continue listening. Now stop interrupting me and let me finish my story."

CHAPTER 11

Facing the Past

Word soon spread that I would be going back to Addis Ababa with the princess for Emama's funeral. I thought I was ready to face my family and friends, but I was gravely mistaken. They were quite angry with me for disappearing on them months before and had no intentions of showing me otherwise.

It started with a call from Saba, who yelled and cried and accused Princess Maryam of lying. She would not speak to me at all. Then Ababa called to tell me not to return and that I was no longer welcome in his home. Yonatan called and simply asked, "Why?" Why had I not trusted him? Why had I felt the need to shut him out? Why? Why? Why? Then came the call from Yeshimebet, who wept, telling me it was my disappearance that killed Emama and how disappointed she was in me. I was struck by how all these people spoke only of themselves and how my disappearance had affected them. Not one of them asked how I was, or what they could have done to support me back then, or even now. I felt angry and hurt, yet I listened to every word and stayed quiet.

I went home even though Ababa had told me not to. Upon arriving at our gates, I saw a huge tent erected in our front yard and people dressed in black. My family was all together, crying and hugging each other, but not one of them looked my way. I felt abandoned even though I was home. It was Berhana who rushed to my side when she saw me, crying and singing, *"The favored one has arrived."* Only Berhana opened her arms and took me in. She walked me to my room, passing Emama's bedroom door. I could still smell her perfume in the house, even with so many people around. Being home made her disappearance surreal. In Asmara, I could deceive myself and say she was simply in a different city, but being here, there was no escaping the truth of her death. There would be no more family lunches with her home-cooked meals, or mornings filled with prayer, or even talks in the garden.

I stayed in my room during the first few days of my trip to Addis. Not wanting to see or talk to anyone kept me from stepping foot outside of the room I grew up in. I felt safe in my own space, away from judgement and persecution. I saw Saba and Yonatan from my window and looked away before our eyes could meet. I passed Yeshimebet in the hallway on a few occasions. Every time I looked up at her with a slight smile, but she looked down and passed me. Her silence killed me the most. I could see the gardens from my window but did not have the strength to go there without Emama. Berhana brought me food and stayed with me when she could, but I was alone for the most part. She gave me an envelope that Emama had prepared for me right after I left for Asmara. She had told Berhana to give it only in the event of something happening to her. Of course, Emama thought of everything.

My Dearest Bella,

If you are reading this letter, it means that I have passed on and that you have somehow managed to return to Addis Ababa. I pray it does not mean you are marrying that fool of a general. So help me God, I will be kicking rocks in my grave if that happens.

I want to take this time to teach you an important lesson that I have been practicing with you since you were a child but never openly discussed it:

God doesn't give you what you want. He gives you what you need! There is a reason for everything he does, and never ever are you to question those reasons. Your task as a child of Our Lord is to obey, and stay on the path he has set out for you. Now, this does not mean that you follow and adhere to what man says, because Lord knows I have never listened to and simply obeyed your grandfather, nor anyone else for that matter. No, this means you follow your instincts always; they will show you the way. God will talk to you through your feelings. You are a smart woman, a brave woman. I know this, Bella, because I raised you and taught you all you know. Now that I am no longer there with you, I cannot have all that time and energy that I spent on you gone to waste, so be strong. Cry for a bit if it helps, and do make sure that they bury me somewhere nice and that I look decent. I want to wear my white and silver Ethiopian dress with Lalibela crosses on the bottom that you know I love. Do not let that mother of yours pick something for me to wear; I want to go to heaven looking as elegant as I always did on earth. I trust and love you immensely, Bella, and I know you will accomplish great things if you haven't already. Go, travel the world, meet new people, fall in love over and over again, live the life you want! Not because of your father and mother or even because of me, but because that is what you are destined to do.

Love always,
Emama

I read the letter repeatedly. In the envelope there was a picture of the two of us from our first trip to Paris together years ago. I remember how excited I was to travel with her. As a child, I wanted to be just like her when I grew up. The way she talked, the way she walked, everything so full of grace; even when she danced it was perfect. I remembered that on that trip, she let me stay up late to watch her get dressed for a party and she wore a Dior pendant I picked out for her. Now, all these years later, the pendant was in the envelope, and there was something else as well. I turned the envelope upside down and out came Emama's gold rosary ring, the one that had never left her finger. If she had given the package to Berhana when I left that meant that throughout her sickness, she was not wearing her ring. Even in her death she was telling me something. I felt her presence and her legacy when placing the ring on my finger.

My thoughts were interrupted by a knock on the door. "Bella, open the door." It was Saba. I would recognize that voice anywhere. She hugged me tight and did not say a word. My response to that hug was to cry and cry and cry, only stopping when I saw Yonatan coming down the hallway. He too walked into my room and gave me a hug, holding me so close that I thought I would stop breathing.

The two of them had continued dating and seemed happy together. Any other day, that would have made me ecstatic, but on this day not even love could make me smile. I showed them the picture, the letter, and the ring on my finger.

"Bella, cry today, cry for as long as you need to, but then you have to let her go, just like she let you go when you left months ago. You have no idea how sad, scared, and miserable we all were during those months," said Saba. "When we found out that you were with Maryam this whole time, we were so angry and hurt. Now though, I understand why you did what you did and I am so proud of you. You chose your path and your grandmother helped you follow it. You must respect that. In honor of her, you must now live the life you have always wanted.

I started to cry again and she embraced me tightly. I realized again how much I missed her and how much our friendship meant to me. Saba was not just my best friend; she was the sister I had never had.

"Maryam got to you, huh?" I asked her with a smile, because I knew there was no way she would be this understanding without knowing my full story from the princess. "Yes!" she said, hugging me even tighter. "I want to know what happened. No one told me anything!" said Yonatan, and I could see he was genuinely hurt. "I will tell you later," responded Saba, saving me from the ordeal of explaining.

There was another knock on the door. This time it was Berhana with food and a request for me from Yeshimebet.

"You are being called, Bella. Go now, Yeshimebet and Ababa are in Emama's bedroom and they are waiting for you." I felt my nerves shaking and thought the very worst. Maybe they were going to exile me or even worse: force me to marry the general.

I slowly walked into my grandparents' room and kept my eyes lowered, focusing on the red and cream carpet. Ababa spoke first: "What you did is unacceptable, unthinkable, and disgraceful. As your grandfather and the man of this house, you have shamed me and you have shamed this family. What is worse is that I hear your grandmother had a huge part in this adventure of yours. I will not speak ill of the dead, but shame on her and shame on you. I do not know how you did it, but per the emperor's orders, you will no longer be marrying General Kebede. I hope you understand what this means for your future."

I was boiling with anger! He had called me into my dead grandmother's room to talk to me about how shameful my behavior was. We had not even buried Emama yet and he was giving me a lecture about family pride. I could not stay silent.

"Ababa, what about love? Don't you want me to love the man that I marry?"

"Love?" he smirked, shook his head, and said "Love as you young people call it, that comes later in life. What do you even know about love? Love is making sacrifices for the people you care about. Love is thinking of others before you think of yourself. You are so selfish; how can you possibly understand love?"

"I never said I understood it. I simply asked that I should be allowed to marry a man I love. Should I not be allowed to determine how and with whom I spend the rest of my life? And while we are on the subject, I would not have had to leave and Emama would not have had to do everything she did if you had not been so stubborn. Your way is not the only way. I am not you. I am not her. I am not Yeshimebet, nor anyone else for that matter. I am Annabella Lorenzo and I refuse to live out a life that someone else has planned for me. I came home to bury my grandmother whom I loved dearly. If that is all you wanted to discuss, then I would like to go back to my room and mourn in peace." I did it! I said it! I told him how I felt and it was freeing. This is what Emama meant in her letter; this is why she left me that envelope. I would be strong and fierce like her.

I turned to walk away when Yeshimebet said, "Bella, sit down. Baba, tell her why you called her in here. She needs to know."

"No, let her go. Selfish little girl. I have nothing to say to her."

I closed my eyes and shook my head. He still did not understand.

"Baba, please. This is not about you or Bella, it is about Emama. This is what she wanted, which is why she wrote it out so specifically."

"Your mother was sick and probably even dying when she wrote this letter, so how can you deem it serious?" He was upset and waving a letter in the air.

"Baba, stop, please! Do it, or I will."

"Calm down, *eshi eshi*. Bella, you stubborn child, it is no wonder you and your grandmother were so close. You are the same. At any rate, she wrote us both letters with clear instructions of what she wanted after she was gone.

"What did her letter say, Ababa?"

"She explained why you left and how she encouraged you to go. She demanded that I forgive, understand, and bless you. She wanted you to be free to live your life, one that you choose for yourself. She demands that I accept it, that we all accept it. Therefore, against my better wishes, Bella, I am going to give you my blessings and let you go.

I smiled and moved towards him to give him a hug, holding him tight in my arms. From over Ababa's shoulders, I could see Yeshimebet smiling. "Okay, okay, enough, I am too old to be hugged and as I said before, I am doing this for her, not you!" he grumbled.

"Ababa, you are never too old for hugs!"

He straightened up and looked at me. "We can discuss your plans and what you need after the funeral. Your mother will need help with the planning. I want to make sure all of your grandmother's crazy requests are met and that we send her off with the most beautiful and elegant funeral."

"Of course, Baba. We will take care of everything. Do not worry."

"There is more, Bella. While you were away a letter came for you from Montpelier University. It was attached to your grandmother's letter. She wanted me to give it to you and let you know that whatever you decide to do, we would support you. You fought hard and you won the battle for your right to marry, now go to Montpelier and get that law degree. Do not stay in Asmara doing nothing."

"Thank you, Ababa. I will think about it."

I set about planning the funeral and told Yeshimebet exactly what Emama had wanted. She was pleased and agreed with it all. Planning the service made me feel useful and distracted me from my grieving, which was a blessing. I wanted to make sure her funeral was as beautiful and elegant as she was.

My desire to have white doves released at the ceremony and an open casket so we could see Emama and say our goodbyes was not generally accepted in our culture, but I planned it nonetheless. Many in my family felt that I was too westernized, and I wondered where I would ever fit in. In London I was the privileged black girl from East Africa. In Addis I was the spoiled child of Lorenzo. I longed to start my new life in Asmara. There I would simply be me — Annabella!

The day of the funeral came; we were all composed and felt as ready as we could be. The ceremony was magnificent, and I felt Emama smiling down on me from heaven. As her casket was being lowered into the ground and people were weeping and crying her name, I looked up and saw the clouds shifting to reveal the sun. A dreary, cloudy morning became a sunny, warm one. With Saba to my left and Yonatan on my right, I smiled up at the sun and squeezed their arms. "That is Emama telling us we did good. She loved the warm weather. This is a sign from her." They both nodded and we hugged. There were thousands of people there to pay their respects. Next to Papa's, this was the largest funeral I had ever seen. She was buried not so far from him at the cemetery in Kidest Selassie Orthodox Church. Even though we were Catholic, she loved this church, and she came to visit and pray often.

Per our usual customs, our friends and family came home after the funeral to pay their respects. I was greeting people at the main gate with Yeshimebet, when I saw Kasahun enter with his head down and dressed in a black suit. It had been five months since we last saw each other, and unfortunately, neither of us had kept our word to stay in touch. He greeted Yeshimebet, offering his condolences. When she asked how he had known Emama, he said, "Only by word of mouth, but it was almost like she was my grandmother as well." He looked at me, nodded, and went to sit down. There was something different about him. He had gotten a haircut and was dressed differently as well. His suit seemed expensive, almost as though it was tailored for him. He did not seem like the same person he had been during our road trip to Asmara. I waited for five minutes, then excused myself and went to find him. In the early months, I had often thought about what I would say to him when given the opportunity. Recently though, he seemed more like a dream than reality. The more time passed, the less I thought of our time together with hopes of a future.

He was sitting in the corner eating kolo and looking like a lost puppy. I sat next to him and said hello. He offered his condolences while looking away from me, scanning the crowd. "Are you looking for someone?" I asked.

"No, why would you ask me that?"

"Well, I am talking to you, and you are looking somewhere else. It is actually rude and annoying."

He laughed and looked at me with his beautiful smile.

"*Yekerta.* I am nervous being here with you. I have thought about you every day since I left you in Asmara. I wrote you letters with my updates, and never found the courage to send them to you. Now seeing you here next to me seems unreal. Why did you return? How did you return? What about the marriage to the general?"

"If it was not for me, who did you come to see?"

"Bella, do not respond to my question with a question!"

I smiled. "Oh Kasahun, it is nice to see you! You look and seem different though. Is everything alright?"

"*Ende.* Again, with the question over my question. Please, you answer me first. Then I will tell you everything about me."

I rolled my eyes but decided to have a little fun at his expense. "Well, let me see. First I created a plot to have the general assassinated. I worked with spies from Yemen but the mission failed. Then I was kidnapped and brought back to Addis Ababa in the back of a truck." His eyes widened as I went on. "I was brutally mistreated mentally and physically, but never sexually. They refused to feed me and then they unleashed their worst by releasing their big German shepherds on me." He was gasping and making faces that showed he was sympathetic, amazed, and mortified. "Bella, oh my Bella — I am sorry! I am so very sorry. I should never have left you there alone," he said. "This is all my fault. Here I was, living a good life while you were suffering. What kind of human am I? What kind of man am I?"

"Let me finish please, and how is this about you? You did not ask me to kill the general, you did not tell me to go to Asmara. Stop trying to be the hero. I do not need that. So right when the dogs came to eat me, a miracle happened! Do you know the story of Daniel and the miracle in the lion's den?"

"Yes, what does that have to do with you?"

"Well, that is my miracle. God saved me from the dogs and sent an angel to close their mouths because I never did anything wrong to my kidnappers. So, like Daniel, I was saved." I could not help myself any longer, I started laughing so loud that people began to stare and shake their heads in disapproval. I covered my mouth to stop, and Kasahun got up and walked away towards the main exit. I stayed back for a while, wondering what he was doing, and watched him get closer and closer to the main gates. The more he got closer, the more I realized he was not going to turn around and come back, so I quickly got up to follow him.

It took me a while to catch up to him, and I was out of breath after just a short jog. "Kasahun, please wait. I am sorry. It was just too good of an opportunity for me to miss." He finally stopped and turned to walk towards me. "Oh, thank God, I can stop running now," I said.

"What was too good of an opportunity? You finding a chance to laugh at my expense, or treating your life as a big joke?" he said angrily. "I was being serious with you, Bella. I told you I loved you and wanted you. And now after five months, all you can do is play games."

"Wait, am I missing something here?" I looked around to make sure the man was talking to me. Well, I knew he was talking to me, but I was taken aback by his tone and demeanor. "Who do you think you are, judging me? You came to my grandmother's funeral. You asked me what happened. If I want to have a little laugh and create a story, then I have every right to. You do not get to come and start acting like I owe you anything because I do not."

There was clearly something else that was bothering him. He was looking for ways to fight with me as he had done in Asmara. "This is not about me at all," I said. You are using my story as an excuse, a way out, which is funny because I never asked you to come to the funeral in the first place. What I said to you in Asmara is still valid, Kasahun. I have accepted our fate. I am okay with what happened between us, and I wish you nothing but the best. If our paths cross in the future as they did today, then so be it. If not though, I walked away a much better person after meeting you and experiencing what we had."

"I am not okay with that, though," Kasahun was close to tears. "I wanted you. I still want you. I made stupid mistakes thinking I would never see you again."

There it was. The real issue was coming out.

"What do you mean, *stupid mistakes*?" I asked.

"I slept with Lemlem when I got back. I missed you so much that I even called out your name during our intimate time together and that one night has ruined my life. She is pregnant now and claims it is my child."

I was shocked, and for unlikely reasons. "*Ende,* had we become a couple, you would have cheated on me because you missed me? What kind of backward thinking is that? Is that how you show your love to someone? By sleeping with someone else, and then calling out my name? How insulting! How degrading! Not for me, but for Lemlem. I feel sorry for her, but I wish you both well.

I pray she delivers safely and that you are happy together."

"No, Bella. You do not understand. I am miserable with her. I do not want this!"

"I knew something was wrong with you the second you walked into our compound today," I said. "It was written all over your face and you have changed. Shame on you, Kasahun. I hope you at least used the money I gave you to go to school and make something of your life. If not for you, then for your child."

"Yes! Yes! That was the news I wanted to tell you. I enrolled in flight school and have been attending classes. I also paid for both my sisters' education. Thank you, Bella. Thank you so much. I love you."

I was shocked once again at how easily he used those words, especially under these circumstances. "Please do not use those words so lightly, Kasahun. Clearly you do not understand their value. Have a good day, and do not come back to my home, please. If it is forgiveness you are looking for, you are forgiven."

"So why are you upset then?" he asked, holding my hand firmly and refusing to let go. I shook my head. "If you cannot see that, then you clearly are not worth my time. Loyalty is a trait no money can buy, my friend. Remember that." I yanked my hand away and ran home. When I got to our open gate, I pulled my scarf back on and walked in like nothing happened. Because nothing had happened. He was nothing.

CHAPTER 12

Taking Charge

I had promised Ababa that I would think about law school, but my heart was not pulling me in that direction anymore. I felt like there was more for me to do in Asmara. I stayed home for a few more days and then Ababa, Yeshimebet, and I flew to Asmara to get me situated in my new life. It was time for me to move out of the palace and they insisted on coming to help me establish a home of my own. Maryam found me a beautiful, small villa not too far from the palace and in the heart of the city. Ababa wanted to pay for everything, Yeshimebet wanted to be a part of all the decision-making, and Maryam wanted to have it all decorated for me to her perfect standards. I was grateful and overwhelmed at the same time. The home was exactly what I wanted and needed. It had a little front yard with a fountain and garden where I could sit and enjoy a cup of tea or coffee. It reminded me of Emama's gardens at home. The main house had three bedrooms and there were service quarters in the back. It was perfect for me, and the previous owners were delighted to sell. They were an older Italian couple who ran a cinema house next door, and they wanted to retire, which meant going back to Italy. Ababa offered them more than they asked, and within days, the house belonged to me and my grandfather was back on a plane to Addis Ababa.

Walking into my own home, I felt grown up. When I met my neighbors, they were shocked that I would be living alone with no husband or children, just a maid and a guard. "Mama, do you think Berhana and Marcos would want to come and live here with me?" I asked Yeshimebet. I wanted people I could trust living in the house and there was no one I trusted more than Berhana.

"No, *Yene Lij*, as much as I know that would make you happy. Berhana has children and a life in Addis Ababa. How would that work for her? We will find you someone."

During those early days of owning my new home, I thought of Daniel a great deal. I remembered how he called Asmara *La Piccola Roma*, and that everyone knew everyone. I experienced this first-hand when shopping for my furniture. Yeshimebet and I planned to go to Europe, to Rome, Paris, or even Istanbul to shop for items for my new house. But Maryam asked that we give local carpenters a chance. She wanted to introduce us to a company in town that could create beautiful pieces, and with only one look at their designs, I was sold on the idea.

The local company I hired was able to create all the designs I wanted for my house. Working together, we tore down walls to make the house feel more spacious and redid the kitchen cabinets, the bathrooms, and the bedroom closets. They took my vision and made it real. The best part was the fish tank in the kitchen. Throughout the building process the company owners, Signore Mebrahtu and his wife Tsega, kept telling me to dream it and they would make it happen. Signore Mebrahtu was a carpenter, as was his father and grandfather. They were all gifted and self-taught, which made me admire them even more. While he was talented beyond measure, his wife, Signore Tsega, was the brains behind the business — she took care of the budget, and in her free time created décor ideas for their clients. I loved spending time with them, and they treated me as though I was a part of their family. Often during the weeks of planning and building, they would invite me to dinner, introduce me to their friends and family, and on several occasions, insist I go on weekend trips to the beach with them. They reminded me of Papa and Yeshimebet, so loving and supportive with abundant kindness in both of their hearts.

Though I now owned my first home, was about to start living alone, and was finally free, I still felt that there was more I should be doing. The work I was doing with Princess Maryam in ensuring education was available to all was meaningful, but it felt as though there was more I could be doing. My dreams of running the Ministry of Foreign Affairs were a part of the past I left behind in Addis Ababa, but I still wanted to do my part in making change happen. After the dreadful ordeal of a forced marriage with a man I did not even know, I wanted to focus on preventing this from happening to other women. In Addis, Prince Addisu was working towards the same thing. When I spoke with the princess about my ideas, she was beyond happy to assist and we started working on several initiatives right away. Still, again, I felt like there was more I could be doing.

Yeshimebet decided to go back to Addis for a while and be with our family, and one question that she asked me helped me realize why I still felt so uncomfortable. "Bella, how much money should I leave for the renovations and furniture?"

"What do you mean?" I said.

"Well, how much money will you need? Should I leave cash here or place it in an account for you?" That was it. I was a grown-up renovating my own home, but I still took money from my family. That was the void. I believed I was free, but how could I be when I was still relying on my family for help? "Mama, I think it is time for me to start working and paying for the house myself. You and Ababa have done more than enough for me. Let me finish it. If I feel like I need help, I promise I will ask. Until that time, trust me please, Mama. I can do this. I must do this."

She pulled me towards her, gave me a hug, took a deep breath, and said "Well, I guess all children must grow up at some point and I do trust you. I am very proud of you, Bella, and I know Lorenzo would be too. If this is what you want, then so be it."

Just like that, Yeshimebet left, and within days and Maryam's help, I had a job interview at *Banco di Roma* for a bank teller position. I took the same advice Emama gave me about meeting with the emperor to my interview. I was on stage and gave the best performance so much so that the hiring professional Signore Antonio offered me a position as the company spokesperson. He said it was because he was impressed with my language skills, educational background, and grace, but I had a feeling it had more to do with my last name. "*Grazie mille signore*, but what does that job do?" I asked. I needed to know exactly what I would be doing before I became too excited. He laughed at my question and told me the job was very prestigious; that I would run a small team of three and would be responsible for all the press relations with regard to the bank. He then mentioned that, along with the financial spokesperson, I would present at the annual banking conference in Rome. "You will be working a great deal with your counterpart on the finance side," my prospective new boss told me. "Let me introduce you two now," he said, dialing a number on his phone. "Daniel, Daniel, *vieni qui, per favore*. I want to introduce you to your new counterpart." Moments later, in came none other than the same Daniel from the café. I was glad I was still sitting down as my boss said: "Daniel Kahassay, meet Annabella Lorenzo. Annabella, meet Daniel Kahassay. You two will do great things together. I love this," Signore Antonio said, getting up from his seat and clapping his hands. "For the first time ever, we have not one but two leading Eritreans in our bank. This makes me so happy." he said. I looked at Daniel as he closed his eyes and shook his head in a gentle way that told me not to say anything just yet.

As soon as Signore Antonio left the room, I brought up the awkward comment Signore Antonio had made: "Let me ask you a question. This is our country, and yet a white man is excited that he has hired two black people. That does not feel wrong to you?"

"Bella, calm down. You are either very naïve or very entitled," Daniel said, offending me even more.

"Excuse me, I am neither of those things. I am straightforward and demand respect," I said.

"Which you have earned, obviously. He hired you, did he not? All he said was that there will be two Eritreans leading the bank. That is a good thing! Do you know how far we had to come for this to even happen? Do you know what this means for our people? This is a sign of hope. Eritrean children will see this example and be able to say, 'I want to be educated and work in the bank like them.' Listen, you clearly are not from Asmara, and wherever you have lived, maybe you never saw white people or even foreigners in general running the show, but around here it has been happening for a very, very long time. First the Turks, then the Italians, the British, the Americans, and now the Ethiopians. Let the fat white man talk all he wants. At the end of the day, I am the one, the black man who signs the documents whenever funds leave this bank. I am the one who processes all the payments, and I got here because I deserved it. I worked hard for this and I earned it." He looked at me and smiled. "You, on the other hand, I do not know about. Did you go to school? Are you experienced? Do you deserve this job? I would hate to learn that he hired you simply because you are beautiful, because then my entire speech would go to waste."

I laughed and said, "Yes, you can relax. You are right. I graduated from King's College in London last year with a degree in Political Science. Signore Antonio said it was that, and the fact that I spoke multiple languages that inspired him to give me the job." Out of fear of being judged and ridiculed, I did not want to overshare information with him about my family.

"Political Science. Hmm — I would have never guessed. So why come here?" At this point we were on the main street in front of the bank.

"I thought I told you once before that I do not give information to people I do not know." I smiled and walked away, secretly hoping he would follow me. To my surprise, all he did was yell out, "Until we meet again, Bella!"

I had a job, and not just any job, but one with an important title in a prestigious bank. Things were looking good for me, and I made a note to call and tell Saba and Yonatan the news. I also wanted to invite them to the house once the renovations were complete. I decided to stroll through the neighborhood around the bank and found myself admiring each storefront and café. There were many different types of people out walking with me. There were mothers holding their children's hands, men in suits walking to lunch, kids laughing with friends, beautiful women in elegant clothes walking to different stores or to the beauty parlors. Life was simply happening to each of us in our own way. I noticed that no one stopped to look up at the palm trees or the sky, no one paused to admire the breeze that we were all feeling. They did all stop to greet each other, or to make the sign of the cross when they walked past the cathedral.

Without realizing it, I walked all the way to my new home, which took me all of ten minutes, even with a stop at my new favorite bakery that had the best bonbolinos in town. I picked one for me and some for Signore Mebrahtu and his work crew. It was the least I could do for them.

I walked in through the renovated main gates and admired my fountain and the brightly colored mosaic wall. Apart from the currently loud construction work, it was a very peaceful place. I found Signore Mebrahtu in the kitchen installing my cabinets and yelling at one of his workers in Tigrinya mixed with Italian: "*Atay stupido donkoro wedi*! What are you thinking? This is the top, not the bottom. *Oh, dio mio!*" He was surprised to see me and quickly calmed down enough to say hello. I offered him a bonbolino and told him in a joking way that it would calm him down. "I want it all to be perfect for you, Bella, just perfect. My wife will kill me if it is anything but." I smiled, thanked him for everything, and told him the house was looking outstanding already and that I could not wait to move in. "It should be ready in three weeks at the most. Well, that is if my men can understand the difference between the top and the bottom drawers." His eyes shot directly to the employee who had made a mistake, and I could tell that the man was deeply embarrassed. "*Spiacente signora*, I am very sorry." I made a face that said everything was fine and then smiled at the poor boy.

"Signora Tsega and I have created some of the best designs I have ever seen for the furniture. Has she shown you the drawings?" I asked.

"Ah, yes she did. She is currently at our workshop showing it to the crew so they can begin the work."

"Her style and attention to detail are impeccable," I told him.

"It truly is. I would love to say that she gets it from me, but I would be lying," he said laughing. "We will miss working with you when the project is complete. You must always continue to design your home." I gave him a hug, promised him I would, and said my goodbyes. I had to get back to the palace to tell Princess Maryam about my interview that morning and spend time with the girls when they came home from school.

The princess was waiting for me in her office and had a worried look on her face when I arrived. "Oh, there you are! What happened with the interview? What took you so long? I have been thinking about it all morning. Come, come, look at these drawings for our school project and these that just came in as well for the women's initiative. These are your designs. They look great!"

There were so many questions that I did not know where to start. "What do you want to hear first?" I asked her.

"Well, the interview went quite well. You are looking at the new official spokesperson for all non-financial matters at *Banco di Roma*." She screamed out of happiness for me. "I cannot believe it! Our Bella is all grown up, owning her own home and working a real job that she earned without her title."

"Well, I got the interview because of you and I have a feeling that my title had something to do with my offer."

"I did not tell them who you were. I simply told a friend of a friend that I had someone in mind for a job at the bank. I thought they would give you the bank teller job, not an official spokesperson position. That is amazing and I am so happy for you. Stop overthinking the small details, because you earned that job."

"I am very excited. Also, guess who I will be working with? That man, Daniel Kahassey from Alba Ristorante. Do you remember, he paid our bill months ago?" I could tell she did not have the faintest clue who I was talking about.

"Never mind, just know that I will be working with a very handsome man." She burst out laughing and I joined in. "I went by the house today, which is actually what took me so long. The improvements are outstanding. I cannot wait to see it finished. I am thinking of inviting Saba and Yonatan for a weekend once I am settled in."

"That would be great. If you can get Saba to come here, I will be happy. I have invited her many times but without much success."

"Well, that is because you are not her best friend." I smiled and continued, "I love these new designs, Maryam. We are going to bring so much change and good to people's lives. I can feel it."

"So, when is your first day at the bank and what do you want to do to celebrate?"

"Monday morning. I was thinking of celebrating by going shopping downtown and getting some work dresses and suits made. Do you want to join me?"

"Of course! Who says no to shopping? But you know I have people who can do that for you, right?"

"Yes, but where is the fun in that?" I said.

That afternoon we spent hours at all the best tailor shops and boutiques. The stores were clustered together in one area downtown, just as they were in Rome. You could find anything from perfumes, shoes, handbags, and dresses to undergarments. Many of the tailors offered services where they could create sketches for you and design a dress exactly to your liking, whether it be traditional Eritrean dresses or something more western. By the end of the day, I had purchased a handful of beautiful new dresses and suits, two pairs of shoes, and ordered three additional outfits I could wear to work.

CHAPTER 13

Banco di Roma

The weekend quickly went by. I woke up bright and early on Monday, showered, had eggs and firfir with hot tea, and then headed out of the palace at 6:30 a.m. before the kids got up for school. I wore my favorite purple blouse that by now qualified as my lucky blouse, with a black pencil skirt that flattered my figure. My low heels showed that while I meant business, I also believed in comfort. My hair was pulled back in a bun, and to finish the look, I added Emama's Dior pendant and rosary ring, and a pair of simple gold earrings.

I took one last look in the mirror from bottom to top, and with each inch I took a deep breath and told myself that I would do great. By the time I reached my forehead, I was convinced that I was going to be the best spokesperson that bank had ever seen. I grabbed my favorite Coco Chanel perfume, spritzed my neck twice, and walked out the front door.

Maryam insisted on the family driver taking me to work on the first day at least, and against my better judgment, I agreed. The second I entered the car, all my confidence dissolved into fear. I was scared. I had never worked a day in my life, not a real job at least. What did I know about banking apart from how to spend the money in my bank account? The conversation I had with Daniel kept replaying in my mind. Yes, I went to school and had a degree, but my degree had nothing to do with banking or finance in general. What could I possibly bring to the table at this bank? The dreaded thought of being hired because of my title and looks kept resurfacing. Daniel was right — I was both naïve and entitled and had no business taking such a prestigious job and thinking I had earned it. As we approached *Banco di Roma* and the car started to slow down, I hid my face and asked the driver to pass the bank and drop me off three blocks away. The last thing I needed was for people to see me getting dropped off by an imperial car and driver. At that moment, hiding in the back seat, I realized two important life lessons. The first was that saying I want to live the life I chose and actually living that life were two very different things. Second, I honestly wasn't sure what I wanted in life, and this was terrifying.

In those moments huddled in the car, I saw myself for who and what I really was. I wanted to be strong, yet I was scared. I wanted to be independent, yet I relied heavily on my wealthy and powerful family. I wanted love, yet I had no idea what love really meant for me. I said I wanted to bring about change, but my actions showed otherwise. Honestly, I did not know what it was that I wanted for my life. At this point, the driver, Ahmed, was staring at me as politely as he could, trying to figure out what was going on with me. "Signora, are you okay? Should I take you back to the palace, or maybe to a doctor?" he asked. "No. No, Ahmed. I am fine, thank you. You know what, though? Can you go back to the front of the bank, please? I changed my mind. Drop me off by the bank." And that was that! I might not have known what I wanted but I was not going to let fear stop me. I was going to thrive! In anything I did, I would thrive. My past, who I was, where I came from, all of that was part of me and I was proud of it. So what if I went to school with royalty, so what that I grew up in palaces and traveled far and wide, so what that I lived with the crown royal princess and her family, and so what that I was being dropped off at work in one of their vehicles? So, what! If anyone had a problem with that, then the problem was theirs, not mine.

With that confidence I opened the car door, said goodbye to Ahmed, grabbed my purse, and walked right into the bank with my head held high. People were staring at me, and I was fine with that. I walked past the guards, said hello, and opened my purse for them to search. Then I walked past the bank tellers and through a set of doors that said "*Fermate Solo I Dipendenti*" and "Stop! Employees Only." I noted that the signs were written only in Italian and English, even though we were in Eritrea. That would be something I would change soon, I thought. I walked down a long bright skylight hallway. With each step I heard people speaking different languages, many of which I understood: English, French, Tigrinya, Amharic, Arabic, and Italian. Towards the end of the hallway, I heard some Russian and was reminded of Papa. I was sure he would have been so proud to see me in Asmara, creating, helping, and doing what I thought was right for myself. With all those feelings whirling around inside of me, I took a deep breath and walked right up to the manager's office, announcing my arrival: "*Buongiorno* Signore Antonio, how are you?"

"Ah, Bella. *Buongiorno, Buongiorno.* Welcome to your first day at *Banco di Roma.* I trust you had a wonderful weekend. My wife and I went to the beach and enjoyed the sun. You like my tan?" He got up from his desk and walked toward me. I smiled but told him the truth: "It looks more like a sunburn, are you okay?" He laughed, "You sound like my wife. I told her the same thing I will tell you, it is a tan and I am sticking to that story. *Va Bene?* Follow me and I will show you to your office."

We walked back down the same hallway before he stopped and waved his hand, "After you, Signora." My office was gorgeous and bright, with one wall of exposed stone and the others painted a beautiful cream color. There were three large curved windows on the wall opposite the exposed stones, and one panoramic window across from the door that let in tons of light. In the middle of the room stood a large, dark wooden desk with three drawers on each side flanking an elegant cream-colored chair. There were two lavender-colored chairs and a sofa for guests. I looked down and noticed that the floor was all marble, with flecks of cream and grey that complemented the furnishings beautifully. "Do you approve?" Signore Antonio asked. "You can put some of your favorite paintings or your degree up here if you like."

"Thank you. This is perfect."

"I am glad you approve. Daniel's office is right across from yours. He should be in shortly, and he can introduce you to your team. They are all excited to meet you. I will also have him introduce you to our board of directors. I will be back to check on you before the day is done." He smiled and walked out, leaving me alone in my office. I noticed that I could see the palace from my window. Past the downtown area, I could even glimpse parts of my new neighborhood.

"Am I interrupting something?" I heard Daniel's voice before his knock on my door. "So beautiful!" I said, still looking out the window.

"I have never been called beautiful. People typically say I am handsome, but there is a first time for everything." I turned and rolled my eyes at him. "You are quite full of yourself!"

He walked into my office and joined me at the window. "Simply breathtaking. What moves me even more is the people. Here in Asmara, the people have a unique and proud bond. That is what makes this city so special to me."

"What bond is that?" I asked.

"It is hard to explain, but if I had to try I would say it is the feeling of pride for our country and its people. The gratitude that we get to wake up to another day alive in this beautiful place. And these days there is much hope for change. It was not long ago that my father had to flee Eritrea for Somalia because of the Italians. So many of us continue to have to leave because of work conditions and racial conflicts. Those of us who stay behind must work extra hard to create change. But that is a longer story for another time. Come, let me introduce you to your staff."

He walked me down the hall to a large room that had a sign on the door *Ufficio di Comunicazione* and I could see seven people sitting at their desks.

"*Dahando Hadirkum Good morning.*" Daniel smiled and waited for everyone to look up and return the greeting. He went around the room and asked each of them about their weekends, how their families were, and listened attentively as they responded. I could tell they were very close and treated each other more like family than co-workers. Everyone smiled cordially and continued to talk to him as I awkwardly stood by his side. When Daniel finally introduced me, he spoke of the first day we officially met at the café opposite Cinema Asmara. He spoke of how consummately professional I was and then ended by telling them that the first person who could get any kind of personal information out of me would get 100 birr from him. Then he moved to the side and said "Everyone, meet Signora Annabella Lorenzo, or Bella. She will let you know which she prefers. Bella, meet everyone."

Introducing myself to a room full of people was not easy. I did not know where to even begin, and I did not want to tell them everything about me. Fear started creeping into my mind again. I looked at everyone and could not summon a single word to my mouth. At that moment, Daniel saved me by getting extra close, holding my waist, and whispering in my ear, "Show them the *Capo* I met at the café." I looked at him and he smiled at me. There was something powerful and moving about him, yet calming at the same time. His supporting words helped immensely. I gathered up the confidence to introduce myself and went full force with the intention to make a great first impression.

"Dahando Hadirkum. I am incredibly grateful and happy to be here with you all today. As Daniel said, my name is Annabella Lorenzo, but everyone calls me Bella. I guess Daniel will owe everyone 100 birr today, because I am about to share my personal story with all of you. I was born and raised in Addis Ababa, but I have lived in different parts of the world for various reasons. My favorite cities are Paris, London, Cairo, and Rome, and I recently just graduated from King's College in London with a degree in Political Science. Although I studied politics in school, I have always been interested in the banking system, and I am even more excited to create new initiatives that can help our community and ourselves as well.

Let's see, what else is there? I love reading and writing in my journal, and learning about new cultures. I speak six languages and am always striving to learn more. I moved to Asmara to learn more about my father's home and I am pleased with that decision. I cannot wait to start working with everyone and learning from you as well."

I had already made the decision to keep my name but share very little about my family. The more information I gave about myself and my educational background, the more I hoped they would simply accept me for that and not ask questions. I was determined to accomplish the job on my own merits.

The second I finished my introduction speech, I heard Daniel's voice from the back of the room: "Are you married? Do you have children?" Of course Daniel would ask me that. "I'm sorry sir, but as I have told you before, I do not give personal information to people I do not know." I smiled, looking back at the group of people I was about to start working with. I asked them if they had any serious questions for me, and when no one said anything, I responded with, "Okay. I would love to spend time with each of you this week and get to know what you do and how it all relates to communications for the bank. We can start today." Daniel came back to the front of the room and interrupted me. "Around here we like to do things differently than you uptight people from the south. Around here we discuss business over food and drinks. Everyone, Bella will take us out for lunch today and we can all tell her about our duties. I tried buying her a coffee once and she refused, so today the meal will be on her, per her wishes to pay for everything herself." I could not help but laugh. "Sounds like a plan. Everyone, lunch at Alba, my treat."

Daniel and I walked out of the office together, and he took me upstairs to meet the board of directors. There were five in total, and each of their offices had floor-to-ceiling windows and beautiful views of the city. Everyone was polite and welcoming, but it was the one female director, Signora Lucia Barattolo, who seemed the happiest to meet me. *"Grazie a Dio!* Finally another woman in a leading role! Welcome, Annabella. You have no idea how much I have prayed to have another woman to work with. All these men do is talk loud, smoke cigars, and discuss women as though they were meat. No offense, Daniel." She smiled at Daniel, who was embarrassed and shook his head. "We will have to chat more. I would love to know how you got here. Where did you study? I heard you graduated from King's College. I went to their sister school in Rome years and years ago. You must come for dinner at my house. Please, I insist! Does tomorrow work for you?"

This woman just had an entire conversation with herself, I thought, but instead said, "On a work night, I do not know."

"Why not? Dinner will be at 6:30. You will be home early. Come on. Daniel, you must bring this dear one, please."

"*Si, Si,* we will be there, Signora. Thank you for the invitation."

The second we got back to Daniel's office, I made sure to speak my mind. "What was that? First of all, I do not go places I do not wish to go. Secondly, why did she tell you to bring me? What are you, my driver? Am I the bank's new pet? Is this how things are around here? Am I supposed to jump every time the white people say jump, because I am telling you, that will not work for me."

With pursed lips, he heard my complaints, nodded his head, and made serious faces as I was getting upset. I felt he completely understood until the second he opened his mouth. "You do not like getting dressed up and eating dinner with nice people?" he asked.

At that point, I could tell he had been holding back laughter throughout my entire speech.

"What is so funny?"

"You. You are funny. All she did was offer you dinner, and you made it about white people this and white people that. Just go! She is your new boss. It will be fun and her cooking is outstanding. Do not burn bridges you have not even built yet." He laughed some more and then said, "Thank God, I am here to save you. You would not last two days here with your attitude. Now fix your frown, smile, and let us go to lunch with our staff. And another word of advice; you will have to win these people over. To them you are the new person who came out of nowhere and was handed a position that many of them have been working years to attain. Go easy on them."

His advice came from a good place. He wanted me to succeed. Watching him throughout the morning, I noticed how free and confident he was. His swagger and charm were not reserved only for women, they were for everyone at his workplace and I liked that very much. He had the ability to make people feel special. People felt free to laugh around him and be themselves while still showing him the utmost respect. He reminded me a great deal of Papa.

I was intrigued and secretly looking forward to spending the evening with him at Signora Lucia's house.

Banco di Roma *Asmara*

September 2019

"Wait a minute! Let me get this straight. You, Weizerit Annabella Lorenzo, worked for someone else? No way! Now I know you are adding tales to your story," said my granddaughter Awet.

"I wasn't always an entrepreneur, my dear," I responded patiently. "My start in the working world was at this bank. Remind me to take you all there next time we go home."

"Okay, but at least tell us, is this Daniel, our Grandpa Daniel? asked my other granddaughter Bilen.

"Listen and you will soon find out," I said.

CHAPTER 14

Lunch Meetings

The walk from our office to Alba was five minutes yet felt like an eternity. I took Daniel's advice to heart and because of it, I did not know how to act with my new team. I made conversation by asking questions and being attentive, and even when their responses were short, I continued to try and somehow bond over details in their life.

At the restaurant, Daniel was greeted at the door by the owner and taken to his favorite seat in the house. *"Ciao, Daniel, Come stai? Tutto bene?"*

"Ciao Mario, va tutto bene. Grazie. É Tu, tutto bene?" he responded in impeccable Italian.

"Si, Si. Va tutto bene. Come, I have your usual table ready for you. Ah, the whole team is with you today. What is the celebration? Silvia, come add chairs," he yelled.

"We are celebrating the arrival of our new spokesperson, Bella."

I said hello and smiled at Mario, who in turn took my hand, kissed it, and told me I was very beautiful. I could tell the entire staff was looking at me, which made me feel uncomfortable. I withdrew my hand and said a quiet "Thank you."

"Your restaurant is beautiful, Mario," I recovered enough to say. "How long have you been open?"

"You are new to Asmara, I can tell — everyone knows about Alba. The best Italian food in all of East Africa, maybe even all of Africa. We've been here for over 20 years, *cara mia.*"

By this point we all had menus, although I was the only one that needed to read it. "You must try the lasagna," said Daniel. Before I could say anything, Mario responded with, "No. She will love the Alba special bistecca."

I was not in the mood for meat in the middle of the day, so I said, "I think I will try the tagliatelle pasta with your best sauce."

"Wise decision, *cara mia.*" Mario took everyone's orders and came back moments later with antipasto dishes for everyone to share. We enjoyed bruschetta, focaccia, and different Italian cheeses with charcuterie and olives. Mario brought his best wine, a Barolo, my favorite. It reminded me of my vacations in Italy. "Only the best for my favorite customers," Mario said as he opened the bottle. He poured wine for all of us, as our plates started coming out of the kitchen. My pasta was divine and took me back to cooking with Emama.

Over a plate of pasta, Daniel suggested that everyone introduce themselves to me and tell me of their duties at the bank. One by one, our staff informed me of everything they did at the bank, how their roles were important, and how it all tied into what Daniel did and what I would be doing. Nigesti, the press writer for the bank, mentioned, "Up until now, Daniel has run everything by himself, with our help, of course. You have big shoes to fill, Annabella." She was beaming at him as she spoke to me. "It seems I do," I answered. "So why did the bank decide to separate financial matters and public relations?" I asked.

"Management thought it was best that the person who spoke on behalf of the bank not be the same person who signs the checks," Daniel said.

"That makes sense. So how is everyone's workload divided then?" I asked the team.

"Well, Nigesti, Saba, and Gebremeskel are on the press side, and Tekleab, Asmara, Teclino, and Alem are in finance. As you saw earlier, they all work in the press room at the bank. We hold our staff meetings together as well. Typically, those happen on Monday mornings, as you saw today. Our biggest reports are due at the end of every month, and then annually for the banking conference in Rome. Any other questions, I am always here to help," said Daniel. The team all started asking me questions and Daniel sat back in his chair to watch as I answered queries about where I was from, where I went to school, and what I was doing in Asmara. I left out who exactly my father was and the real reason why I was living here." I came to Asmara to learn more about my Eritrean father, my culture, and to live amongst my people."

Daniel jumped in and said, "You could not say all this when I met you, but here you are telling your life story! Now I have to pay all these people 200 birr each!" he exclaimed.

"Two hundred? I thought the deal was 100 birr!"

"He upped the price earlier," Asmara said laughing. She extended her hand to Daniel and said, "Pay up, sir."

"You did not leave me much choice Bella," said Daniel. "It was either this method or send out spies." They all laughed and I smiled, but only out of politeness. As I looked up at Daniel, I saw him staring at me, the way he had weeks ago when I first met him in this restaurant. Normal people did not just sit and stare at other people, and it usually made me very uncomfortable to be looked at like this. With Daniel though, there was something I trusted. His confidence level sometimes annoyed me, but nevertheless I felt he could be trusted. I could see that he had good intentions and a big heart. I liked that, and of course there was the handsome face and tall lean body. It was the smile that got to me the most. His deep dimples and the way his entire face lit up when he smiled delighted and even thrilled me a little bit.

Dating was the last thing on my mind. I wanted to work hard and succeed in my new job, make normal friends, attend parties, write in my journal, and maybe read some books. I knew I did not want to spend my time working on a romantic relationship. Now, nothing held me down to anyone, and I loved the freedom of it. On multiple recent occasions, I had been introduced to eligible bachelors, and if I did not feel intrigued by them, I would simply and politely walk away. Maryam kept telling me I was never going to find a husband with my attitude, and my response was always, "I am not looking for a husband at the moment." Daniel though, Daniel was different. There was something that intrigued me about him, but I was also very cautious. He was clearly a ladies' man, and now that he was my counterpart at work, I wanted to keep our relationship professional. The last thing I wanted was a scandal at the office. "Nothing good could come out of us dating," I told myself over and over again, even as our eyes locked at Alba.

When Mario brought the bill to our table, he handed it to Daniel. In response Daniel looked straight at me, gave me the bill, and smiled. He told Mario and the staff "This one is on Bella, Mario. You do not want to tangle with her and ask me to pay the bill." I said, "Yes, today is indeed my treat and it has been a pleasure. Thank you." I paid, left a generous tip, and we all got up to leave. It was only then that I realized how the team was watching our every move, especially the women. Asmara and Nigesti were eyeing me with a look of annoyance. It was the same look the waitress from a few weeks ago had given me. Aha! This was the look of jealousy! Daniel had the gift of listening well and showing interest in what people were talking about, whether it was a man or a woman, and I realized that many women mistook his attentions as being romantic. I took note. I would be Daniel's friend and co-worker and that was it.

The walk back to work was quick and entertaining. Teclino and Gebremeskel, two of the leading men on Daniel's staff, offered their guide services if I ever needed a tour around the city. They insisted that they knew all the best cafes, restaurants, night clubs, and shops. I asked Teclino and Gebremeskel what they were doing Friday night, and as soon as I mentioned it Daniel jumped in. "I heard Friday night — what are we doing? We can make it an office outing." I saw the two men's faces drop as Daniel's lit up. It was almost like they knew how the story would end even before it had begun. Poor guys. "Actually, I just remembered Friday night will not work for me after all. Teclino, Gebremeskel, let me know what your schedules are like next week.

Maybe the three of us can do something then." I winked at the guys and started to walk ahead a little faster, leaving Daniel behind with his mouth wide open. I wanted the entire staff to know that we were not going to date. This way, the ladies could be more at ease with me and the men would not give up on pursuing a friendship with me.

CHAPTER 15

True Identity

My first day at work went quickly and soon I was walking out the bank doors headed home. It was still daylight outside and the sun was shining brightly on the city. I closed my eyes and took some deep breaths, enjoying the crisp clean air. I was proud of myself! I had a job and I liked it! When I opened my eyes, I saw Daniel in his car looking at me. He jumped out the moment our eyes met and walked towards the passenger side of the car, opening it for someone. I looked behind me, thinking a co-worker or even a director was coming out to join him, but there was no one there. I looked back at Daniel, who was laughing.

"I am here waiting for you, Weizerit. I will take you home."

"How did you know my name was Weizerit?"

"What are you talking about?" he asked me with a confused look.

"How did you know to call me Weizerit?" I asked again.

"I was under the impression that Weizerit meant 'Miss' in Amharic. I was being polite and trying to speak your language. Did I offend you?"

"No, I am not offended at all. More confused," I said.

"Confused how?"

"Some of my family members call me Weizerit."

"Why do they call you that?"

"I do not know. It is a name that has just stuck with me, I guess, and I am not married as of yet, so it suits me in many ways. Weizerit meaning 'Miss'." I gave him a smile hoping he would not ask additional questions.

He smiled back and looked into his car and back at me with the intent to take me home. I had to end this conversation somehow.

"Oh, thank you for the kind offer, but I prefer to walk. I have a few errands to run before heading home anyway, and I do not want to take up too much of your time."

"You would not be taking up anything that I am not willing to give you. Please let me take you, it will get dark soon," he said.

This was a dilemma. I did not want this man knowing where I lived and I did not have any errands to run! I had to think fast. What if I took him to my new house? No, I did not want him knowing that house either, and I could not risk him knowing Signore Mebrahtu and then asking questions about me. There had to be something else I could say that would make him go away.

"I prefer to walk, actually, but again, thank you very much for the offer."

I saw his mouth drop in shock. Clearly, he was not used to rejection.

"Well, how about I park my car and walk you home? We can talk about your first day."

This man was certainly persistent! Was he serious? Walk me home!

"Daniel, clearly I do not need or want an escort home and it is too far in your designer shoes anyway. If you are simply trying to spend more time with me, then maybe you should simply ask?" I needed to stall until I could come up with a better way of saying no.

"Okay, then. I would like to spend more time with you. May I please take you home?"

I smiled at him, and with one hand on my chest said, "My apologies. I do not spend time with people I do not know well." And with that I walked away. I heard the car door slam shut and the engine turn on. Just to be on the safe side, I took the long way home and kept looking back to see if anyone was following me.

The next morning, I found Ahmed standing by the car waiting for me with his full uniform on and a smile. "Ahmed, thank you, but unless it is raining, I think I want to walk to and from work going forward."

"But why, Signora?"

"I like the fresh air and it gives me time to think. Plus, I am trying to stay healthy like you." I winked and smiled at him.

"Well, indeed it is a beautiful day to walk. Enjoy the sunlight."

"Thank you! *Arrivederci!*"

I took the long scenic route through downtown to get to the bank. I loved feeling the crisp morning breeze and the rays of sunlight on my face. The streets were filling up with people, all heading to their workplaces or running various daily errands. Early in my time in Asmara, I had created a game for myself where I looked at everyone who passed by and tried to imagine what they were thinking, where they were going, or what their story was. Sometimes I thought of things that were so funny that I would find myself laughing on the streets alone. Other times, I would see a sad face and imagine terrible events that would bring tears to my eyes. The more I played my game, the more compassion I felt for the people of Asmara, for people everywhere, the world is full of so many wonderful stories and difficult struggles at the same time.

I got to the bank and found Daniel sitting on my coach and waiting for me with a cigarette in his hand and a frown on his face. "We need to work on the talking points for our upcoming meeting with Parliament. What time works for you? If you prefer, your staff can handle it and you will do the final edits before it goes to the 4th floor for approval."

"Good morning to you too, Daniel!"

"So, what do you want to do?" he asked me, completely bypassing any kind of small talk.

"About what?"

"About the talking points. Please pay attention, Bella."

"Oh yes. Well, how about we start over lunch today? My treat of course."

"I have plans for lunch today," he said gruffly.

"Is everything okay? You seem rather off." I asked, "Have I offended you somehow?"

I knew the answer to that but asked it anyway. He knew that I knew and said,"No! I am fine. Why? Do you think you have done something that might have offended me?"

He looked straight into my eyes and waited for an honest answer.

"No, not that I can think of." I noticed his demeanor changing as I gave my response, and after a few seconds, he changed the subject and showed me a side of him I had not seen the day before. This Daniel was all business and no pleasure.

"Regarding talking points for the meeting? I think we should start by telling the bank's story, why they chose this location for their East African base, and why the structure is the way it is. That will resonate with Parliament more than us simply showing them our numbers," he said.

"Good point, but I think our numbers should still be a huge part of our presentation. People are always in need of a good bank. You want to leave them asking informed questions and thinking about moving their money from other banks to ours. Whoever gives the speech should also talk about how Eritreans have been working here since the first day the bank opened. Parliament will be pleased that the bank is providing jobs for the local people. Parliament will also want to see numbers, especially since that will determine the bank's tax amounts," I said.

"How do you know so much about what Parliament will want?" Daniel asked me with a look of disbelief.

"I know a lot of things." I smiled, but he did not smile back. Instead, he got up from his seat and called for Asmara to come in and take notes on what we were discussing. When she walked in, we went straight to business and came up with a great presentation that the bank directors would surely approve. It showcased the bank as having humble roots and wanting family and the youth to thrive. We highlighted our mentorship opportunities and how we worked to teach the youth not only how to save their money, but also be smart and creative about it. We talked about being the trusted bank for Eritreans and expatriates living in Eritrea. Daniel incorporated our current numbers and future statistics as well so that Parliament could see that, although our bank was owned by Italians, it was helping Eritreans in Asmara and even Keren and Massawa. Our first draft was ready to be reviewed just before lunch. I wanted to present it to our staff and get their feedback and input before submitting it to the board of directors. Being so new to the job, I also wanted the staff to know that I trusted them and valued their contribution. Daniel did not seem to think that was a good idea.

Asmara said, "How do you know they are not trying to hurt or sabotage you?" I was shocked. "Why would they? If I excel as their leader, it means I have a great team supporting me, and if they are excelling in their positions, that means I am doing a great job in leading them."

To end the discussion, Daniel got up from his seat and asked Asmara to lunch and they left. Just like that. I could hear them laughing as they walked away down the hallway.

After reviewing the last few minutes in my head, I left my office to find lunch somewhere close by and clear my head. I wanted to think about what I could have done differently to prevent building the wall between Daniel and I. Before leaving the bank, I walked past our common office area where only two of my staff members were sitting and having lunch. I had every intention to walk in and say hello, when I heard one of them say my name in a way that made me stop to listen rather than interrupting.

"Who does she think she is? Why must we continue to deal with these unfair circumstances? I have been working here for more than 10 years and never even received a raise let alone a promotion. When I went to Signore Antonio for a promotion, he simply said there was nothing available within the bank, then two weeks later, she came and is now my boss," said Nigesti.

I felt numb just listening to her speak. No wonder the staff were not welcoming. I was a threat, instead of an ally. I knew I could prove myself to them if they only gave me time. I left the bank not only thinking about Daniel but also about my colleagues.

I walked to a small downtown café, about two blocks away from the bank, that was located right in front of the cathedral. I took a seat by the window so that I could see people passing by, and when a waiter came with the menu, I ordered the first thing that I saw — a club sandwich with fries and a Coca Cola. Emama would have a fit if she saw me eating mortadella and cheese from just anywhere, she was always particular about that kind of thing back in Addis Ababa.

Lost in my own thoughts of the day's happening, I did not realize my food had arrived until my waiter came back to check why I had not taken a bite of my meal. The food was delicious, although it would have been even better with a touch of Emama's spicy awaze sauce. I ate and headed back to the office, still not clear on the morning's events or my strategy for the afternoon. Daniel and Asmara were still gone, so I took the opportunity to fine-tune what we had created and then went to talk to our staff. I gave them the idea, ran each concept by them, and asked for their feedback. They had great suggestions and added key points to the presentation. Halfway through the meeting, Daniel and Asmara walked in and joined us. They jumped into the conversation as if they had never had hesitations about it. We spent the rest of the afternoon putting the final touches on our first draft and then I took it upstairs to deliver it to the directors. I ran into Signora Lucia as soon as I got to the fourth floor.

"Do not forget dinner at my house tonight. Daniel said he will gladly bring you over." I had forgotten all about her dinner invitation.

"Of course, although I believe I overheard Daniel saying he had plans later. I will check with him and let you know."

"Do not worry about it. I will have my secretary call his office now and find out."

Daniel answered his office line and told Signora Lucia that he would indeed love to attend her dinner this evening but that I would most likely be finding my own means of transportation. She told me that he said that I had refused his offer of escorting me. She did not ask *why* and I did not offer any explanation. I asked for directions to her home and told her I would be there at 6:30 as discussed the day before. I asked if there was anything I could bring and she said, "No, no, just come. We will have a lovely evening."

I arrived home to find Maryam in the office helping the girls with their homework. The family had tutors, nannies, cooks, and housekeepers, but Maryam was an amazing mother and incredibly involved with all the details of her daughters' lives. She almost always did homework with them, had dinner with them, and usually gave them a bath before tucking them in for the night.

I knew exactly what I wanted to wear to dinner: a light blue silk dress that had a fitted bodice and a full and fluid skirt. It was purchased on a trip to Paris during my university days, and I loved how it made me feel and look. I added a pair of beige high heels and a matching clutch. To top it all off, I wore Emama's pendant and rosary ring. One final look in the mirror and a small private pep talk and I was out the bedroom in hopes of finding Maryam and the girls. They were all together in the kitchen, helping bake cookies for an event that Maryam was hosting at the palace.

"So how do I look?" I asked them. Everyone looked up and gasped.

"You look so beautiful, Bella," said Zewditu, clapping her hands. "Where are you going? Can I come too? Will there be a prince there? Will you marry him? Is it a ball? I want to come with you."

"Zewditu, darling, I am not going to a ball, but the next time I do, I promise I will take you with me and we will find my prince together, okay?" Makada joined in with her usual seriousness. "Only a princess can find and marry a prince, Bella. What you are saying is incorrect." We all rolled our eyes and started laughing. "I do not care what Makada says, Bella, you are a princess to me and you will marry a prince. Right?"

"Right." I said and gave them both a kiss before turning to Maryam. "What do you think, Princess? How do I look?"

"You look stunning, dear, absolutely stunning! Where are you going? Is it with that Daniel fellow?"

"I meant to tell you earlier, but you were busy. I am going to have dinner at one of the board director's home, Signora Lucia Barattolo. She is an impressive woman — very commanding and assertive. She reminds me of Emama."

"I know Signora Lucia, she is indeed a strong woman. I have heard she is an excellent hostess, so enjoy yourself. Have you called for Ahmed to take you? It is quite a long walk and those heels might be a problem."

"I told him on my way in earlier. Okay, I love you all. Goodbye. Wish me luck!"

I got in the car and thought about telling Ahmed to drop me off a block or so away from Signora Lucia's home. I felt like my emotions were on a carousel; one second I was proud of my past and heritage, and the next I was hiding it, embarrassed because it made me feel different from everyone else. I did not like this carousel ride. I felt dizzy going around and around, up and down.

Before I knew it, we were at Signora Lucia's front gate. I told Ahmed I would be ready to leave at 8:30 and stepped out of the car. I rang the bell and an elderly gentleman peered through the small window on the gate and asked who I was. When I told him my name, he opened the door and escorted me onto the property. There were three cars in the driveway, and one of them was the car I had seen Daniel in yesterday. He was already there.

The house was beautiful and grand, with lavish gardens and a long driveway. It reminded me of our family home in Addis. Signora Lucia and her husband, Signore Roberto, met me at the front door and greeted me warmly. "Thank you for having me as your guest. Your home is beautiful," I said. "I like to believe it is nice as well," said Signora Lucia. "We took our time and designed every corner of it. It feels a bit like Italy, yes? Signore Roberto is very well-known around here for this kind of architecture; he designed most of the homes in this area and in similar neighborhoods in Keren and Massawa. Some of them are quite grand. I must take you to see his other projects." She lit a cigarette as she was talking to me, asked me if I wanted one, and I declined. Then Daniel entered the room and asked Signora Lucia for a cigarette, followed by Signore Roberto, who took one out of his pack. He turned to me and said, "Are you sure you do not want one?" before he lit his. "Well, sometimes I smoke on special occasions," I said. "Why not?" Against my better judgement, I took the cigarette Roberto offered me. That was the first time I had ever tried a cigarette, and while I did not much like it at first, I did enjoy the way it made me feel connected to the conversation. The four of us strolled into the living room for drinks and appetizers and began talking about the ways that life had changed since the Italians had left the country. In Signora Lucia's opinion, Eritrea was much better off with the Italians than the Ethiopians. She gave examples of flourishing cities and abundant resources being available during the days of Italian rule. I listened attentively, looking at her, her husband, and then at Daniel, who appeared to be paying close attention. "I must disagree with you on this topic, Signora Lucia," I said. "I do not see how any nation feeling superior to another and forcing that nation to act as they act, speak as they speak, and change their cultures and traditions is beneficial. In fact, I feel that colonization is something we should all work hard towards ending. What right does anyone have to go to another country and dictate how those people must behave? No right at all. If we look back historically, colonization has never ended well, neither for the colonizers nor the people who were colonized."

My audience was now awkwardly silent. Daniel was the first one to say something. "Bella graduated from King's College in London this past summer with a degree in Political Science. She passionately wants to save the world." I gave a weak smile, to which Signora Lucia said, "So do you think Ethiopia is doing a better job at running Eritrea than the Italians did?" Obviously, she was still startled by what I had said, but the fact that she focused on that one point from my entire speech stunned me. I had taken her for a modern woman and an intellectual, but clearly I was wrong. I thought about how I had compared her to Emama earlier and realized she was nothing like her.

I looked straight in her eyes and said, "I do not think anyone can run Eritrea better than an Eritrean, just like I do not think anyone can run Italy better than an Italian, and the same goes for England, France, and Ethiopia."

"But how can you say that when your own father helped the emperor restore the crown in Ethiopia, and you yourself are part of the royal family?"

"That is my point exactly, Signora Lucia. My father helped return Ethiopia to the Ethiopians. My father died while working towards ending colonization by the Italians and other western powers in Africa. He believed Africa
should be run by Africans. It is called Pan-Africanism. Have you heard of it?" I
was getting upset. How did this woman even know who my father was? Her husband spoke next, "I agree with you, Bella. We should put power in the hands
of the people who will truly understand and care for their own. Instead, most
African countries are now dealing with power struggles, poverty, and greed. I
pray this does not happen to Eritrea."

"I pray for that as well," added Daniel.

Dinner was by now ready, and we all walked to the dining room where
I saw a stunning wooden dining table that was large enough to seat a dozen
people. The amount of food laid out on the table could feed three times that.
I wanted to mention that the spread reminded me so much of home, yet home
was the last thing I wanted to discuss after the conversation we had just had.
Instead, I kept myself and my mouth busy with all of the delicious food and
tried not to say too much. We talked about anything and everything but colonization, and then at exactly 8:30 I thanked them for a wonderful evening and
said good night. Signora Lucia thanked me for coming and asked me to come
again soon, while Signore Roberto got up from his seat to walk me to the main
gate. "I must apologize for my wife's behavior. She is not used to being told
things that she does not want to hear."

"Please, no need to apologize. It is her home. I was her guest. Perhaps I
should have held my tongue. But I would like to know how she knew who my
father was. I never mentioned that in my interview nor to anyone at the bank."

"My dear, have you not noticed how small Asmara is? One can easily
find out information on anyone. Not to mention your last name carries great
weight around here, some of it controversial. Your father is seen as a legend by
some and a traitor by others. Do not worry, though, in my family we have always
respected him. That includes Lucia Barattolo," he said with a smile. "She is a
good person, Bella. She even put in a kind word for you with the board. I think
you two might be friends one day."

"Well, thank you again for a wonderful evening Signore Roberto. I hope we will all become good friends."

"*Basta* with the 'Signore,' we are already friends so you must call me Roberto. Besides, Signore makes me feel old."

I laughed. "Okay. Thank you again, Roberto. Good night."

Ahmed was waiting outside the gate with the car door open. When I got home, I asked Maryam if she had told anyone about me, and she said no. But then we both remembered that she had told her friend who I was, the one who recommended me for the job at the bank. I realized that, at the end of the day, it was probably my title that had landed me that job. I felt sick just thinking about it, and the more I thought about it, the more my head hurt, then my stomach hurt, and finally I ran to the bathroom where I vomited every last bite of my dinner.

Downtown Asmara

CHAPTER 16

First Kiss

The next morning, I thought of calling in sick to work and then got mad at myself for even thinking that. I thought of quitting and then got mad at myself again. Finally, I got out of bed, put some clothes on, and left the house for work. That morning I did not care about what I was wearing, I did not give myself the pep talk in the mirror before leaving my room. To the contrary, I looked at myself with disgust, utter disgust. I was in a leading position which I had not earned. I had sneered at the entitled white people and yet I was practically one of them. I was not happy with the person I saw in the mirror, I left the house and interrogated myself all the way to the office. What had I earned? What had I done with my life? Was my degree from King's College even real? Did people just agree with me because of who I was? Was this job fake? Was I even capable of having a real job? I walked into the bank with all these thoughts swirling in my head and forgot to open my bag for the security guard. He did not stop me, and the second I realized it, I turned around, opened my bag, and asked him why he had not stopped me. "I know who you are," he stated with a smile. He knew who I was, and because of who I was, I did not need to get stopped at the door of a prestigious bank. I wanted to cry right there in the lobby. What he had just done was confirm everything that I had been wrestling with all morning. While he thought he was actually doing a good deed, it was, in fact, devastating. I needed air and walked right back out of the bank. I marched in circles in front of the building until Daniel stopped me.

"Is this another thing people in the south do?" he asked with a smile, but I wasn't in the mood.

"Not now, Daniel, I need to think."

"Walking in circles helps you think? Interesting. Personally, I prefer to write my thoughts on paper. Have you ever tried that?"

"Why are you walking with me? Why are you talking to me? I told you I was thinking. Please leave me alone. I prefer to think alone and in peace."

"Two heads are always better than one, that is what I say. What are you thinking about? Whatever it is, I am sure I can be of help. As you know, I am a very skilled problem solver. Tell me your problem and I will most definitely help you find a solution."

I rolled my eyes to show him that his comment was annoying. "I'm serious, Bella. Give me a chance. I just want to help, and I am tired of walking already. Why don't we go talk in your office, or even better, let's go have some coffee? I know a place not so far from here that has the best cappuccinos."

"I thought you said you were tired of walking."

"I am. That's why we will drive there."

I reluctantly agreed and we walked together to Daniel's car. The café was next to a beautiful small park that was full of lush greenery and had several fountains with benches arranged around them. We placed our orders and went to sit on one of the benches.

"Let me hear all about what has got you upset enough that you feel the need to walk around in circles outside of your place of employment. Some people might find that behavior disturbing," Daniel said.

"I do not care if people judge me. Walking helps relax me and I told you, I think better when I walk."

"Is that what you learned living in Addis Ababa?"

"Why do you ask me so much about life there?"

"I don't know. I'm just curious, I guess. Why? Does it upset you?"

"No. I was simply asking." I laughed, thinking of Kasahun. He would have hated that I had just answered a question with another question.

"What's funny? I want to laugh as well." Daniel looked confused.

"Nothing, I was just thinking of an old friend. Whenever he asked me a question, I always answered him with another question, and he hated it. He used to tell me that that was his trick and that I should not abuse it."

"But yet here you are doing it."

A waiter came with our two cappuccinos and Daniel was right, they were made perfectly.

I decided to have a little fun and steer the conversation away from what was really bothering me.

"Does it make you mad that I am talking about another man?"

"No. Not at all. I just do not find the topic amusing. Was this man your lover?"

His reference to Kasahun as my lover made me spit out my cappuccino in laughter.

"*Besemam*! I have never been asked a question like that so directly."

"Well, is he, or was he?"

"Am I on trial here? You keep asking me questions."

"Oh, you are doing the question over a question thing now. I get it. Well, was he?"

"*Uff*, you are very annoying," I said.

"If you answered, I would not have to be. It's quite simple. You either say yes or no. That's all."

"Will you define 'lover' first, please?"

"Again, with the question over a question. I can see why your friend or maybe lover would get irritated. A lover is someone you make love to. Someone you kiss, someone you hold dear to you."

My face felt hot, and I could tell it was turning bright red. I had never had a conversation like this before, not even with Saba. Daniel took my hand in his and looked straight at me, saying, "A lover is the person who takes your hand in his like this, and when he does that, your insides melt. You feel warm, and all you can do is smile. You feel like you can achieve anything, be anyone, and you want to keep that feeling forever. That's what defines a lover, my dear." He was still holding my hands and his gaze kept me speechless. I liked him. I liked him a lot. My insides might have been melting a little bit. But, I did not want these feelings. I did not want to like him at all. I slowly took my hand back and said, "I have never experienced anything like that before. Have you?"

"No." I was shocked. "Ata, do not joke with me. How can you know so much about love and lovers and not have experienced it?"

"Great question. I do not have an answer for you, though. I have never felt anything even close to what I just described to you, but all the Italian movies I see and the books I have read prove that what I have told you is a fact."

I laughed. "Daniel, now I know you are joking! You are basing your theory of love on movies and books? I cannot believe I just sat and listened to you."

"At least I got you to laugh for a moment. Now let's talk about what is really bothering you, and do not throw in any more diversionary questions. I think it has something to do with our conversation at dinner last night. I am not sure why this would be upsetting. If it makes you feel any better, I have known who you are since I met you, but I wanted you to tell me yourself when you were ready and trusted me enough. I wanted to respect your privacy."

I instantly thought of our staff. "Do they know?" He knew who I was referring to and said, "I believe so but I am not sure. Why does that matter to you?"

"How? I mean why? I mean..." I stammered.

"Well, for one there are not that many Eritrean families with the surname Lorenzo, and for another you are so well-educated and well-traveled and I saw you with the princess. It was not that hard to put the pieces together. May I be honest with you, though?

"Yes, please. I want you to be."

"Okay. Well, to me it seems like you are somehow ashamed or embarrassed of who you are. Like you are, as though struggling with your past and trying to change it. Is that why you came to Asmara? To run away from your past?"

"In a way yes, but not for the reasons you are probably thinking."

"What do you think I am thinking?" Even though it was a question, on a question I knew he was being sincere. The jokes were over and we were two people finally having a real conversation, a serious one.

"I think you are thinking that I am a spoiled, ungrateful brat and that this is all a game to me."

"That is not what I am thinking at all." He took my hands in his without taking his gaze away from mine.

"What I am thinking is that you must be scared, lost, sad, and feeling very much alone. Even in a room full of people. You feel this way because that room full of people are not your people; they are not your friends, your family, they are not the people who know you and love you. These are all new people, new places, new everything. Whatever happened to you in Addis Ababa must have been massive for you to decide to move hundreds of miles away. I am thinking of how brave you are, probably the bravest woman I have ever met. I am thinking you are courageous and beautiful and smart."

"Daniel, if that is a line from a movie, then so help me God, I will kill you," I laughed, keeping my hands in his and my eyes locked on him.

"*Giuro su Dio.* I swear to God, it is the honest truth and I have only said it to you."

I released my hands from his and began to tell him my story, the whole thing from start to finish. I began with the nuns at Saint Thomas and then being raised by Papa and Yeshimebet until Papa's death. I told him about my fierce and wonderful Emama and our beautiful days together in Addis Ababa. I explained Yeshimebet's role in the royal family and what it was like to receive a telegram from the emperor's office informing me of my wedding to an old general I had never met. I explained how my grandmother, along with Princess Maryam, created a plan to get me out of the city and to live safely in Asmara. I told him about Kasahun and how I thought I was in love but now knew I was not. I told him how I convinced Prince Addisu to buy me more time, and ultimately get the marriage proposal thrown out. I described how I was working with the prince to help prevent other girls from being forced into marriages they did not consent to. With tears in my eyes, I told him about how on the day of learning about my own freedom, I had also learned that my beloved grandmother had died, how I could no longer be with her, and that now I felt utterly alone in the world. My sense of home and love existed now only in memories. "Addis Ababa will never be the same for me," I said, while the tears came gushing out. Daniel held me throughout the story. He rested my head on his shoulder, put an arm around me, and listened quietly to everything I shared, all the way up until the part from that very morning when the security guard had not checked my bag.

I took a deep breath at the end of it, lifted my head off his shoulder, and looked at him. "Well, you asked for it all, and there you have it." What happened next is something I did not expect at all and will never forget. He put his hands on my cheeks, then leaned in and kissed me softly on the lips. We remained seated quietly on that bench until I said, "Daniel, is being such a good listener one of the ways you get women to kiss you?"

"Bella, stop that. It is only you."

"Only me what?" I wanted to hear him say the words.

"You are the only woman I am interested in. Yes, I go out and socialize with different ladies, what man does not? But conversations are sacred. Conversations are for friends, family, and people I genuinely care for. My time is something I cherish, and I want to give you my time. I want to give you my everything."

"You do not know me well enough to be that interested in me, I said.

"I feel like I have known you for a lifetime."

"Well, that is very flattering, although I feel like that story took a lifetime to tell! I appreciate you listening, and I am happy you know the truth, and I trust you with it. I think we should be friends for now. I need real friends right now more than I need romance! Plus, we work together and that alone would cause problems."

"I do not agree, but I will respect your wishes. Trusted friends it shall be."

September 2019

"That's it! It's confirmed. You kissed him in broad daylight! You will definitely marry him! That's it guys, this is Grandpa Daniel. Yuck, I cannot picture you two kissing. I cannot picture you kissing any man, Grams," said Natsenet.

"The next person who interrupts me will get kicked out. Do you understand?" I said.

"Yes, Grams," they all said.

CHAPTER 17

Love on the Streets of Asmara

I got up from the bench and offered Daniel my hand to shake in the most professional way. "Co-workers and trusted friends. Deal," I told him with the utmost seriousness. Part of me wished he had protested a bit more, somewhat wanting a romance with him. He shook my hand solemnly and said, "I am going to enjoy being your friend."

We returned to the car in silence, and the quietness stayed with us as we drove to what I thought was going to be the bank. Instead he parked his car in a neighborhood that I had been to a few times before.

"Whose house is this? Where are we?" I asked.

"I forgot an important document for work. It will only be a minute. Would you like to come in?"

"So, this is your home as in family home, as in your family lives here?" The man took me to his house after telling me we were just friends. I did not know whether to feel honored or disturbed.

"Yes, come in," he said, leaving the car. He opened my door for me and pulled out a key to open the front gate, walking ahead of me as though he was sheltering me from something. I looked up to see an older woman sitting on the front porch drinking coffee along with two younger ladies. Terrified of linking eyes together, I looked everywhere but their direction. The house from the outside was beautifully kept and had a remarkable garden full of vegetables and flowers.

"*Selam*, Mama," I heard Daniel say, greeting his mother with a kiss on each of her cheeks and a pat on the two younger ladies' heads. "This is Annabella Lorenzo, who works with me at the bank."

I looked up, greeted his mother with the utmost respect and turned to the younger ladies once Daniel introduced them as his sisters.

I could feel his mother looking at me as I waited for him to return. I was used to being in rooms with royalty and dignitaries. I had given speeches at school and was easily able to start a conversation in a room full of people, yet for some reason I could barely open my mouth to speak to his family. I could tell just by looking at her that she was a force to be reckoned with. Tall, with broad shoulders and very distinctive features, she was beyond beautiful.

"Annabella Lorenzo, an interesting name. Are you Italian?" she asked.

"No, I am from here, just born and raised in Addis Ababa, among other places too," I replied.

"What brought you to Asmara?" Her eyes showed concern, and I could tell she wanted to protect her son.

"No reason in particular." As I opened my mouth to elaborate more, Daniel came out of the house, saving me from further explanations. He hugged his mother, and told her that he would be home for dinner. Seeing their interaction made me miss my family back in Addis Ababa. There would be no more porch coffee drinks with my family now that Emama gone.

In the car ride back to work, as much as I wanted to talk to him, I could not find the right words to explain how I felt. So I left the matter of "us" alone and so did he. The next few days were awkward. I went straight to my office, met with staff, worked on different projects, and saw Daniel to discuss work matters only. Neither of us knew how to approach each other and discuss what had happened between us. I was the one who had told him that I wanted to be friends, and he agreed to it, but now it seemed like we were not even that. We both went about our days, stubbornly pretending as if nothing had happened. The only problem was that something HAD happened, and I, for one, could not get it out of my mind. I dreamt about the kiss every night. I envisioned his hands holding mine, his body close to mine. Day after day it was the same routine at work. We were civil and polite to each other, even laughing at work -related jokes brought up by staff or one of us. We kept our lives separate and cordial, especially when attending different bank events and lunches. Somehow, we made sure there was always a group instead of going alone, and I could tell that we were both in agony.

Days turned into weeks, and weeks turned into months before something would change for the both of us. It came in the form of a work meeting on the 4th floor to discuss the talking points we drafted together months earlier.

Daniel and I entered a large sunlit conference room where the only furniture was a massive, carved, mahogany table and chairs. Signora Lucia sat at the head of the table. I was proud to see a woman sitting there. I respected her, but a warm friendship had never grown between us. There was something that I just did not trust about her. Daniel and I were requested to sit down, and were shown to our respective chairs. Signora Lucia spoke first. "Great work, you two. You obviously make an excellent team. This is very well done." She was pointing to our draft talking points. "What would you think about presenting to Parliament yourselves? The board and I have discussed it at great length, and we feel confident that you two would deliver a much more convincing argument than we could. With your combined skills, you two will ensure that the bank receives the full government approval it will need to succeed this upcoming year."

I got excited and looked at Daniel, hoping he would be excited as well, but his face looked pale and numb. He said nothing, so after a few seconds of pure and awkward silence I chimed in for both of us. "Thank you so much! We would be honored to present to Parliament." I looked at Daniel again, this time telling him to back me up with his eyes and maybe a nod. When he finally spoke up, he said, "Yes, yes. Thank you very much. As Bella said, we would be

honored to go to Addis Ababa and represent the bank in front of Parliament."
Signora Lucia clapped her hands together excitedly. "*Perfecto!* It is settled then.
I will have my secretary make all the arrangements for you. You will both leave
on the 15th and stay in Addis Ababa for one week. Bella, are there any particular hotels you prefer? Please be sure Meheret gets the information."

"I can stay at my family home, but of course I will give her all the information she will need for the both of us. Thank you again."

I got up to leave thinking that was the end of the meeting, but no one else
rose from their chairs. Daniel nudged me to sit back down and that is when
it hit me. The meeting was indeed over. However the head of the table, who
in this case was Signora Lucia, had not adjourned the meeting, and everyone
at the table was waiting on her to dismiss us. I shook my head in apology and
smiled lightly while laughing inside, wondering what the men in the room
must be feeling. It felt good to know that a woman held this kind of power.
I was proud of her, although I still did not like her very much. She looked at
everyone and finally announced: "Meeting adjourned." When she stood up,
everyone else in the room then got up and started trailing out behind her. I
watched in awe, and after she left, I caught Daniel staring at me and quickly
looked away.

We were going to go to Addis Ababa together. The 15th was only a week
away! My hometown! My city! I felt excited and nervous at the same time. I
loved that I would get to show him all the places I loved as a child and introduce him to my family and friends. At the same time though, things were not
the same between us since "the kiss" and I hoped it would not get even more
awkward while on our trip.

"Bella! Bella, slow down," I heard Daniel calling from down the hallway.

"Sorry. I was just thinking about that meeting. This is amazing."

"What were you thinking?"

"Well, that we get to go to Parliament! And the details of our trip and all
I need to do to prepare for it." I was not about to tell him that I was thinking
about introducing him to the most important people in my life.

"Honestly, I am kind of nervous about the whole thing. I have never left Eritrea and going to Addis Ababa was not the first place I envisioned traveling to. I am glad that I will be experiencing it with you, though." He smiled at me.

"I am happy too. But no funny business, sir. We are going as business partners. I will gladly show you around the city though. You will like it, trust me, and you have nothing to worry about. Think of it as a big Asmara, but less organized and not nearly as clean. The people, the food, the culture, and even the music have a lot of similarities. Come on, we can talk more about the city and our presentation over coffee. My treat."

"Sounds like a date."

"Just two friends having coffee together. Come on!" I hit his shoulder lightly, grabbed my bag from my office, and then we walked out together. We went to the same little café near the bank where I had been going almost every day since I started work.

While we were waiting for our coffee, he asked me if I had thought about him at all during the last few weeks. I blushed and thought about how to respond, especially given the fact that he had not divulged any information on his feelings for me.

"Not necessarily, why? Have you?" I stalled. He said, "Yes. I think of you when I wake up and then again when I go to sleep." I smiled, "Well what about during the day?"

"No, during the day, I am fine for the most part." We both laughed. Since he was being honest, I decided to follow suit. "Well, I think about you sometimes. It's your laugh that gets me, your smile that I think about the most."

"I knew it! I knew you thought about me just a little bit! Maybe you like me just a little bit?"

"Slow down! I like you as a friend. I did not say anything more than that."

"Okay, okay. I will continue to respect your wishes. I hope that one day they will change."

We drank our coffee and started talking about our upcoming trip. "This time next week, we will be on a plane heading to Addis Ababa."

"Do not remind me. I think I am more nervous about the trip than I am about talking in front of Parliament," said Daniel.

"It will be fine, you will see. You will love traveling so much that you will start going farther and farther away from home. There are so many places for you to explore. I was just as nervous as you are now when my grandmother took me on a trip for the first time, but after a few days of exploring Paris, I was already excited for my next trip. Trust me, you are a born traveler."

I had been all over the world, but this was the first time I would be traveling for business and I was excited.

The fact that the bank trusted me to go on a very important mission like this for them helped to heal the insecurities I had about my job. They valued my work, they valued Daniel's work, and now we were being given a chance to prove ourselves. Going in front of Parliament was a tremendous opportunity that would let me put my degree in political science to use.

The best part was that I now knew somewhat how Daniel felt about me. For weeks, I had been replaying our kiss in my head. Now I knew that he thought of me, too, and it made me happy. I wanted to share something with him, something that was not romantic but sentimental.

"What are you doing after work today?" I asked him.

He looked at me with concern. "Should I be worried? First a coffee date, then an honest conversation, and now an evening date? Have I died and gone to heaven? I think so! Pinch me please, I want to make sure I am alive." He was teasing and it made me smile. He could be very charming.

"Do not make me reconsider. No one said anything about a date. I am simply asking if you have plans after work."

"The answer is no. I do not have any plans, Signora Bella. How might I be of service to you?"

"I want to share something I am working on with you."

"Boring. I thought you were planning a fun evening, not a work project."

"Who said anything about work? Just come with me, please."

He rolled his eyes and said okay.

The rest of the day went by slowly. Daniel kept popping into my office to ask me questions about my mysterious project. He was concerned about his attire, if there would be food, if he would need his dancing shoes, how we would get there, if I was working with other people. He asked dozens of questions over the course of the afternoon, so that by the end of the day, I almost regretted asking him to join me in the first place. I told him we would walk, but did not tell him where to.

I was taking him to see my new house.

My home renovations were finally complete, and Signore Mebrahtu had just finished putting all the finishing touches in place before the furniture was delivered. I would have only a few days in my new home before I had to pack up and leave for a week. I still had much to do to get ready, but I could not wait to see my new sanctuary.

On the way to my house, I stayed quiet, lost in my own anticipation, plans, and schedules. Daniel chattered on about different subjects regarding our upcoming trip and mentioned his love of surprises.

"For a man who says he loves surprises, you ask a lot of questions."

"What can I say, I am a curious human. At the very least, tell me where we are headed."

"We are just about there, and you will see for yourself in three, two, one."

"See what? All I see are gates and houses. Are you working on someone's house?"

"Yes. I am. I am working on my own house and have been for months now. I just finished it and I wanted you to be my first guest."

He looked shocked and proud at the same time. "Bella. I am honored and quite impressed. Thank you for sharing this with me." He gave me a hug and I hugged him back. I liked it. I liked it a lot. He leaned in to kiss me. My heart wanted the kiss, but my mind rejected it. I drew back and looked away. He did not say anything, and I changed the subject to focus on the house. I pushed the unlocked gate open and led Daniel inside.

"Come on in, watch your step." His first view was of my garden, which, with the help of the palace gardeners, had already produced beautiful flowers. My fountain was in the middle with two benches and a side table. One entire wall of the garden had a colorful floral mosaic that resembled the one we had at home in Addis Ababa. He took a seat in my oasis and seemed mesmerized.

"Imagine sitting right here and drinking your morning tea or coffee with a good book," I said, pointing to the bench where he sat. "Picture having a cocktail party and entertaining your friends out here. There is so much I plan to do with this space. It reminds me of home and my grandmother. I do not know if I told you this before, but she had a magnificent garden in our home. She had a little bungalow there where we would spend our afternoons talking and drinking tea. My family would sometimes gather there on Sundays to drink coffee after lunch. It was her favorite place to be, and building this feels like I get to keep a small part of her close to me here at my house. My house — that sounds good! Daniel, I feel like such an adult. I have a home, a job, friends, you." I looked at him. He looked at me. He drew in closer. This time I allowed it, as mind and heart connected, giving me the courage to accept this kiss. I wanted it with every inch of my body and soul. He put his arms around me and our kiss became more passionate, each of us wanting the other more and more. "I think now, with me, here in my arms, you can feel like a happy adult," he said as he kissed my cheeks, and my neck. Suddenly I felt warm and short of breath, but I did not need air. I needed him, more of him. As I leaned in to kiss him again, Signore Mebrahtu walked out of the house with his team and Signora Tsega. I could feel my face turn hot and red. How embarrassing!

"Daniel? Daniel, is that you?" Signore Mebrahtu shouted across the garden. Great! Just my luck! Not only was I with a man here in front of them, but they also knew that man. "*Aboye* Mebrahtu, how are you doing?" said Daniel, relaxed and cheerful.

"I'm doing good. Not as good as you, I think. What a small world it is. I have been trying to introduce you to Bella for months now and you kept saying you were not interested in anyone. Now I see why."

"*Elelele.* God answered our prayers in his own time. We wanted you two to meet and here you are together on your own timing."

"Bella is our favorite and most valuable customer," said Signore Mebrahtu. "She is also quite creative. All the designs you saw at the shop? Well those are hers and Tsega's. They have been working on them for months now, for this house."

"Great Work! Your color selections and designs are outstanding. Both of you." Daniel looked at Signora Tsega and then at me.

"You have been to the shop?" I asked.

"Yes, of course. We are old neighbors. My family home is next door to their workshop and store, which is also their home, as you know."

"That's right. Daniel here used to come help us after school when he was little. I take pride in saying that he learned all about business and numbers while working with me," Signore Mebrahtu said. Signora Tsega hit him lightly on the chest and said, "Mebrahtu, do not lie. The child was always smart. You did nothing but make him work extra hard."

"Children have to work hard if they want to succeed in life. Daniel is a prime example that hard work pays off. We are a prime example. See that, boys? When you work hard, you become successful." He was talking to his three workers now, who were listening to his every word as though their lives depended on it.

"Bella, *zagualay*, the house is finally done. We were hoping to surprise you tomorrow, but it looks as though you, my darling, have surprised us all. Come, look inside," Signora Tsega said with pride.

I pulled on Daniel's hand and told him to come look with me. He smiled and followed me in. The house was even better than I had imagined. Everything had come out perfectly. Upon entry, there was a small but elegant foyer with two doors. The door on the left led to the living and dining rooms. On the right was the door that led to the rest of the house. We had converted a three-bedroom house into one with two spacious bedrooms with separate bathrooms and generous closet space. I wanted something similar to what I had back home. The kitchen had oak cabinets and white marble countertops. There was a path from there to the backyard which had a second beautiful herb garden and the service quarters. I was unsure of what I was going to do with that space, being that I was the only one in the house. I knew I would need help with certain responsibilities, but could not see myself hiring more than one person. The space could go to a needy family that could help around the house while living for free, or I could use some of the space for the girls Miriam and I were trying to save from forced marriages. The options were endless and I was happy knowing I could and would bless others with my good fortune. My mind was far in the future, but Signora Tsega brought me back to the present with a conversation about furniture.

"Your furniture will all be delivered first thing tomorrow morning and placed according to your instructions. Congratulations, *zagualay.* It's a beautiful home. We must be off now. You two enjoy yourselves," Signora Tsega said as she hugged us both and left. I walked the team out and returned to find Daniel in the living room looking into the fireplace.

"Well, what do you think? Do you like it or is it not up to your standards?" I asked Daniel.

"I am speechless. It is truly one of a kind, Bella, just like you." He pulled me into his arms and started kissing me again. He knew exactly where and how to hold me. I loved that I had to stand on tip-toes to reach his lips. I loved that my head rested on his chest when he hugged me, making me feel secure and desired.

We sat on the marble floor of my empty home with him leaning against the wall and me nestled into his chest. His arms were around my waist and our hands were locked together.

"What are you thinking about?" I asked him.

"I knew you were smart and strong, but what you have done here is like nothing I have seen before. You never cease to amaze me."

Although I loved the compliments, I wanted to be honest and as open as possible with him.

"It is not all my doing. My grandfather bought the house for me. All I did was redesign what was already here and make it look more appealing."

"Stop doubting yourself. Regardless of who paid for the house or the redesign, it looks impeccable and that was all you. It is a dream house." He kissed my cheeks and lifted my hands to kiss them.

"Daniel, when you think of the future, what do you imagine for yourself? What do your dreams look like?"

"*Wey Gud...*" he was trying to speak Amharic to me. "I have never been asked that before. Is this a question you ask all your boyfriends?

I laughed. "No, just the ones I do not particularly care for, and who said anything about a boyfriend?" He nudged my shoulder,hich made me laugh even more.

"I dream of one day opening my own import-export business and doing some kind of consulting with different banks in Eritrea. I dream of marrying a woman who will be my equal. She will be beautiful, smart, kind, humble, God-fearing, and adventurous. This amazing woman will become the mother of my children and grow old with me. I dream of owning a house on Tiravolo Street. I dream of traveling the world with my family. I dream of buying a bigger house for my parents and making sure my entire family is well taken care of. There is so much more I can say, but I will not bore you with my thoughts."

"No, please continue. I love hearing what you want for your life."

"Okay, well, I want to buy property all over Eritrea and become a success-ful businessman. I want to create what the Europeans call generational wealth. If you notice, the white man always has money to last multiple generations. Why do you think that is? In all my years working with Eritreans and Europe-ans, one main thing separates us from them. We think of ourselves only. How to better our own current lives. We think about how to get ahead immediately. The problem with that is that once we see a little money, we think we have made it and we cease to dream of bigger and better things. Europeans though, they think ahead. They create and build with the future in mind so that they, their children, and their children's children will continue to enjoy the fruits of their labor. That is generational wealth. I want that. I want generations of my family to be comfortable. I also want to teach other Eritrean businessmen how to do the same, so that one day we will have a wealthy Eritrea that sustains itself for generations to come. How about you? What are your dreams?"

I was nervous that he would ask me that. My dreams were big for me, but after listening to him, they felt so small that I was hesitant to share.

"My dreams. Can you define, dreams?"

"Is this you, asking a question over a question? Do not try to change the subject, tell me your dreams please."

"Well, I must admit that after listening to your dreams, it is hard to share my own. I have never met a man who knew exactly what he wanted."

"A wise woman once told me: 'I am not like other women!' Maybe she should take her own advice and see that I, Daniel Kahassay, am not like other men." "Well said, Daniel. Well said."

"Tell me about your dreams, please."

"Had you asked me five years ago, even one year ago, what I wanted for my life, I would have told you that I wanted to run the Ministry of Foreign Affairs like my father had before me. God had other plans for me, though. He wanted me to come home to Eritrea and learn more about my people. Had it not been for the marriage proposal, I would have never come to Asmara."

There was a long silence between us until Daniel spoke.

"I have learned that in life we all go through seasons. A season where you plan you will become one thing and maybe end up becoming something else. There is a season where you are becoming a husband or a wife, and a season where you are parenting children. The key thing to remember is that nothing can or will stay the same, nor should you want it to. Spring, summer, autumn, winter — you must be open to change, because it is unavoidable, and because that is when you grow."

"You are full of wisdom today," I said, turning my face to kiss him softly.

"What can I say? You bring out the best in me. Now, tell me more about how you see your future."

"Well, I see myself living happily here in my little home. I see myself working with the bank on all political matters and helping them grow their presence in Africa. I see myself traveling between Addis Ababa and Asmara a great deal and possibly purchasing my own home in Addis Ababa. I also want to build churches and give to the less fortunate in any way I can. One of my biggest dreams is to abolish arranged marriages. No one should be forced to marry someone they do not love."

"How about a husband and children? Do you not see any of that in your future?" he asked.

"Honestly, until today, I cannot say that I have. I mean, I have dreamt of the man I would marry and have a general sketch of him in my head, but until this conversation, I cannot say that I have thought about what I want my family to look like."

"What does that sketch look like?" Daniel asked me.

"Well, he is tall, handsome, strong, and has a great sense of humor. He is smart, successful, or at least working towards something. He has faith in God. Strong faith. I want a man who will become a great father to our children. Lastly, I want to wed my best friend and grow old with him."

"You just described me perfectly!" Daniel said it jokingly, but I took it very seriously. He was everything I wanted and I had not seen it until that moment.

"We should get going, Daniel. We have been here for four hours and the more we stay, the more clouded my mind becomes."

"We should definitely stay, then. I am in no rush to get home."

"Well, I am. Come on, let's go."

I got up first and gave him my hand to help him up, but he pulled me back down and began kissing me all over again. His lips were soft and warm, his strong arms were holding me tight, and it felt good. It was as though our bodies were made for each other.

It took me a while to compose myself and finally get him out the door.

We walked to his car talking about our upcoming trip to Addis Ababa and about us. I wanted him, but I was also nervous about it. We were colleagues and I did not want our relationship to impact our work. I also wondered if my family and wealth would intimidate him. Would I be able to take him to the palace with me and introduce him to the princess and her family?

We reached the car and he opened the passenger door for me. "Where should I drop you off, Signorina?" Daniel asked. It occurred to me then that I had never disclosed where I lived.

"Daniel." I looked up at his face and waited for him to look at me too. I was sitting in his car and he was still holding on to the passenger side door.

"Yes?" he replied with a look of concern.

"I live at the palace, Daniel, with the imperial family. One of the princesses is my best friend." There! I said it.

"Well, I guess I should get the *principessa* back to the palace before the royal guards come looking for me." He smiled, closed my door, and came around to the driver's side.

"I am not a princess, Daniel. My best friend, Saba, is. I am a simple woman."

"Who lives in a palace."

"Yes. Until tomorrow, when I will move into my new home."

"Define simple, please?" he asked me.

"Simple, meaning I will never become a princess, unless of course, I marry a prince. Simple meaning that I am not of royal blood."

"How does that sound simple to you?" he asked. "You are anything but simple. You do not have to be a princess or royalty to be extraordinary."

The rest of the drive was quiet. When we got to the main gates of the palace, he kissed me on my forehead, then got out of the vehicle — even with the guards yelling at him — opened my door and said, "Good night, my *principessa.*" Then he showed his hands to the guards and yelled, "Only delivering the most beautiful woman in the world." The guards relaxed when they saw me and opened the gates. As I walked to the palace doors, I thought about how Daniel's gentle touch had left a mark on my heart, and I could not wait to spend more time with him. I felt free from the secret I had been holding as well, and happy that he was not intimidated by my title and wealth. I went to bed that night in a haze of feelings that I had never felt before.

The next morning, I woke up wanting to look extra-special. I was excited about going into work and then spending my first night in my new house.

Once I was showered and dressed, I gave myself the usual pep talk in the mirror.

"You are beyond capable of everything you are doing. You are strong, you are brave, you are great!" I kept repeating myself while heading to the dining room to have breakfast with Maryam and the girls.

"Are you ready for today?" the princess asked me.

"I think so. My clothes all seem to be packed and Signore Mebrahtu is moving all the furniture in today. Thank you so much for helping me with the move. I know how busy you are, Maryam."

"Speaking of busy, you have been working a lot! When are you going to have time to help me with our project?"

"I promise once the move is settled and I am back from Addis Ababa, I will make time to work on our initiatives."

"What do you mean, back from Addis Ababa?" said Maryam.

"Oh, my goodness, I have not had a chance to tell you!" I said. "This all happened yesterday and I got home too late last night to share the big news! The bank offered Daniel and me a great opportunity. Remember months ago, I mentioned the talking points we created and delivered to the board of directors? Well, they asked us to present it to Parliament on their behalf! That is fantastic news, right? I get to go home and speak in front of Parliament like Papa did. My dreams are coming true."

"Bella, that is wonderful news! Daniel is the man you liked, correct?"

"Yes, he is. I still like him. I like him a lot Maryam."

Her eyes softened and I could tell that she was about to give me some motherly advice.

"Bella, please be careful. You might be out of my father's sight, and you have been given a chance to create a life of your own, but do not push your luck. You know the rules in your family."

"I know, I know. I promise I am careful and will continue to be."

I guess bringing Daniel to the palace was not going to be an option any time soon. Luckily, I was moving out today, so for now I could spend more time with Daniel without everyone knowing.

"I am off to work! See you all later. I will stop by for dinner."

The walk to work was especially enjoyable that morning. I saw couples holding hands, walking towards work, school, cafés. I saw friends talking and laughing. I saw families of all colors walking with their children and everyone just seemed happy. Maybe it was because I was happy.

I got to my office to find the door slightly ajar. In my hurry to show Daniel my new house, I must have forgotten to close it the night before.

I walked in and found a large bouquet of white and red roses on my desk. On the couch sat Daniel, cigarette in hand. He took one last puff, then used the ashtray on my table to dispose of the cigarette. The whole time our eyes were locked. There were no words spoken between us; we both knew what would happen next. He got up from the couch and walked directly towards me. I stood frozen. He took me in his arms and kissed my lips with passion as though we had not seen each other in ages. I felt my knees get weak and only stopped when I had to gasp for air. I stayed in his arms as he gently kicked the door shut. He moved me to the couch and sat down with me on top of him, straddling his body. Until that point, I had never had the desire for sexual relations with him or any man for that matter. I had planned to wait until I was married to have anything as sacred as sex with a man. I felt differently now. With Daniel I felt grown up and free and wanted to experience everything.

We continued to caress and kiss each other until Daniel stopped and asked me if I had ever been with a man. When I said I had not, he moved his hands from my back to my face and sighed, "Oh, my *principessa*. You are truly my *principessa*."

I did not like the phrase at all; what suddenly made me 'his'?

"What does that mean?" I asked in annoyance. "I am yours now? Is my innocence some kind of trophy that is now yours?" I disentangled myself from him and straightened my dress. I walked first to the door to open it and then went to sit behind my desk so I would not be tempted to go back to the sofa.

"How have I offended you?" he asked.

"Please do not answer a question with a question."

"I was merely saying that I feel deeply connected to you. You are a princess to me. I was expressing admiration, not ownership. Have you ever felt like this for anyone else before? I haven't."

"Explain more in depth, please," I said. I liked where the conversation was headed.

"I do not know how to describe it, Bella. My brain respects you tremendously, and my body is full of passion for you. Ever since the first time I saw you at Alba, there has not been a day where I did not think about you. The more I got to know you, even though you irritated me with your stubborn ways, I still could not ever seem to get you out of my mind. There is something special about you, and I feel strong and proud when I stand by your side."

"So, would you call that love?" I asked.

"I do not know what to call it. I have never loved a woman before apart from the family love I have for my mother and sisters. This is different."

"Thank God! I do not want to be compared to your sisters or your mother." I smiled at him and he laughed back.

"What about you?" he asked.

"Well, I do not have as much experience in this field as you do. However, I have never felt these types of feelings before either. Just so we are both in agreement though, I do not belong to anyone but God. How can someone belong to someone else? People are not objects. Even children do not belong to their parents. Parents are blessed with children in order to teach and love them and then set them free," I said.

"Now you are talking like the white people. That is a very western way of thinking, Bella. Parents give everything they have to their children because they love them and because they belong to each other. It is their responsibility, and then in return it is the child's responsibility to take care of the parents. What kind of world would it be if children just left their parents and never looked back?" he said.

"I did not mean that they should never look back, I just meant that parents should not expect them to."

"I beg to differ, but this is a conversation we can save for a later time. Why did we even bring it up in the first place?" he asked.

"Because I never want to be told that I 'belong' to someone."

"Can I at least please call you my *principessa*?" He smiled, making my heart and all the tension I felt melt away.

" I am perfectly fine with that nickname. Now let's get to work. We have a lot to do before our trip. I want to make sure you are well informed on how Parliament works and who we will need to please in order to get our funding approved. In order to gain the right support, we will have to convince the members that it is in their best interest that our bank stays open. Papa always said that although those men were representing the nation, they were always very quick to consider their personal gain first. They must see how it will benefit them personally before they see how it will benefit Ethiopia. Back when Papa was part of Parliament, there was an upper senate composed largely of nobility, ministers, and distinguished members of the military. The lower chambers were all members chosen by the emperor. Things have changed and I believe that as of two years ago, members are now elected to the lower chamber, and their numbers have increased. I will not know many of these new members because they are not of the nobility. They are mostly rich merchants, and maybe some high-level members of society. While that might hurt us a little, we can also use it to our advantage. The merchants will want whatever benefits their pockets. Once we show them our numbers, they will agree with our proposal. While you do that, I will work on the high-level members and the upper senate. I have already asked my cousin Yonatan to give me a list of who they are, and he will have it ready for us upon arrival in Addis Ababa."

"What can I do to prepare in the meantime?" Daniel asked me.

"Well, to start we should go over basic Amharic terms that you can use to show them that you respect their language, their city, and their time."

We reviewed the basic words and customs Daniel would need to know and he was diligent in taking notes and paying attention. He asked questions and made comments. He practiced his speech repeatedly for days while I listened, corrected him, and gave examples of when and how to use different Amharic words. We practiced our presentation, gathered notes, and became thoroughly familiar with our mission. We practiced during the short time before our departure date. I was confident that Daniel would do well, and even more confident that we would return to Asmara with an approved proposal and funding for our bank. What I was nervous about was introducing Daniel to my family and friends. As the date got closer, my worries multiplied. What if Ababa, Yeshimebet, Saba, and Yonatan did not approve of him? I had asked Saba about her relationship with Yonatan since he was not of royal blood, and she had confided in me that the emperor was making plans to augment his title. Yonatan belonged to that world; he was born and raised in it. Daniel, on the other hand, was not. If Princess Maryam had advised me to be careful, I could only imagine what my family and friends would tell me.

CHAPTER 18

Work Trip to Addis Ababa

On May 15, 1958, Daniel and I flew together to Addis Ababa. Though he did not want to reveal it, he was nervous. He held my hand and asked me if I was scared, only to have me tell him over and over again that everything was fine. The flight was roughly two hours and we spent most of it holding hands, with me doing a lot of calming and talking, and him asking technical questions about the flight. As soon as we arrived in Addis Ababa, he claimed that he had been pretending to be nervous in order to distract me from my own worries about flying. He knew very well that I had none.

"*Uff*, why can't you simply admit that you were scared?" I said.

"How can I claim something that I am not? I assure you, *principessa*, I was not afraid."

"Well, we will have to return to Asmara on the same flight, so we will see who was scared and who was not."

He quickly changed the subject.

"It seems rather cold here. We have much better weather in Asmara."

I laughed. "Yes, my dear, the weather here is slightly more chilly than what you are used to in Asmara. Due to the city's geographical locations, it can get very cold in the morning and evenings and rather hot in the afternoon. It is similar to the temperature changes in Asmara, just a slight bit colder. Look! There is Yonatan!"

I waved at my cousin and ran to greet him. I had missed him dearly. Daniel walked slowly behind me and greeted Yonatan warmly, telling him that he had heard a great deal about him and was pleased to finally meet him. Yonatan teased Daniel and told him that he, too, had heard a great deal about him and was pleased to meet the only man that had stolen his cousin's heart. I punched him gently in the stomach for that comment.

"Well, it is true! Just the other day on the phone you were going on and on about how much you liked this man, how maybe you were in love…"

"Okay. That's enough. Those were private conversations." I thanked God that Daniel did not understand Amharic very well.

"It is good to have you home, Bella. We have all missed you dearly," Yonatan said as he gave me a hug.

" It is good to be home. How are Saba, Ababa, and Yeshimebet?"

"Everyone is doing well. You will see them at lunch today."

We walked to the cars and I saw Tadasse waiting for us. I ran to give him a warm hug and greeting and heard Daniel ask Yonatan:

"Is that her grandfather?" Yonatan laughed. "No, that's their family chauffeur. You will hopefully get to meet the family on this trip. Fair warning though. They will not be as friendly and loving as Annabella. They expected quite a different life for her than the one she has chosen."

"Noted. Thank you for the warning."

We put our bags in Tadesse's car and headed to Ghion Hotel with Yonatan in his car. As we drove, I enjoyed showing and explaining the history behind the different neighborhoods in Addis. Daniel was fascinated by the vastness of the city and wanted to know about everything he saw. I promised him I would show him around after he rested and got some food.

"Let's get you checked in and then you can come to lunch at our house," I told him, which caused Yonatan to cough and almost choke.

"Bella, I think Daniel should rest today and maybe eat at the hotel. What is the rush? You both will be here for two weeks, correct?"

"Well no, actually only one week, but…" Yonatan did not give me a chance to finish my sentence.

"Still, you have plenty of time to bring Daniel home. Let him rest today."

"Well, what would you prefer to do?" I asked Daniel.

"I am not too tired, but I also do not want to intrude on your family time. I am sure they are all excited to see you. Yonatan is probably right. I can come by any day this week. We are not presenting to Parliament until Monday."

I could sense that he was nervous about meeting my family. Yonatan's suggestion was probably a good idea after all. I could go home and tell my family about Daniel and hope that they would be on their best behavior when they eventually met him.

"Okay. Well, rest up. I will come by after lunch and check on you. We can walk in the city or I can come with Tadesse and drive you around, if you prefer."

"No need to bother Tadesse. I am at your disposal, Daniel, and I would love to show you around," Yonatan said.

We arrived at Ghion Hotel and parked our vehicle in front of the reception area. Moments later, Tadesse drove up behind us with our luggage. Daniel grabbed his bag and handed it to the bellboy before giving me a hug and telling me that he would miss me while I was with my family. I told him I would return shortly and gave him a kiss on the cheek.

"Until later then, *principessa*. Ciao," he called out as I got in the car.

"Are you speaking Italian these days?" asked Yonatan as soon as we got in the car. "Do those fascists Italians still live in Eritrea?"

"You have some nerve, you know. What is wrong with you? Why would you tell him what I said to you about him? Why would you want to embarrass me like that? And why don't you think he should come home for lunch? You take Saba for lunch at our house, right? It is the same thing. And yes, he calls me *principessa*, because I am his princess and they do speak Italian in Eritrea.

There are still plenty of Italians living there, and whether they are fascists or not, I have no idea, but I enjoy living there and speaking Italian occasionally. I can do as I please." I could not believe the bold words that were coming out of my mouth. I had definitely changed since moving to Eritrea.

I took a deep breath, looked at Yonatan, and said, "Daniel is a good man. He is kind, sweet, funny, smart, charming, and I like him. I like him a great deal and I need you to respect my feelings about him and support me, or…" I was interrupted by him stopping the car quite suddenly. He turned to face me. "Or what, Bella? What? You will run off again, because you do not agree with what our society expects from you? Or what, you will disappear, letting all of us think you are dead? You have already done those things and we have already suffered the consequences. There is nothing you can do that will be worse than what you have already done."

Trembling with emotion, I said, "Yonatan, I cannot expect you to understand why I made the decisions I did. But trust me when I say that it was the only way. I would have put both you and Saba at risk if I had shared my plans with you, and I could never knowingly hurt either one of you."

"Well, you did hurt us. You hurt us a great deal. You never call, you do not write, and when you do, it feels as though we are strangers. It seems like we have lost you, Bella. You went to Eritrea to figure out who you are, who your father was, and escape that horrible marriage arrangement, and we were all happy for you. But now I feel like you are not the same person."

I knew Yonatan well enough to know when he was truly hurt, and I could count only a handful of times I had seen him like this.

"Please, Yonatan, you must know that I would never ever turn my back on my family, especially not on you. I have an entirely new life now in Asmara, and it has been hard work to make that happen. Now I have a new job, a new house, and I am just sorting things out. I have been very busy."

"Yet you have had time to date this fellow Daniel."

I sensed a hint of jealously coming from Yonatan that I had never seen before.

"We work together. That is very different and you know it. If I have offended you I sincerely apologize, I love you dearly and I meant no harm. I will talk to everyone in the family and explain my choices and apologize if necessary.

"Apology accepted," he smiled and started the car back up so we could go home for our family lunch.

I worried that everyone would feel the same way as Yonatan did, primarily Saba, but it was the exact opposite. My family was genuinely happy to see me and I received a very warm welcome. Everyone was on their best behavior until the topic of Daniel came up. First Ababa asked in detail what brought me to the city and then Yeshimebet continued by asking questions about Daniel. I told them he was my colleague from work and would be giving the presentations with me. It was in my description of Daniel that they all sensed the feelings I had for him.

"Bella, please be careful, *Yene Lij*. That is all I will ask of you, *ebakish bakish*, do not do something that will bring further disgrace to the family," Ababa said.

There it was.

I got up from lunch, threw my napkin on the table, excused myself, and left the room. Saba ran after me, stopping me right before I got to the front door. "Bella, please, what has gotten into you? Where is my best friend? What happened in Asmara? We are all worried about you!" She sounded just like Yonatan, or was he sounding just like her? "Nothing is wrong with me. I am the same person. We can talk later. I have things to do." I could tell she was hurt, but I knew if we talked now, our emotions would get the better of us, so I did what I knew would be right, even if it felt wrong, and I left.

I found Tadesse cleaning the car out front and asked him to take me back to Ghion Hotel. Throughout the entire ride, all I could think about was how narrow-minded my family was, starting with Yonatan, who I thought would always understand and support me. Had courting my best friend changed him? The power and notoriety that came with dating Her Royal Highness Princess Sabework could be intense, but I never thought he would become so cold and

petty. I thought maybe this had nothing to do with Daniel, and everything to
do with my defiance of the family's culture and rules. That had to be it, me
being with Daniel was just another example of my not fitting in. In the family,
it was only Emama that knew and understood me. I had thought that Yonatan
and Saba did as well, but I guessed we were all different now, grown up and
going our separate ways. Emama would have loved Daniel, and I decided at
that moment to go and see her. I reached Daniel's hotel and told Tadesse to
wait outside. I wanted to take Daniel and introduce him to the most important
person in my life.

Ghion Hotel *Addis Ababa*

CHAPTER 19

Ghion Hotel

I asked at the front desk which room Ato Daniel Kahassay was in, walked up the stairs, knocked on his door, and was stunned by what I saw when it opened. He was freshly out of the shower with steam still coming off his body and had only a towel wrapped around his hips. I froze completely.

He opened the door even more and asked me whether I wanted to come in or not. He reached out and pulled me in by my waist and began kissing me, one soft kiss at a time. He moved his hands from my waist to my hair back and forth slowly as though he knew I would melt away and he would be there to pick me up. He led and I followed him to the bed. I wanted him to touch me, to kiss me everywhere. I began to take off my blouse but he stopped me.

"No. Not like this. I want to wait until the time is right. I respect you too much. I want a future with you. Being with someone in that way changes a person, Bella. It's something that you will hold onto forever and if I am blessed to have you in my life and get to experience that with you, then I want it to be as special as possible. Not rushed by lust, but because we love each other and want to commit to one another," he said.

"Well, when you put it like that, I guess I want to wait as well. How long are we thinking, though?" I wanted him and did not care what he thought about it. He smiled and told me that when it was right, I would know.

I gave him a soft kiss and thanked him.

"I almost forgot. Get dressed, please. Tadesse is downstairs waiting for us. I want to take you somewhere special."

"Does this special place have food as well? I did not get a chance to order anything and I am very hungry."

"I will not let you starve. We would not want you to think we do not treat our guests with respect here in Addis Ababa." I smiled as he got up to get dressed for the afternoon.

There was so much I wanted to show him, but first we went to eat at a small café that made the best kitfo and tibs in the city. The car ride was full of lively conversations between the three of us. Tadesse tried his best to speak Tigrinya, while Daniel practiced his Amharic and I almost cried with laughter listening to them. We drove down Arat Kilo, and as Tadesse made the same right turn that he had been making for years, my stomach began to swirl. I had been coming to this area since I was a child. I knew all the roads that led to Parliament. What was once a building of power and prestige to me was now reduced mostly to memories of my father. While his office was not located in Parliament, he spent a great deal of time working on different projects in that building. I associated positive things with the building because I always saw him doing good there. Even after his death, I continued to work hard with the goal that I, too, would be in that building bringing change for our people. Moving to Eritrea might have changed my goals, but the building was still a symbol of promise and greatness for me; it was Papa's legacy. With him gone, I never went back, but every time I passed it on my way to visit his grave at Kidest Selassie, I felt his presence. Daniel sensed something was wrong and I told him it was nothing. There was so much to tell him, I had no idea where to even begin. Luckily, the outside appearance of the café quickly captured his attention. He was surprised by the tiny hut with a long line of people out front.

"You want us to eat here?" he asked me.

"Trust me, their food is amazing! The owner just refuses to renovate; he likes the old style and believes that there is nothing wrong with it. Look at that line. If the food was bad, these people would not be waiting for so long to place their orders. Tadesse, please order us the kitfo and tibs special. Tell Ato Fisseha that it is for me and I would like it cooked the usual way. Order whatever you like for yourself as well, and two Coca-Colas, please."

"Bella, where are you going?" Tadesse asked as I got out of the car and pulled Daniel by the hand.

"We will be back. I am going to introduce Daniel to Emama."

"Should I bring the food to you?" he yelled out.

"No. We will come back and eat with you here. I want to say hello to Ato Fisseha as well." With that, Daniel and I started walking towards Holy Trinity.

"What is that building?" Daniel asked me, pointing at Parliament. He wanted to know everything.

"That is our Parliament. That is where we will be presenting next week," I said in my best tour guide voice.

"That is why you eat at that café all the time, and why you brought me here, yes?"

"Yes and no. I also wanted you to meet the most important people in my life."

He was astounded by the ornate beauty of Parliament and kept stopping to stare at the building.

"Daniel, the guards will think you are a threat, come on let's keep walking." I pushed him up the road and into the main gates of Kidest Selassie.

"Welcome to the most beautiful church in all of Addis Ababa. Kidest Selassie, built by Emperor Haile Selassie in 1942." I continued to explain the importance of the church to the Ethiopian people. "Built after the Italian invasion, it symbolized freedom, God's strength, and His mercy for our people." As we walked towards the back of the church, I told him why the church meant so much to me.

"Papa is buried here, Daniel, and so is my grandmother. They are the two most important people in my life and both are here, close to each other and close to Parliament. I know Papa loves that," I said, smiling.

"Tell me about them." He grabbed my hand and led me to the garden benches that faced both my father's and grandmother's graves.

I told him all about Papa. How gentle and loving he was with me and Yeshimebet. She was the love of his life and I was his only daughter. He shared his dreams, hopes, and aspirations with us freely. He loved to laugh, dance, play cards, and tell stories and jokes. He was a free spirit and so full of life. I told him story after story of our travels together and how things were at home. Then I shared all about Emama and how she always advocated for me. The more I shared with Daniel, the freer I felt, like there were now no secrets between the two of us, at least not on my side.

With each story I told him, Daniel leaned in closer to listen, interested in what I had to say. He could feel my joy and my hurt and held my hand tighter when I needed it most. I remembered our first interaction and how I had told him that I did not share information with people I did not know. Much had changed since that day. Now here I was, sharing intimate details of my life with him, and just as he had predicted, he was here for me, listening as though his life depended on it.

"We better get back to Tadesse and our lunch. I want you to try your food while it is still hot." I got up and started walking towards the cafe.

Still sitting on the bench, Daniel said, "I have one question."

I turned around and walked back towards him.

"What would you like to know?" I asked him.

"Why did your family bury him here instead of in Eritrea? He grew up there. That was his home."

"I do not have a good answer for that question." My father had lived most, if not all his adult life in exile here in Addis Ababa, fighting the Italians off. After they left, he never discussed going home. I wondered if it was because he wanted to return to a free and independent Eritrea.

"I do, however, have an answer for your hunger demands. Come, please let us eat."

We walked out of the church and back to the café where Tadesse was waiting with our meals. Daniel loved the kitfo and tibs and praised the meal that Papa and I used to enjoy as a special treat. It meant a great deal for me to share this experience with him.

The three of us laughed together as Tadesse told Daniel stories of how mischievous I was as a child. Blessedly, Daniel's limited Amharic only allowed for him to understand certain parts and when Ato Fisseha joined our table and added more details, I could feel my face getting warm with embarrassment. These were people who had been in my life since childhood and knew almost everything about me, at least the young me. As they continued to enlighten Daniel, I thought about how much I had changed and matured. Now, I had a prestigious career, owned my own home, and was falling in love with a man instead of the boy crushes of my past. I caught myself mid-thought. Love! I had never loved a man before. Never before had I felt the feelings I had for Daniel. When I was with him, I felt unstoppable, unreachable, almost like I was walking on clouds of joy. The second we were apart, that cloud opened to drop me into the unknown. That scared me and excited me at the same time.

I told Tadesse that we would walk back to Daniel's hotel and gave him a time to pick me up from there. Daniel was interested in seeing the city and the best way to do that was on foot. We walked the opposite direction from his hotel so that he could see more. On our way, I showed him the Haile Selassie University, which was once the emperor's palace. I explained how the emperor had moved to the Jubilee Palace and gifted this building to the students of Addis Ababa. I talked about it with such pride, yet Papa would never have allowed me to attend classes there. Although he would never say it, he believed a European education would offer more opportunities for me. We walked past other buildings, and through different neighborhoods and sections of the city.

As we walked back towards his hotel, I showed him Liberty Square and told him the story behind the monument there. Emperor Haile Selassie had it built in honor of Ethiopian liberation after the five years of Italian occupation in the late 1930s. Any kind of history fascinated me, but this artifact brought pain to Daniel.

"Ethiopians will never know what it is like to be under someone else, to be considered a second-class citizen in your own home, to fear what will happen to your children, your wife, your family. How can they understand what the rest of Africa has succumbed to if they have never experienced our struggles?" He looked down at the ground with pain in his eyes. My heart ached for him. I wanted to place my hands around his face and have him look at me, but I knew that doing that would look inappropriate in public. So instead I spoke from the heart and hoped that my words would make a difference.

"Do not think that because we were not colonized we have never experienced the pain of white domination. Remember that Ethiopia was occupied by the Italians for five years, and even before and after that, the people here faced domination from within. Did you know that until recently, there were slaves in Ethiopia? Every country in Africa has experienced its own version of enslavement, be it from an outsider or from its own people."

"You are right, but also wrong, Bella. The people here are free, they understand what freedom means - they breath it, they feel it, they know it. There is a big difference in having your own people dominate you and having a stranger do it." He was right, and sadly, there was nothing I could do at that moment to change those feelings for him.

"Enough talk about the past, let us walk into the future. Tell me something no one else knows about you," I said, trying to change the subject.

He looked at me with one eyebrow raised. I noticed that he did that anytime my questions were very serious and thought-provoking.

"There is not much about me that you do not already know," He said.

"Do you mean to tell me that my knowledge of you is the same as everyone else's? That does not make me feel special at all."

He rolled his eyes and thought some more of what to say to me. "Here is the one and only thing that no one in the world knows. I am afraid of heights. Especially flying. That is why I never left Asmara. The opportunity of being with you, however, made me face my fears and I am grateful for that." He looked at me for a response as we walked further and further away from the church and closer to his hotel. I did not know how to respond. I felt warm and started blushing right away.

"Why so distant?" he asked.

"I was thinking how much I enjoy spending time with you. I was also thinking about how wrong my family is about you. I want them to see what I see, instead of judging you without giving you a chance."

"I am guessing they do not like me because I am not from the same class, speak the same language, nor have the resources that you grew up on."

I had said too much already.

I tried to correct my earlier the statement best I could, "What I meant was, I cannot wait for them to meet you."

"No, Bella. Please do not lie to me."

"It is my turn to tell you something that no one else knows about me," I said, hoping to change the conversation yet again.

"That can wait. I would like to know about the conversation you had with your family. I had a feeling your cousin did not like me very much and was going to ask you why. Am I missing something here?"

"Honestly, their feelings regarding you as of now have nothing to do with you and everything to do with me. Remember how I told you about my journey from Addis Ababa to Asmara? Well, they are disappointed in me. Apparently, I embarrassed the family when I decided not to marry a powerful general and then I had the nerve to make my own decisions for my life. According to Yonatan, I added insult to injury by leaving Addis Ababa even after my marriage proposal was thrown out. I have not been here in months and honestly, I do not feel this place as home anymore. Without Emama here, how could it be? Then here you are with me, someone who is not from a prestigious family, and

I am reckless enough to fall in love with you. I do not know how things work in Asmara, but here class matters, especially to my family. Who you are is determined by who your family is or was, and the elders are determined to keep things that way. If you and I were to, let's say, get married, then it would cause havoc. It is all rubbish, if you ask me. Pure rubbish and I told them as much. I will not be forced into any relationship or be with someone who I do not truly love just to preserve the status quo."

He kept quiet.

"Say something, please," I begged, keeping our hands locked together. I looked up at his face.

"You love me?" he asked.

"Did I say that? Wait a minute, I poured my heart out and all you took from that entire conversation was that I love you, and I would like to add that I did not mean to say that," I said.

"No, no, no. You said it. You meant it. It is okay, Bella. I love you too."

"You do not have to say that just because I did. Let's wait before we say that to each other. I was merely explaining myself. Back to my family issues, please."

"You want my honest opinion?" he asked me.

"Yes. Always!"

"Family matters. My mother always said that family either turns your marriage into a nightmare or the best dream ever. I can understand why your family is concerned. If they were going to wed you off to a general twice your age just for prestige, then can you blame them for not wanting you to be with a simple banker who did not go to a university overseas, speaks two languages, and does not come from money? They are only trying to protect you, so do not take it personally. I am sure once they get to know me, they will change how they feel. If not, that is okay, too. Our lives are based in Asmara, we will make our own way and create the life that we want. That is, if you will have me. You must not let such things get to you though. They love you and want the best for you, but they are also stuck in their ways. Do not fault them for that," he said with a smile, squeezing my hand. He was right.

"Are you telling me, without really telling me, that I need to apologize to them?" Now my eyebrows were raised.

"Yes, *principessa*, that would be the right thing to do." He kissed my hand and changed the subject by asking what was the one thing about me no one knew.

I told him about my collection of dolls from every country I had ever visited. It made sense when I was a child, but now as an adult, I often lied about my collection and pretended I was purchasing souvenirs for my younger cousins. He laughed at my secret, telling me that I better not get on his bad side or he would exploit me greatly. I rolled my eyes at him, saying I would do the same with his fear of heights. We finally got back to the hotel with our feet aching from all the walking we had done. We both needed to rest and decided that we would go through the final practice for our meetings with Parliament the next day. Daniel kissed me goodbye and went to his room while I waited outside for Tadesse.

I fell asleep in the car listening to Tadesse tell me how nice my new friend was. That evening, I did not eat dinner with my family; instead, I went to bed early and woke the next morning to get ready and head to the hotel. To my surprise, I found Yonatan sleeping and snoring on the edge of my bed. I gave him a light kick to wake him up.

"What are you doing in my room? Does privacy mean nothing to you?" He rubbed his eyes, yawned, and stretched awake. "What are you doing here?" I asked again. "There are other rooms in the house."

"Ever since you left, anytime I stayed late, I would stay here. It reminds me of you."

"Okay, now that is just creepy." Another kick.

"I wanted to make sure I was here when you woke up. You and I are going to hang out today. If you want we can invite Saba and Daniel, but I would prefer it if it was just the two of us."

"Yonatan, as much as I would love to hang out, today is not a good day. I have to focus on my meeting with Parliament."

"I can help with that."

He was going to be hard to get rid of. As much as I wanted to spend time with Daniel, I owed my cousin a day at the very least, but we were going to spend time together on my terms. He would be a great asset to have for our meeting with Parliament, and so would Saba.

"Okay. How about I make you a deal. We will spend the morning together, and then you can come with me to meet Daniel for lunch and even bring Saba. Then the two of you will help us with our briefing. What we will not do is ambush Daniel, or make him feel like an outsider. Deal?"

With a firm look, I gave him my hand. I could tell he was not happy, but he shook my hand and said, "Deal."

"Great. So, what should we do? Let's have breakfast in Emama's garden. Should I ask the maids to make your favorites?" I was happy to spend time with Yonatan but also wanted to hurry the visit so we could go and see Daniel. If love meant that all you did was think about the other person and the next time you would see them, then this feeling I was having, the thoughts I kept thinking, were all about love. Yonatan would be the best person to talk to about these matters, but I would have to be careful. The conversation would have to be in regard to his relationship instead of mine.

I was happy to see Emama's gardens kept so nicely even after her death. Yonatan made a point of telling me that Ababa spent a great deal of his free time out here now. I knew that would make Emama happy. In the cool morning air, we wrapped ourselves in warm blankets and settled into two chairs in the garden.

"How are things going with Saba? Are you happy? What is the future looking like?" I asked him.

"Things are going well. I must admit that my education in France has made it a bit hard for us to stay in touch, but she visits often and I come home more than ever. I am here for the entire summer now and will graduate early in December."

I had missed so much. How did I not know that she was in France a great deal now or that he was graduating early?

"Why did you not come to Montpelier University when you got your acceptance letter? I do not understand, Bella, you were so determined to bring change, to follow in your father's footsteps, and then you just left. When I found out you were alive and well, I thought you would join me in France. Every time I wanted to bring it up on the few occasions that you called, you sounded so happy with how life was going that I did not feel it was right to inquire. Help me understand, please."

My acceptance letter. I had not given it much thought since the day Ababa told me about it.

"How did you know I got accepted?" I asked him.

"Ababa told me and asked me to speak to you, and then the university called me and asked if you were coming. You must have put my name down as a reference."

I remembered the day I applied and the thoughts that were passing in my mind. I remembered how it felt to write why I believed I would make a great candidate and how important it was that I attended my father's alma mater. I wrote about wanting to bring change to Africa and lead us into the future. How naïve I was back then. I knew so little of what was to come after graduation. I had no regrets, but wondered how my life would have been had I gone ahead with law school when Ababa first mentioned it to me.

"Yonatan, by the time Ababa told me about the acceptance letter, I was already starting to question all my life plans. The things that had once seemed so important meant so very little to me in the face of having to flee Addis Ababa. Life in Asmara changed me, Yonatan. I cannot tell you exactly how, but it is for the better. I might not be on the path we talked about, or that I dreamed about growing up, but I am on a path that makes me happy and I feel free. I never even knew freedom like this existed."

"Would this have anything to do with a certain man?" he said, smiling.

My grin said enough but I still felt the need to respond. "No, Daniel is a wonderful man and I enjoy his company a great deal, but I was determined to start my life over before I even met him. He just happened to be in the right place at the right time. I have a question for you, though. Do you love Saba?"

"Yes, very much."

"When did you know you loved her?" I asked. Subtle probably was not going to work with Yonatan; he knew exactly where I was going with the conversation.

"It was not a matter of when really, it was a matter of how much. I have loved her since we were children. The feelings only grew over time. You are falling in love with him, Bella! Affairs of the heart have a way of showing up when we least expect them. Just be careful. You might think you love him, or maybe you really do love him, but there is no need to rush it. You say you are happy in Asmara, you are working and living in your own home. You are finally free to do whatever you choose with your life. Do not rush anything."

"Would you be saying the same thing if he was Prince Addisu, or someone else in the royal family, or even one of the men we grew up with? I think that you are being hard on Daniel because he is not from our world. To be completely honest, that is what attracts me to him. He is not consumed with status. He does not care what people think of him, and he works genuinely hard for everything he has and believes in. I have never met a man like him, nor have I ever felt these feelings before, whatever they are."

"He seems like a good man, Bella. But what happens when the infatuation fades? Because right now you are clearly infatuated. Right now, you are only thinking with your heart. You two have yet to experience real struggle or adversity. Are you sure that in difficult times he will be there for you? I know our world seems unrealistic and maybe even fake to you now, but the people here respect you and will be here for you always, no matter what. Can you say the same for him?"

He had a good point. In the short time that I had known Daniel, everything had been good in my life. We had not been challenged, but I wanted to give him a chance. Fear of the unknown would not hold me back.

"Yonatan, that is good advice, you wise old man! Thank you. I promise I will be on guard, but I need to see what the future holds for us."

"Good. That is all I ask. Now tell me all about your work and the house. You shared very little in your letters."

We talked for what felt like hours before I was summoned to the house by Berhana for a phone call. "The man says his name is *Principessa*," she said, with a disapproving scowl.

"Good morning, Ato Daniel." I said, without even hearing his voice.

"*Buongiorno, Principessa.*" I loved hearing his voice. It excited and calmed me at the same time. "Did I call at a bad time? I worried about giving my name. How are you doing? Did you talk to your family? When can I see you today?"

I did not know which question to answer first.

"No, you called at the perfect time. Yonatan stayed over and we were just finishing breakfast." I could see Yonatan walking back from the garden. "I am doing well, thank you for asking. Did you sleep well?" I could not answer the question about my family with Yonatan so close by.

"Apart from missing you all night, I slept very well. I was tired from our walk."

"I fell asleep on the car ride home and went straight to bed. Yonatan and I will be coming over to pick you up in roughly an hour. I think he can be helpful to us in preparing our presentation. Will that be okay?" I wanted to make sure he knew I was not coming alone.

"Sure. I think. Unless, of course, he is coming to kill me," Daniel said jokingly.

"For his sake, he better not be. See you in a bit. Grab something light to eat while you wait."

I hung up the phone and noticed I was sitting in Emama's chair. The last time I was in this room with her, we were doing one of our many Novenas together.

"You are sitting just like her, you know?" Yonatan said as he walked into the sitting room.

"Do you miss her? She was such a big part of this house, of our lives. I think, living so far away, that part of me could pretend that she was still here," I said.

"Did that work for you?"

"Yes. I believe it did. Somehow it gave me the strength I needed to move on with life. She always pushed me to do better, be better, want better, and I would not have been able to do that had I stayed in this house, in this city even. I needed to close this chapter of my life and start a new one. Now that I look back at the time following her funeral, I did hold back from all of you. I owe you an apology, Yonatan. I am deeply sorry if I hurt you or made you feel un-loved. It was truly nothing against you. I needed the distance and time to heal."

"Thank you, God!" Yonatan yelled, clasping his hands together. "It is good to have you back, Bella! We all just want what is best for you and to be a part of your life, that is all. Speaking of your life, we should get going. There is a tall and handsome *Asmarino* waiting for you at Ghion Hotel."

Yonatan and I drove over to the hotel to find Daniel at a café table by the swimming pool. It reminded me of our first encounter, except that this time it was I who was blocking his sunlight. "I would say 'Excuse me' and ask you to move, but in all honesty, I prefer this view," he said. He stood up to embrace me and gave me a gentle kiss on the forehead.

Yonatan grabbed a chair and said, "I hate to interrupt you two, but we have work to do."

We ordered coffee and I pulled out our briefing notes from my bag. "Just like your father, always so organized and professional," said Yonatan.

"You should see her at the office. She even has the security guards working when they see her. No one messes with the great Annabella Lorenzo," Daniel added.

"Gentlemen, I simply prefer to utilize my time efficiently. We will have time to lounge and chat later," I said.

I handed Yonatan a copy of our proposal and gave him time to read through it before jumping into our briefing notes. I could see his eyebrow raise now and then, and he occasionally stroked his chin in deep thought. I was wondering what he was thinking when I looked up to see Saba walking towards our table. I waved and smiled vibrantly, hoping she had forgotten our exchange from yesterday. She waved back, but I could tell her smile was not a sincere one.

Saba greeted Yonatan and me warmly, then gave Daniel her hand as if to remind him that he was the stranger at the table and she was a princess.

"Daniel, it is with great pleasure that I introduce you to my best friend, the love of Yonatan's life, and the Royal Princess of Ethiopia, Her Highness Princess Sabawork." Saba's genuine smile appeared. "Saba, it is with great pleasure that I introduce you to my colleague, friend, confidant, and, dare I say, suitor — Daniel."

We all blushed and laughed together.

"It is wonderful to meet you, Your Highness. Bella speaks fondly and often of you," Daniel said.

"Thank you. It is nice to meet you too. I come with a warning though. If you hurt her in any way, I will have you found and killed." Leave it to the princess to be forward with words.

"I promise, if she allows me, I will take care of her until the day I die."

"Great. Now that we understand each other, I would love to get to know you better. Tell us, where were you raised? What do you like to do for fun? Do you enjoy badminton or tennis? Trust me, I will be the only one asking these good questions. When you meet the family, it will be serious talk all the time."

"People, please stay on track here. Remember we have a Parliament presentation to prepare for," I scolded everyone. "Yonatan, what do you think about the proposal? Be honest, please." Saba took it to read while Yonatan gave us his feedback.

"It is very well done. The numbers alone would be sufficient, but if you really want to win them over, you should add personality and get the members to resonate with everything you tell them. For example, you talk about giving back to the people, right? Well, remember you are speaking to ministers and other nobility. Will these men care about funds going to the people? I doubt it. Most of these people only care about how they can benefit personally. Hence, in addition to saying 'giving back to the people,' how about you word it in a way that will seem as though some of that funding is coming back to them," Yonatan said.

"I see. Leave the briefing as is and present stories that show the individual benefits."

"Exactly. This is where Saba and I can help. We know each of the men that you will be meeting with on Monday. Let's go through the list and discuss a way for you to speak on something that will attract each of them specifically." Yonatan said.

Saba added, "Your status as Lorenzo's daughter could be seen as a good or bad thing. On one side you will have the backing from his friends in Parliament, but do not forget that there were many against him. The mere fact that you moved to Eritrea and declined General Kebede's proposal can be seen as a threat to their way of life. Do not forget that these men are loyal to their pockets, to my father, and to Ethiopia. Be smart. Do not let your emotions get the best of you. Stick to your briefing notes and let Daniel do the rest. They will try to attack you so you must stand strong."

She was right. I had to be prepared for the worst while hoping for the best. It would not be just the bank on display, but me as well.

Ethiopian Parliament Building *Addis Ababa*

CHAPTER 20

Beginning a New Life

The day of our briefing was finally upon us. I got up early with knots in my stomach and sweaty palms. It took me back to the day I received the telegram about my marriage to the general. In other words, I was a wreck.

I dressed in my professional best with a white blouse and a long black skirt. For good luck, I pinned Emama's brooch on the left side of my blouse and added pearls as accessories. One last look in the mirror and out the door I went to meet Tadesse.

Daniel was waiting in the main lobby of his hotel. We had breakfast together while going through our briefing notes for the last time before heading towards Parliament.

"Are you nervous?" I asked.

"A little. So much is on the line," he said, taking my hand into his.

"Are you nervous?" he asked.

"Yes, very. I am nervous not only for the bank, but I will have to see General Kebede as well and other people from my past."

"We will do it together and we will prevail. Do not worry."

When we arrived at the main gates of Parliament, a rush of memories came to my mind, mostly all dealing with Papa and the time we spent together within those walls. I remembered naming the two golden lions and saluting them instead of the guards. What I would give to go back in time and walk through the gates with him again. I heard my name called and came back to reality. Daniel was standing by the car, with one hand holding all our briefing notes, and the other reaching out for mine.

A part of me wanted to stay frozen there in my thoughts of the past, frozen with Papa, while the other half wanted to run to Daniel — my future.

"Bella. Bella, we really must get going." I grabbed Daniel's hand and walked through the gates that had once meant so much to me.

We were searched outside and again inside the building and were told to wait while badges were prepared for us. I got a feeling that someone was staring at me from behind and turned around to see General Kebede walking toward me.

"Young lady, you have a lot of nerve coming here today after the trouble you put your family and all of us through last year," the general said.

"Hello, sir." That was all I could think of to say to him. He was on the board of members that we would be presenting to today. I remembered what Saba had said to me. I could not let my emotions show here.

"I look forward to hearing all about your little bank. We fought the Italians and sent them packing. It is a shame the people in the north could not do the same," he said, and I immediately understood that he was trying to test me. I would not fall for his tricks. I was there to do my job.

"General Kebede, this is Daniel Kahassey, my colleague from *Banco di Roma* in Asmara. We look forward to sharing our proposal with you."

Just then, our badges were ready, and we left the lobby.

"Was that him? Daniel whispered.

"Yes," I said.

"No wonder you ran away. He looks like a black version of Mussolini." We laughed together and I felt my courage coming back. I knew that so long as I had him by my side, things would be fine.

The presentation room was windowless and dingy. I had never seen this side of the building before. All of Papa's meetings were in bigger and elegant rooms. The table was circular and held about fifteen people. According to Yonatan, there were fifteen people invited to the meeting, so it was expected that Daniel and I would stand the entire time. I placed a copy of our proposal by each person's chair and looked up to see a huge map of Ethiopia on the wall, showing its different regions, including key-shaped Eritrea at the very top of the country. As I pondered the map, the ministers, generals and other nobility filed into the room and took their seats. General Kebede was the last to enter. Daniel politely waited for him to sit, and then closed the door. We introduced ourselves and thanked them for taking time to meet with us, and then we dove into our presentation. I told the story of the bank from the roots up and explained what it meant for Ethiopians living in Eritrea. Daniel explained the bank's holdings and how it would continue to be a huge source of income for the Ethiopian government. I looked up from time to time throughout the presentation to see everyone at the table nodding in pleased agreement.

"While the bank is owned by Italians, Ethiopians in Massawa, Keren, and Asmara have invested in our bank since the day it opened. We offer mentorship opportunities that teach the youth how to handle funds, and assist them in finding jobs in the cities where we have locations. Our way of giving back reaches everyone from the wealthy to the poor and provides stability within the cities. We are one of the only banks that keeps our revenues high and expenses low, allowing for higher taxation, which will benefit the government greatly." I concluded by showing them pictures of projects the bank had funded in various cities. Heads were still nodding and I knew without a doubt that we had won them over. All but one.

"This is all very good but it does not take away from the obvious fact that the owners are white Europeans, Italian fascists to be exact," said General Kebede." Why should we support them?"

Daniel opened his mouth to respond, but the General interrupted. "No, sir. I would like her to answer the question." Everyone in the room, including Daniel, was now looking at me.

"Most of you know me. I grew up in this building, running up and down these hallways. I used to think like you, that all Italians were bad, fascists even. My father left his home because of them. He was your colleague and your friend. While what the Italians did in Eritrea and Ethiopia is wrong, and no words can repair the damage that they have caused so many families, not all of them are bad people. The owners of *Banco di Roma* genuinely care for the people of Eritrea and they bring business into the cities. Through taxes the bank can provide opportunities for each of you to grow your ministries and military bases as well. Think of all the renovations we can provide for our government buildings and how we can build up many different cities in Ethiopia with this money."

"We have heard that they are helping the people mobilize towards fighting for an independent Eritrea. How can we be sure that that does not occur?" another general asked.

This time Daniel responded.

"I grew up scared of Italians, running away whenever I saw them coming. That fear was instilled in me as a child when one night they came to arrest my father because he had taken a second job to provide for his family. While he was imprisoned, my family and I suffered greatly."

He continued, "So why would I, why would we, want to do anything with the Italians after everything they put us through? We live harmoniously with the ones that stayed behind because they have denounced any ties to the Italian government and live among us as expatriates. Many of them have married local women, and started families and businesses."

"As a person who lives there and grew up there, do you think Eritrea should be an independent country?" asked another one of the generals. And there it was: the question that would be the difference between our triumphant success or crushing failure. Would Daniel tell the truth?

"Sir, I believe that Eritrea is the best it has ever been. What the future holds, I have no idea."

Good answer! I was nervous and satisfied at the same time. General Kebede rose from his seat first. He thanked us and asked us to wait outside while they discussed their final decision.

"Well, regardless of what happens, I think we did great," Daniel said, smiling at me.

"Did you mean what you said when you answered that last question?" I asked.

"Let's just say, I know what needs to be done to get what I want and I am willing to do it."

I wanted to kiss him, but just then the door opened, and we were handed a yellow envelope, thanked again for coming, and shown the way out. We did not dare open it while still in the building, so instead we waited until we were in the car and driving away from downtown.

"You have to do it, Daniel. I cannot," I said, looking at the envelope in his hands.

As he opened it, I closed my eyes and did a quick Hail Mary. With my eyes still closed, I waited for him to say something, anything. But all I heard was the purr coming from the car's engine. I opened my eyes to see him smiling at me.

"Did we get it? What does it say?" I said, snatching the paper from his hands.

It was a receipt from Parliament that showed the date and our presentation topic. It had a big red stamp that said APPROVED on it. Just like that! We did it.

I screamed in the car, startling both Daniel and Tadesse.
"*Ere bakish anchi lij*, I do not want to get in an accident," Tadesse said in a stern voice.

"We did it, Bella. We really did it! I had my doubts, especially towards the end."
"Me too. I still cannot believe it," I said, reading the paper again. It felt so good knowing I had accomplished something so big that would benefit countless Eritreans. I thought about the many jobs and families we saved today.

"We must celebrate. Let's go to dinner somewhere nice in the city. I will invite Saba and Yonatan, too. I am sure they will want to join us. Since we are achieving great things today, how about you come home for lunch? Let's surprise my family. I want them to meet you."

"Let's not mess up our good luck, Bella. I do not think your family will want me to come home for lunch without informing them first. I do not want to bring you any trouble."

"I promise it is no trouble at all. Tadesse, take us home please. Daniel, it is settled, you will have lunch with us as my special guest and meet my family. Plus, I can show you Emama's famous garden. Please, we are leaving in two days, I want them to meet you before we go back to Asmara."

"If you say so, *principessa*."

We arrived at the gates, and I saw Daniel's eyes widen. Emama always loved seeing people's faces light up whenever they first entered her home. She used to call it her special experience. Tadesse parked the car in front of the main house and I led Daniel into the foyer, announcing our arrival. Different family members were still trickling home for lunch, but Ababa and Yeshimebet were sitting in the living room discussing something rather important. They stopped talking when Daniel and I entered.

"Hello, Mama, Ababa," I said, giving them each a kiss on their cheeks. "I have some great news and I want you to meet someone very special as well. This is Daniel. We work together at *Banco di Roma* and today we got our bank's yearly proposal approved at Parliament." I was so excited until I heard the tone of Ababa's voice.

"I heard. You two were the talk of the morning in Parliament. Even General Kebede was impressed. As much as I wanted a different path for you, *Yene Lij*, I am proud of you for doing what you think is right. You inspired many of my colleagues today and they called to tell me Lorenzo is not dead, and that he lives through you. This could open so many doors for you here in Addis Ababa now, Bella. You should stay and follow up with the Foreign Minister's Office." Ababa said all this while looking Daniel up and down, trying to read his reaction.

"Ababa, my life is in Asmara now, but thank you for the suggestion." I knew where he wanted the conversation to go and I did not want to entertain it. Not at that time or in that place. We were there to celebrate.

"Daniel, Yonatan tells me you are great with numbers. Do you like working at the bank? How long have you been there? Do we know your family?"

Ababa asked.

Daniel began to answer all my grandfather's questions, and I could see both Yeshimebet and Ababa listening attentively. I could tell they did not want to like him. They were looking for reasons not to, but they would not find what they were looking for. He was hard to resist.

The rest of the family arrived, and lunch was served. We reviewed our meeting with everyone and all faces lit up with excitement for us. Yonatan seemed the most excited. The family talked to Daniel here and there but not with great enthusiasm. After lunch I took Daniel to the gardens while the family sat on our front porch for their afternoon coffee.

"It's beautiful, isn't it?" I said, looking out over the vast flowerbeds.
"Not as beautiful as you are," he responded, pulling me towards him and kissing me softly.
"You know my family is right outside that wall, right? And some of them carry guns and are not afraid to use them," I said, only half joking.
"I will risk it," he said, kissing me on the neck.
I stood there being kissed, loving every second of it, but also fearing that Ababa would send someone to spy on us.
"Come, I want to show you the best part," I said, pulling his hand.
We walked for a few minutes until we reached Emama's bungalow and greenhouse. I marveled at the sight and so did Daniel.

"You know, it reminds me of your house in Asmara. I see where you get your love for flowers and gardens now. This is paradise."

"It is, it really is. Emama used to spend all her time here or in the kitchen cooking family meals. I learned a great deal from her. I will cook for you soon, once I am all moved in. Daniel, I spent so many afternoons right here laying on the grass or reading on that bench, drinking tea with her, talking about my ams, and sharing everything with her. I wish you could have met her."

"I have. I met her at her grave and I see her every day in you."

This time it was I who kissed him passionately, so much so that we both fell to the ground, laughing and kissing. I wanted to tell him I loved him, but the words did not come out. Maybe I was too scared or maybe I decided he just knew it, the way I knew it. We lay on the grass looking at the clouds and talking about random things for what felt like a mere minute, when Yonatan arrived.

"Bella, are you still leaving tomorrow?" he asked abruptly.

I told him the truth, that we would both be leaving in the morning and asked why he needed to know.

"Because I want to take you both out to celebrate. Castelli's tonight, my treat," he said.

"Great idea. I was telling Daniel we should celebrate and we were going to take you out, but I prefer spending your money," I said, smiling and watching Daniel get offended.

"Bella, stop. Yonatan, no. You have done so much for us already. You must let me treat you. Please let us take you and Saba out tonight."

"You two can stay here and argue all afternoon about who will pay. I have to go inside," I said, giving Daniel a kiss and heading back to the house.

"Yonatan, please drop Daniel off at the hotel so he can freshen up. I have to spend some time with Ababa and Yeshimebet before leaving tomorrow."

I went to my room to pack while Ababa took his afternoon nap. Yeshimebet knocked lightly on the door and asked to come in.

"Do you have to go tomorrow?" she asked me. "I wish you could stay just a little longer. We did not get to spend any time with you."

"I know, Mama and I am sorry. It was a business trip. Soon, I will take vacation time and come visit. We can do anything you like then," I told her.

"I fear you are only telling me what I want to hear and not what will happen. Maybe I will come to Asmara and spend time with you there," she said.

"I would love that. Please come. Come anytime you want. We can go to the beach and visit other cities. I can take you to the village where Papa was born and show you where he went to school with the missionaries. You can stay with me in my new house. It will be wonderful," I told her.

"Will Daniel be there, in your new home?" she asked, concerned. There it was, the reason why she was asking all these questions.

"No, Mama. We are courting but of course we are not living together. We are not married."

"Oh, thank you, Lord! I was so worried. Bella, can we talk woman to woman? I want to educate you on a few things regarding relationships. This is the same conversation your grandmother had with me when I first fell in love. Come, sit next to me." She was sitting on the edge of my bed. I sat next to her and she embraced me warmly. "It is nice to hug you again, to even see you in your old room again. I do not want to let you go, but I know I have to." I could see she was trying hard to hold back tears, but could not do it. I did not know what to say to console her. Instead, I stayed in her embrace and let her cry while I held her tightly. Sometimes the unspoken words matter the most.

When she felt ready, she composed herself and let me go. "Love is an amazing thing, Bella, and it seems that you have found it. I will not lie to you, I had and probably still have my doubts about your banker."

"Daniel, Mama. His name is Daniel."

"Yes, yes, Daniel. Do you understand why we are all worried?"

"Yes, I understand, but trust me, it is not like you think it is. He doesn't care about my title or wealth, and honestly, neither do I. Do you know why I am so happy with my life back in Asmara? It is because I am creating the life I want for myself. Not what the family or our society wants for me but what I want for myself."

"I love your strength and determination, *Yene Lij*, but what you are doing now does not ultimately change who you are. If your job were to go away today, you know you could come home, you know you have options. People have worked extremely hard so that you will always have options, and your children and their children will also always have options."

"What are you saying?" I asked, genuinely confused.

"I am saying that as much as you love Daniel, he does not have those same options and because of that, he will always resent yours. Not because he wants to, but because life will force him to."

"How do you know I love him?"

"I can see it all over both of you. I recognize the expressions, the emotions, the way you talk and walk, the way everything is different about you. I know because that was how your father and I were. I loved him very much, so much that when he was away on missions, I could not sleep out of fear that something would happen to him. When he was with me, it was as if time had stopped and the only thing that mattered was the two of us. I can see that in you both and I am terrified for your future."

"But Mama, it is better to be in love than to be with someone because of a title and money! I know Papa was not always wealthy, especially not when you met him."

"Yes, of course I know that. Money is not the only thing I am talking about here, Bella. What about family, upbringing, and education? You have to have some commonalities."

"Papa did not have a prestigious family. He was brought up in a missionary school with Italian priests. He came to Ethiopia to help the emperor get rid of the Italians. He was not from your privileged world. I still do not see how he is so different from Daniel."

"Bella, please try to understand."

"I do NOT understand. I am doing what you did, which is to choose to be with the man I love no matter what. I have decided what I want for my life, and that includes loving Daniel. If you cannot accept that, then so be it. I want to live every day knowing that every decision I make for myself, whether good or bad, is made not because of what people think of me, but because it is what I want. Me! Please understand."

I looked at her with hope and sadness, praying my words would sink in. I could see that they did. She did not like what I said, but she bowed her head and accepted it.

"Just know that I am always here for you, *Yene Lij.* We all are."

I gave her a hug and we went downstairs to spend some time with Ababa, who was up from his nap. We enjoyed laughing and telling each other stories before I went back upstairs to get dressed for dinner with Daniel, Yonatan, and Saba. I knew the night would be special. Tonight, we would celebrate the end of my old life and the beginning of my new one — a new life that involved a tall, dark, and handsome man that loved me for me and made me happy.

As I looked around me, it felt strange that what was once my entire world now meant almost nothing to me. Last year I was in London, graduating from university and living what I thought was a very glamorous life. Emama was alive, and my dreams revolved around going to law school, entering the Foreign Ministry, and then one day running it. A marriage contract with a man I did not know had changed the trajectory of my life forever. Escaping that contract was just the beginning of my adventure.

Later that evening, the four of us gathered together for our celebration dinner at Castelli Restaurant. Saba and I were listening to the men discuss the difference between two vehicles that I personally had no desire for, but simply listening to them go on and on about something they were passionate about made me smile. I sat with my back to the restaurant door. First it was Saba, then Yonatan who noticed General Kebede walking into the restaurant. When I heard the owner of the Castelli raising his voice at an imperial soldier, I immediately turned around to see what the problem was. I noticed the general and behind him I saw two other soldiers. They came marching straight to our table. This could not be good.

Inside Castelli Restaurant *Addis Ababa*

Postlude

I looked up and saw my granddaughters all cuddled up, waiting to hear more. When they realized that I wasn't going to continue, their faces turned from excitement to confusion to sadness. "What! No way!" said Gabriella. "That cannot be the end of the story, Grams! You have to tell us what happens between you and Daniel, I want to make sure this is our grandfather! And tell us why the general came to your table with soldiers? You have to tell us, Grams!" Her sister and cousins all agreed.

"So sorry, my dears, I am tired. This old lady can only do so much talking," I said. The sad look on their faces did not change much. "Can you at least tell us if you marry Daniel or if he gets killed by the general?"

"If you sleep with him?" said Awet.

"What? I will not tell such a thing! I do not know if I should be upset or disgusted by your question, young lady. I shared a lot more than just my love life. Is that all you got from my story? Because if that is so, then this was all for nothing."

"No, of course not, Grams. We got so much more than just your love life. We got how much of a badass you were, even when you were younger."

"Well, thank you very much," I said. "That is true."

"So, what happens to you after that? What happens when you go back to Asmara?" they all wanted to know.

"That, my darlings, is another story that you will just have to wait for. Right now, I am tired and it is time for bed. Let us meet again next week and I will share a few more chapters of my story.

Author's Note

Between Two Worlds is a blend of fact and fiction that tells the story of one truly remarkable woman — Weizerit Annabella Lorenzo (also known as "*Grams*"). The idea of writing my grandmother's story is something I have been playing around with for years but it wasn't until 2020 that I finally put my dreams into action. I gathered all of her stories together, got her blessing, and dove into writing and researching.

I have always heard the glorious stories of the men in my family from loved ones, my community, and society, yet somehow the women who helped those men achieve greatness always seem to be forgotten. I think that is why my grandmother made it a point to start sharing her story with my sister and I when we were young girls living with her in Addis Ababa, Ethiopia. I believe she shared her story with us to not only encourage us to want more from life, to challenge the status quo, to be independent thinkers and strong women, but also so that we would carry on her legacy.

I hope this book inspires you to want more for yourself and to know life is too short to settle.

Thank you to all the experts who helped with research. Any errors are my own.

Acknowledgements

Publishing a book takes a village, and mine is full of amazing people who are always pushing me to do better and achieve my wildest dreams. First and foremost, I want to acknowledge my biggest supporter and best friend — Biniam "Bini" Tesfaye. All of those late nights staying up with me to help find the right words or storyline have not gone unnoticed. I love you, Bini, without your enduring support, love, and encouragement, there would be no Luwame (blog, podcast, brand) and most importantly, without you I wouldn't be the woman I am today. I value and appreciate all of the struggles and all the joyous moments we have gone through in making us who we are, a stronger, unified, and loving force. You have been my number one supporter and backbone since we were teenagers and I pray we stay strong forever. SHMILY!

To my children — Isabella, Lorenzo, Novena, and Lucas, thank you for letting Mommy off the hook when dinner wasn't ready on time or homework didn't get checked because I was working away in my office. Thank you for coming and giving me ideas, hugs, kisses, and leaving me notes under my office door when I locked you out. I hope you read these pages and understand the depth of your great-grandmother's legacy. I pray that I too will leave you a powerful legacy that will make you all proud.

To my sister Rahwa, the only person who knows how important Grams was to our childhood because you were right there with me. This book is just as much yours as it is mine. I said this when we were younger and will say it again and again. Little One — it's you and me against the world. I will always have your back.

To my best friend and editor, Mimi, what can I say other than thank you. You encouraged me when I thought all hope was lost. You offered your time and energy when you had none to give and always answered my calls regardless of how annoying I got. Our friendship pushes me to work harder and strive for more.

I couldn't have finished this book without all the help from my family and friends. Thank you for always supporting my dreams and sharing the stories that encouraged me to keep on going. To my mother Miriam and her sisters, Liz, Ruth, and Christine: you all raised me on such high morals and values. You took time from your own lives to be my role model, mentor, and friend, and offered me a safe space whenever I needed it. To my father Araya: your legacy will forever live in my heart and in the stories I tell my children. Thank you to my siblings and cousins who all chipped in with edits and story ideas so that this book could come to life. To my bottomless books and brunch ladies, thank you for cheering me on and holding me accountable on my goals each month. To my book coach Deborah Haile, thank you for dealing with all of my excuses and never giving up on me. To my author bestie Tarikua Emiru, thank you for all our calls where I was asking you a million questions. Thank you for holding my hand throughout this whole experience. I couldn't have done this without you.

About the Author

LUWAM A. TESFAYE is a devoted wife and mother of 4. A personal trainer/ life coach by day and a lifestyle blogger/podcaster by night. She left her full-time government career in 2019 to follow her dreams and become an entrepreneur. One of her first projects was to start her blog Luwame.com, where she shares stories on motherhood, relationships, empowerment, and healthy living in the hopes of inspiring and empowering women everywhere to live their best life.

Originally from Eritrea and Ethiopia, Luwam is a first-generation American who grew up listening to stories of her family's exile from Ethiopia following the Eritrean War for Independence. Growing up with immigrant parents shaped her life and motivated her to pursue international studies and homeland security during her undergraduate years at Virginia Commonwealth University.

When not working with clients or on the blog/podcast, she loves reading, writing in her journal, meditating, and, most importantly, spending time with her husband Bini and their four children: Isabella, Lorenzo, Novena, and Lucas. Together the Tesfaye family loves to travel, experience new adventures, and enjoy game nights, including the coveted Friday night movie with pizza.

For more information, visit: www.luwame.com

Made in the USA
Middletown, DE
29 April 2022

65006257R00149